Alligator Gar

Alligator Gar

CHESTER L. SULLIVAN

CROWN PUBLISHERS, INC.
NEW YORK

*This book is dedicated
to my mother and father
and the quiet clearwater place
where we lived in Mississippi*

PROLOGUE

EXCEPT FOR THE GULF COASTAL TERRACE, THE SOUTHEAST FIFTH OF the state is known, geographically, as the Piney Woods. Until the commencement of the twentieth century the whole area was covered with virgin longleaf pines. *A Guide to the Magnolia State,* written by the Federal Writers' Project of the Works Progress Administration (WPA) describes the Piney Woods: "Strong men and women have been reared here, but the earth has been neither fecund enough to facilitate their getting away from it nor sterile enough to drive them away. Until lumbering built a few fair-sized towns out of the wilderness, it was a pioneer country; and now that the forests have been ravished, and the cheaply built mill houses are rotting, as the unused mill machinery rusts about them, it is pioneer country once more. Like all pioneers, the Piney Woods people are economically poor, politically unpredictable, and in a constant state of economic transition . . . these people . . . have always been the yeomen—the non-slave owners—of the State, possessed of an inherited distrust of the planter and of the aristocratic system that great plantations breed."

The town of Tongs, Mississippi, is near the center of the Piney Woods, on the Okatoma River, six miles downstream from the county seat, Beauville. Some Tongs people say that the Beauville Funeral Home runs its drainpipe into the Okatoma River, that it empties the blood into the river. But some say that's not true, while others say it's a "true fact," and still others say that it doesn't matter anyway because the slow river filters the water clean before it gets downstream to Tongs. Along the winding stretches between Tongs and Beauville the river is deep and there are good catfish in the blue holes. It widens and becomes more shallow and straight when it reaches the Tongs Bridge, which some old townspeople still call Shiloh Crossing from the time when there was no bridge there, just Shiloh Church. The church is still there, a rotten shell grown over with kudzu vines and sassafras. Dale Pittman has a service station in front of the old church. He built it near the river so that he would get the fishermen's business. The bridge is steel, silver painted, and on the upstream sides of its pylons there are drifts of deadwood that wash away and are replaced each time the river rises but which always look the same, like the external details of people's lives, details which are so unknowable and complex that they are generally dismissed as commonplace effects of obvious causes. Some observers, standing on the bridge, can distinguish many varieties of fish swimming in the eddies behind the steel pylons. Okatoma runs wide and shallow below the bridge for a mile to where she drops over The Falls into a pool which is eighty yards wide and fifty feet deep.

CHAPTER 1

NEAR TONGS ON THE FIRST SUNDAY IN JULY, 1874, SHILOH CHURCH was full. It was Grave Decoration Day. If he'd been five minutes earlier, everybody would have seen him, but when Arez King rode up, the last stragglers had entered the church. Inside, they were singing. He reined his mare at the little oak grove where she eyed the other horses tied there. He held his left forearm tight against his cut. King leaned forward, coughing—he spat. He heard the people singing, "There is a fountain . . . filled with blood." His mare settled next to the other horses. He pulled his rein and jerked her head up and to the left, but she stamped and refused to turn, so he pulled harder, until she turned, took one step, then two steps, ambling back toward the road. The boy hunched forward, his left forearm pressing his belly, his left hand clenched in the slash pocket of the right side of his coat. He was soaked inside the heavy coat with sweat and blood. It was the last blood drawn by a King or a Jacobs. In their fathers' generation, men had been killed, but Arez and Arthur made do with knife cuts, disputing the affections of a girl whom neither of them took for wife. The knuckles of both of Arez's hands were white from clenching, one clenching the pocket—one the reins. For the rest of his life he didn't know why, after riding seven miles with the cut, he hadn't interrupted church. Years later, when he told his son, Joe, about it, he remembered that he had been weak and hot and nauseous but that there had been no pain.

He rode another hundred yards to Shiloh Crossing, where he slumped from the saddle, easing himself to the ground by holding first to the saddle horn, then to the girth, and then to the swinging, wobbly stirrup. He wallowed out of his clothes and crawled into the baptizing pool, where the water was clear and cold. The white underwater sand lay in ridges, and his bare toes looked like Alps to the magnifying eyes of the sandsuckers as he crouched into the water and washed the dried blood-soaked leaves and dirt from his belly. There was still no pain when he scooted himself from the water bare-butted onto the sand. Inching himself along, like a spawning turtle, he kept his hands clear of the sand. Digging his elbows and heels into the sand, he scooted to where he could prop his head on the heavy coat that he'd worn to stop the knife. Then he laced his fingers, locking his hands over the cut, and lay there on his back until they found him, after church, and a doctor sewed him up.

❊   ❊   ❊

In the fall of 1940, Ira King got up quickly from his desk, stood beside it, and rubbed his finger in the smooth pencil-holding groove that was cut into the varnished desk. He looked at the anachronistic hole in the right corner which was cut for an inkwell, but he didn't know that it was for an inkwell. He began a deliberate recital of the forty-eight states, following each state with the name of its capital city, stopping with the capital of Maine. Other pupils raised their hands and spoke out. The teacher glanced at her book, prompted, and after that pause Ira completed his recital easily.

Ira King's hair was dark, combed slick with Rose Hair Oil. He was a thin, straight boy with green eyes. He stood there, waiting to be excused, but the teacher had another question for him. He answered it, "We live on the Okatoma River. It flows into the Bowie River. The Bowie River flows into the Leaf River. The Leaf River flows into the Pascagoula River. The Pascagoula River flows into the Gulf of Mexico—"

"Thank you, Ira." She released him, having tested him beyond the expectation of her other pupils. Book learning came easy to him, and she thought that learning should be difficult. He sat down, her eyes moved to the boy next to him. "What is the world's biggest river, James?"

"The Mississippi River—" An easy answer for this Mississippi school.

Her eyes moved again, searching for answers about the Amazon and the Nile. Ira listened intently, knowing that rivers were important, for the teacher spent a great deal of time talking about them, and she'd read, that term, to the class—twenty minutes each afternoon—from *Heart of Darkness.* Ira thought that every important city in the United States was on a river, and half those rivers ran into the Gulf of Mexico. He could have traced the Okatoma River back to its tributary, Mill Creek, if she'd asked for that detail, for his aunt lived on Mill Creek, and Ira's grandfather, Arez King, was responsible for the creek's having that name. He didn't consciously wonder about water then, but later, in the hot, dry climate of Oklahoma, when he was a soldier in the artillery, and especially after that, in Texas, when he worked nights loading meat trucks for Swift and Company, and when he went to college part-time in the afternoons, after his morning sleep, Ira King grew to respect water. He felt homesick for the soft abundance of it. When he was twenty-six, and a long way from home, he realized that gravity moves water, that gravity is the strongest force to affect man. The movement of water makes the spirit of water. Water is only mysterious because it seems, to man, as if water moves of its own will, about its own primordial business, below the ground, on the ground, even in the clouds of the sky—in rain and hail and snow. Well water is still. To feel the spirit of well water one must feel the pull of the gravity that keeps it in the well. If one doesn't know the feel of the hand windlass or the pitcher pump, one can't know the spirit of well water. So Ira came to believe, in 1955, when he tried to sketch in his mind a map of his own Mill Creek, for it had belonged to him, until he gave it to Melissa Natale, to expiate old sins—

CHAPTER **2**

EARLY ON THE MORNING OF SEPTEMBER FIRST, 1950, TOM DELANEY arrived in the village of Tongs, Mississippi. He stopped for coffee at the Elite Cafe, across the street from King's Store, before calling on his cousin and friend, Joe King. Midge Farley was the waitress, and she wouldn't talk with Delaney. When he winked at her, as he invariably did, telling her that she had a "pretty little shaker," she remembered what she'd heard about him, that he was queer. She didn't know exactly what her boyfriend, Stanley Rawls, had meant when he told her that. Delaney certainly wasn't a sissy, in fact he was just the opposite—a big flirt. He was handsome, with even features and dark hair and blue eyes and a friendly smile. He always wore tailored suits with bright ties and new shoes. She promptly served his toast and coffee, but she didn't look him in the face, and she retreated behind her counter as soon as she could.

While Delaney drank his coffee, he looked at the King Store, remembering how it was before, when it had only one story, with no plate glass windows. That was when Joe King bought it, and it was big now because Joe was a good manager. He built a story of living quarters on top of it with bedrooms and a kitchen. It had the first second-floor plumbing in Tongs, and lots of people had sat in the cafe or barbershop (both of which faced it) debating at length whether or not the water would have enough pressure to force it up to the second-floor kitchen and bathroom. They all agreed that the drains would work without any problem, and the toilet would flush, but there were many people who were genuinely concerned that the water wouldn't make it up that high. Not only was it a two-story, but it also had a false front which stood higher than any other building in Tongs, except for the steeple of the Baptist Church. Mrs. King had insisted that her husband put lightning rods on top of the store, because it was the highest building in town and seemed likely to attract lightning. They were pretty little wrought iron spokes fitted through blue glass globes. Delaney, himself, had bought them for her in Memphis. There was a decorative balcony with a spooled rail that jutted over the street.

From his seat in the cafe, Delaney couldn't see Mrs. King, who was in the rear of the store, dusting. But he saw his cousin Joe standing up by the front door. He saw Joe tug at his vest and turn, looking at himself in the full-length mirror. Mrs. King said, "Come on, Joe. Could you stop preening yourself and help me straighten up? There's a lot of cleaning to be done."

Joe grumbled about the condition of his suit, saying something about the cobbler's children always being barefoot. Then, with as much grace as he could manage, he wheeled to the narrow staircase, grasped both handrails firmly, and dispatched Mrs. King's request with a steady command, "I've got to get the records straight. Today is the first. Delaney will be around here whining for an order, and I want to clap him in the face with this damned phony batch of green suits he sent us!"

Delaney was alone in the cafe, except for silent Midge, so he took a new copy of *Audubon* from his briefcase, admired the cover picture, and started turning the pages, slowly chewing his toast while he looked at the pages. He read an article on limpkins in Florida, and he decided to order a pair of Bausch & Lomb binoculars which were advertised on the inside cover. They were 7×35 Zephyrs, expensive, he thought, but good.

Left alone, Mrs. King dusted her way to the front of the store. When Delaney looked up from his magazine, he saw her. He paid for his breakfast, put the magazine back in his briefcase, and left the cafe, watching her through the window while he crossed the street. By the time he got to the door, she was behind the long counter, dusting the high shelves with her back to him. He opened the door softly, but the tinklebell gave him away. Without looking around she asked, "Is that you, Ira?"

"No. This ain't 'you Ira.' This is me, Cousin Delaney! You little titmouse!"

She fixed her expression before she faced him, made her face pretty, and turned on her right toe as gracefully as if she were dancing. She held the feather duster behind her back with one hand and brushed back her hair with the other. "Yes, Delaney, the bird-brained fool!"

He grabbed her across the counter for a hug, but she pulled away. "We're mad at you, Delaney. You tried to gyp us."

"What, what, what? You can say that to *me,* in my favorite store, my best customers, my favorite account—my own flesh and blood— come come, my ears deceive me!"

"No, really. Joe's hopping mad about those green suits you sent us that we didn't order and we'd *never* sell. He's waiting." She gestured to the room above.

Delaney looked straight into her eyes with his best blank, honest salesman's expression, thinking that by damn he'd like to kiss her. She wasn't half mad at him, and she was pretty. He backed to the stairs and climbed up to the attic office, proclaiming his innocence of any wrongdoing all the way, and as his head bobbed into the room above he kept up his stream of protests, jerking himself into the office step by step.

Joe King sat behind a small round-topped table. There was a pasteboard box at his feet with the three sides of its top neatly sliced open, so that the lid folded back like a trapdoor. A stack of folded green suits lay on the floor beside the box.

Delaney stopped with one foot trailing on the top step, he asked, "What's this, Joe? I hear from Clara that you got a box of green suits, and I never turned in no such of an order." He wet his lips, "Why, in the first place, *why* would I turn in an order for green suits for you, you'll never sell a *green* suit in Tongs?" He dropped to his knees beside the box and riffled through the stack of folded suits, hooking his professional finger under the label of each suit, checking the size, then he mused, "Yeah, they're Houston House, but it beats me, the shipping department must of just got screwed up. I was back there last week, Joe, you know—I was kidding around with the gal who runs the shipping desk, she probably got all flustered, probably got crazy orders going all over Mississippi."

Joe King said, "It's nothing to get all worked up about, Delaney, I haven't paid for them yet. Just so long as they leave the store when you do. Bundle them up and drop them off at the depot."

Delaney got up slowly and reached out to shake Joe's hand. "Sure, Joe, sure." At the same time he flipped a silvered flask from his back pocket.

"Sit down, Tom," Joe said. "But don't be getting overly affectionate until you get your junk out of here. I was afraid you were trying to pull a fast one on me."

"No!"

"Put that flask away. If you go to the trouble of stopping in Tongs to see me, I can at least provide the whiskey." He lifted a bottle from beneath the table, shook it, held it up to the light, and then put it down gently on the table.

"Sure—OK." Delaney smiled at his cousin. "Well, what did you think when you opened a box full of green suits, Joe?"

"Hell, I didn't know what to think. I thought they were blue at first, blue like the ocean, blue like the northern lights, blue as a maiden's blue eyes, blue as the day is long—until I took them up to the front window. Then they turned green as damn clover. They started turning when the light hit them, and they twinkled like a damn fairy leprechaun had waved his beard over them." Then, despite himself, he grinned at Delaney, and then he called down to Mrs. King and had her send a pitcher of iced water and two glasses up the dumbwaiter. They smoked Delaney's cigars and filled the loft with beautiful blue smoke.

"They sure are green now, Joe. No denying that! Never mind, though, I'll have them out of here in twenty minutes," Delaney said. He seemed to be relieved. He leaned his straight-backed chair against the frame of the dumbwaiter. "How about a quick game of cards?"

Joe agreed. Delaney said that he was low on money, so he put the suits up against ten dollars and carefully lost. In the process of winning, Joe asked, "See Ira when you came in?"

"No."

"It looks like he's been out all night, again."

"No lie?"

"He's as secretive as a cat. He got to climbing in and out these second-floor windows so easy I just gave him a key to the front door."

"He's of the wild oats age, Joe. You rambled too."

"Yeah, but things are different with him. I can't figger where he goes. All of the town girls are present and accounted for."

"Well—?"

"Sure I rambled, Tom," he continued, "but I went out nights and worked days. He's graduated high school with honors, and there's nothing for him to do in this town, he won't work in the store, he won't listen to us. What do you think I ought to do with him, Tom?"

"He's a good boy, something will turn up, he'll find a job and get out of this dried-up burg. No place for a young man here."

They finished both their game and their drinks at the same time. Delaney shook Joe's hand warmly, avoided looking at the green suits, and backed down the stairs, carefully.

He was happy when he held the front screen door for the Italian, Mike Natale, because his coup was complete. The suits were part of an order of twenty that had been returned to Houston House by a bankrupt Irish marching band. The sales manager divided them among his salesmen, gratis, and Delaney sent his share to his cousin —just for the fun of it. It was too early for lunch, and he wanted to smoke another cigar and fan his whiskey glow, so he crossed the street and went into Happy's barbershop, next door to the Elite Cafe.

CHAPTER 3

WHILE TOM DELANEY ATE HIS BREAKFAST TOAST AND READ *Audubon* magazine, Mike Natale walked the four miles from his farm to Tongs with the unsure anger of a first-generation immigrant, knowing that his business was with Joe King, the father, even though *Ira King* was the name that his daughter Melissa had told him, slowly at first and then quicker as she repeated it, saying it almost like she was proud—it was her birthday, September first, she was seventeen.

Mike thought that he was unlucky because he had no sons. He'd had to stop in Tongs seventeen years before, with his wife and two daughters. They were travelling with four other Italian families, and they'd stopped because his new baby, Melissa, was sick. After three days the other families went on north, looking for industrial work, intending to find a place called "Ohio," but Mike stayed as a hired hand so that he could keep the sick girl in a bed of sorts, rather than bundled in the backseat of his brother's old car. He'd meant to follow the others, but he couldn't break away. For seventeen years they stayed, living on tenant farms, farming on shares, and Natale never tried to buy a farm. Tongs' people supposed that he didn't understand about land ownership in this country—he couldn't even drive a car. He spoke Italian at home, but they were all women there, and he had no men to talk with. That isolation from men who spoke his own language had made him uncertain, and as a result of his isolation he didn't know for sure whether he should offer a dowry or start a fight.

He was thirsty when he got to Pittman's service station, and when he saw the hose of the gasoline pump, he wished he had a pickup truck so he wouldn't have to walk. He could see the Tongs Bridge, and he knew that he still had to cross it and walk three-quarters of a mile up the steep hill into Tongs.

"Hi, there, Mr. Natale," Stanley said, sitting on an upturned RC case under the awning. He worked for Dale Pittman.

"Hello, Mr. Stanley. Have you got in one of these pipes or rubber hoses some water? I am so thirsty and I think it is very hot for September."

"It's hotter'n a bitch fox! Sure, we got plenty of water, but if you've got a nickel, we've got eight flavors of soft drinks."

Natale smiled at Stanley and handed him a nickel. Stanley raised the lid of the cold-drink box and named off the flavors for Natale, who took a Nehi orange. Stanley got a Coke for himself. They sat on RC cases and drank from the bottles. Natale said, abruptly, that his daughter was seventeen that day, that he was going to King's Store to see Mr. King about Ira and Melissa. He told Stanley that Ira had been secretly meeting Melissa. He felt that Ira should come up to the house and say hello to Melissa's mother—and he should sometimes take Melissa to town and make a meeting with her and his parents in the big store.

Stanley got red around the ears when he heard the gossip. "Do you know this Ira, Stanley? He is about your same age."

"Sure, sure I know Ira King, Mr. Natale. He's a right good boy, and he's smart, too. He finished number one in the senior class. He made the speech at graduation. He likes to read. He likes to study history."

"Well, one thing is strange to me. I don't understand why Mr. King he didn't spoke to me about this. I should have been asked if it was all right. I should have been asked a long time back."

Stanley told himself that he showed his breeding by not laughing in the old Italian's face. He looked down at the oil-soaked driveway of the station and truly said that he knew nothing of Ira's courting Natale's daughter. Mike Natale finished his Nehi and stuck the empty bottle between his knees into one of the square cells of the case that he was sitting on. He smiled at Stanley. The telling of his story to another man made it simpler and more reasonable to him. He was glad to learn that Ira was smart, number one in the class. He gave Stanley a solemn assurance that he would see him again and stepped out into the sunlight. Stanley watched him walk the two hundred yards to the Okatoma bridge, thinking about the news, for it was all news of the highest order—completely unexpected, and he was excited that he'd heard it first from Melissa's father. He said to himself, "Wait until I tell old Ira I know about this! He'd rather keep a secret than eat! He's the secret cat, but this old cat's out of the bag, this old pussycat's *out* of the bag! Wonder which of them gals it is —Melissa—that's the little dark one, I believe, the one we used to call Palmolive. Ira didn't settle for her!"

Mike Natale felt even better when he got to Tongs and to King's Store. He stood in the street and looked up at the two-story building, admiring its fresh paint, its height, and the blue glass globes on the lightning rods. His wife's fears and Melissa's sullen refusal to explain why Ira wouldn't come to the house seemed less important to him then, for he had learned that Ira was a smart boy and he could see that the King Store was big, and clean, and inviting. He walked toward the store, stepped up onto the sidewalk, placed his hand on the handle of the screen door, and he opened the door just as Tom Delaney pushed it open from the inside. Delaney, flushed from drinking with Joe, gave Mike a snappy wink. "Good morning, my friend, are you out to buy a new suit of clothes?"

"No, no thank you. I am but coming to visit Mr. King."

"Well—like we say in the trade, that lets him get his foot in the door, hand in your pocket. If you happen to look at any threads, don't buy unless it's Houston House. Look at the label, here's my card for good measure." Delaney handed him a business card with his name printed on one side and a sexy cartoon on the other side which showed a travelling salesman addressing a farmer whose buxom daughter listened to their conversation from behind a bush.

"Yes, sir," Mike Natale said, "thank you."

"I wouldn't steer you wrong, buddy." Delaney held the screen door open for Mike. While he held the screen he noticed dusty smudges on his trousers. "Must have gotten these," he leaned forward and brushed his knees, letting the screen slam behind Mike, "on Joe's floor. Cousin Joe has a pretty wife and good bourbon, but upstairs the floor sure is dirty."

Mike Natale quickly pocketed the business card, for he could read neither the caption of the cartoon nor Delaney's name.

CHAPTER 4

HAPPY LARSON WAS ACCUSTOMED TO BEING CALLED GAPPY. HAPPY wasn't his real name anyway, his name was Luther. There were four idlers in the barbershop when Delaney got there. He stepped up into the front chair and said, "Just change the oil, Gappy. Give me fifteen cents' worth of that rose water and comb it out. I'm not due (for the benefit of the idlers) a haircut till Shreveport. You know, they've got a woman barber there, blonde, in the Shrevesporter Hotel. I like the way she brushes her tits on my shoulder. You fellas ever have a haircut from a woman barber?"

"Yeah," one of them quipped, "my maw."

The others giggled. Gappy squirted Delaney's hair with Rose tonic and massaged it in. Delaney said, "No shit? Well—when you get loose from your maw's apron strings, and when you know what tits are for, besides dinner, I want you to do me a favor. Sell your 4-H pigs and take the money and buy yourself a bus ticket to Shreveport, that's in Louisiana, and get yourself a haircut. After that, if you're still as stupid as you are now—and if you come back to show it—I'll buy you another herd of pigs."

That drew a bigger laugh from the idlers. Delaney's material wasn't red hot, but he had good delivery, so he continued, "You know, Gappy, that's a pretty safe offer I just made this young pecker. If these unlettered boys ever stuck their nose out of the Piney Woods and saw the rest of the world, they'd be long gone, and Tongs would really die on the vine."

"I'm sure you're right about that," Gappy replied. "I wisht I'd of gone somewhere before I settled down, somewhere else besides Camp Shelby for six months."

Then, while he combed Delaney's hair, there was no conversation. The air grew thick. Gappy stuck his OUT TO LUNCH sign in the window and washed his hands at the basin. He sat in the other chair and wiped his hands on the towel hanging through a chromed ring on one arm of the chair. He pressed the handle that allowed the chair to swivel freely and kicked himself around to the cabinet so that he could reach his lunch. Then he turned the chair to face the street and carefully unwrapped the *Beauville Clarion* from his lunch. The idlers shuffled out of the shop. They all muttered "see ya," all except the boy who said his maw cut his hair. He tight-lipped it out the door. When they were on the street, beyond hearing, Delaney gave them his benediction: "Go forth, Young Man, and Troll your Pecker in the Stream of Life—Amen."

"There's a new teacher in town since you were here last."

"Oh, yeah? Where did she locate?"

"What makes you think it's a she?"

"Why else would you mention it?"

"Well, you're right, she is."

"Good."

"Is she?"

"Ha hah! Gappy, that's right—keep on your toes!"

Gappy smiled at his own joke, then he said, looking out the window, "Say! What's that going on over on King's balcony? Strange proceedings." He leaned forward, to his right, so that he could see better past the OUT TO LUNCH sign. "That's Joe King, and it looks like the big fellow is Mike Natale. Talk about green! Look at that damn suit of clothes! Do you reckon that's the kind of clothes Eyetalians like to wear?"

"I dunno," Delaney murmured.

"I bet he got some Eyetalian to send him that material and got Joe to tailor it for him. You know, Joe is a right good tailor."

Delaney smiled at Gappy's mistake, for Gappy thought that minor alterations were tailoring. He called his own Houston House suits tailor-made, because Joe had taken up the cuffs and the back seam of the jacket. "Maybe so, but they look drunk to me," Delaney replied.

"Uh-oh, Joe went back in the loft, but that Eyetalian keeps standing there, flapping his arms. There! He's got a glass of booze setting on the banister railing! Look at him strut!"

Delaney, shifting the cigar to the other side of his mouth, said, "Gappy, I bet you ten bucks Joe comes out wearing a green suit just like it."

"Now, what makes you say that?"

"Nothing, just a hunch."

"You're on, it's a bet. A white man wouldn't wear no such of a thing!"

"Think so? Get ready, here he comes!"

"I'll be a monkey's uncle. Would you look at that."

"Don't be a monkey's uncle, just pay up!" Delaney beamed. They watched Joe smooth the wrinkles out of his own green coat. Then, as Natale had done, Joe flapped his arms a couple of times. They both strutted in the noon sun. Like two green praying mantises they squared off in opposite corners of the little balcony, and then came together to smooth each other's suits and exchange admiring gestures. After more turns, bends, and arm-flaps they looked up and down the street, waved and threw kisses to the people on the sidewalks, and went back into the loft. "Give me ten, Gappy. I'm gone for lunch. *Now.* Come on."

Gappy stopped chewing, got up from his barber chair, walked to his big National cash register and pressed the "no sale" key. When the cash drawer opened, he laid the remains of his sandwich on the marble shelf above the open cash drawer and plucked two fives from one of the narrow compartments. He closed the drawer and picked up his sandwich, inspecting the underside of it. "Here, Bloodsucker. You was just over there. You and Joe King probably set up this whole thing!"

"You think I planned for that What's-His-Name fella to come walking up just as I was leaving, be serious."

"Dunno. That's the trouble with barbering. You gotta be a sport, gotta take people's bets, and no matter how clean you keep a place, you still get hair in your food."

*   *   *

Joe collared Ira as soon as Mike Natale left the store. They passed Mrs. King, sitting on her high stool behind the long counter. She had some pencils stuck in her hair knot, and she was looking down at the floor, her eyes red from crying; she didn't look up as they passed. When Ira started up the narrow stairs Joe kicked at him, but Ira, like a squirrel, scampered up into the loft, where he saw the bottle that Joe had started with Delaney and finished with Mike Natale standing empty on the round-topped table. Ira dodged around the table and waited for his winded father to flop in the straight chair by the dumbwaiter.

"I must be getting too old to drink with Tom, so early in the morning, whew, I felt it, coming up those stairs. Well, Son! You fixed it now! Your mother down there almost fainted when that damn idiot Eyetalian came blabbering in here! I had to drag him up here—talk sign language to him—almost had to draw him pictures! Got him drunk, gave him a free suit, listened to his life story —all to plan your wedding—all to get him calmed down!"

"I'm sorry."

"You damn well are. Why couldn't you find a decent girl? Any girl in town would go out with you! You do realize that we're a leading family in Tongs? Don't you?"

"What do you mean, decent girl?"

"I believe you know what I mean. That old man didn't come here because of any Valentine note. He didn't *say* she was in trouble, from what I could make out of his jabber, is she?"

"What do you mean, in trouble?"

"Now goddamnit! Don't play dumb with *me!* You know what I mean."

"No."

"No what?"

"No, she's not pregnant."

"Well then, what are you going to do about this mess?"

"Why's it a mess? I can't see it's a mess. You're going off the deep end."

"OK, Son, OK. You think it's not a mess? You think about it for one minute. You think real hard. Think about all your friends, and think about this is a small town, everybody knows everybody here. You *tried* to keep it a secret! Think about your mother. You're old enough to fly the coop, anyway. I was talking with Delaney about you this very morning, before that Wop came in here with his sob story. Delaney thinks nineteen is the age to move out. I do too. You'd do best to leave quietly, if you go."

"I'd like to try the university. It's just the first of September, there's still time—"

"Go to Kansas. There's some Kings there, no, they're all dead now. But there's schools all over the country. You think about it. There's nothing here for you now, nothing but being married to a Wop."

"I might—"

"You might die trying! My father had seventy acres and a team of mules. He built a dam, he built a mill, he cut every board in this town, before he died. I started this store with a good decent girl and three hundred dollars. Now, by God, if you want to go to college, get your ass to college! But do it on your own!"

Later that day, at dusk, Ira used his key to open the front door of King's Store. He waited inside the doorway for James and Stanley, feeling the hot excitement of indignation. When he'd walked about town that afternoon, he saw people look at him as if they wanted to ask or tell him something, but nobody made the little gesture or took the half-step to initiate a conversation. His friends turned the corner. Stanley carried a black octagonal ladies' hatbox under his arm, trying to make it as inconspicuous as he could. They followed the sidewalk, passing the Rex Theatre, the Elite Cafe, and Happy's barbershop. Then they cut directly across the street and glided in the door while Ira held it open. He gently closed and locked the door, and they went up to the low, windowless room in the loft that had been Ira's nursery and playroom, hideout and clubhouse, workshop and retreat.

James Goff was a birdlike boy with thin features and small, round eyes. When he was twelve he read from Longfellow's *Evangeline* at school assembly, and when he was a junior they asked him to write verses to go under the class pictures in the yearbook. He sent poems to the Beauville newspaper. He gestured to Stanley for him to open the hatbox and said, "Ira. How could you keep such a big secret from your best friends?"

Stanley interrupted, "This is the most exciting day of my life, Ira." He took three cans of beer from the many in the hatbox. "Everybody's talkin' about you! Boy, you *should have heard* that old Mr. Natale. He just walked up to the station as pretty as you please and asked me for a drink of water. Well, I talked him into a Nehi and got him to sit down. Then he just come right out with it and told me about you and his girl in the barn! But I was good—I didn't act none surprised. I just nodded at him, like it was *the* thing to do. Then he come on up here. A couple of boys stopped for gas and I told them about it, tried to get one of 'em to work for me so I could come on into town and see you get shot, or whatever was going to happen to you, but they wouldn't. Then, around noon, I get this call from T. J. Pittman. He was at the Elite, and he said that Mr. King and Mike Natale was all dressed up in green suits and was dancing up on this here balcony! Well, I knew right then that you was going to have a Polack wedding for sure. When Mr. Pittman come in to check the register, he asked me to work the night shift too. I said, 'Hell no!' That's just what I said. I told him, 'There's something big going on with my best friend and I got to get out of here at six and find out about it!'"

"Thanks, Stanley. Thanks a lot!" Ira said.

James said to smiling Stanley, "Sure. Thanks especially for the beer, but I think Ira was being ironic. Ira, are you going to light out?"

"Yeah!" Stanley said, "light a shuck out of this town! Everybody says you'll be leaving. They say Mr. King won't let no son of his marry no Eyetalian girl, and they say you can't stay here without Mike Natale killin' you if you don't marry his girl, after what you done. They say he'd about as soon shoot you as not—if he finds out Joe King tricked him with that green suit!"

"That's what they say, huh? Who says that?"

"Just about everybody." Stanley grinned, "Course I ain't asked the Baptist preacher—I ain't asked the Sheriff of Chambers County —I don't know *what* they say."

"Well, I haven't decided what I'll do, maybe I will leave. If I do, it'll be like a night rider. There won't be anybody to know it except the taxi driver and me. I'll get up before day and take the taxi to Beauville and get that seven o'clock Trailways to Jackson."

"Why Jackson? Ain't you going to the university?"

"No. No money. Probably go out west, Texas or Oklahoma."

"Cowboy King!" Stanley slapped his leg. "That do sound good." He opened more beer and passed the cans around.

"Maybe I'll work some cows, drive a cattle truck, maybe work the wheat harvest up in Kansas. This store isn't making money like it used to. I'll have to save up a grubstake before I can start college."

Stanley pursued the idea of cows and cowboys. "Maybe you could keep right on going till you hit California—Hollywood. They need a lot of movie stars out there. You ain't *bad* looking, least somebody, I ain't naming any names, don't think so. I wouldn't mind getting all slicked up some Friday night to take Midge down to the Rex and watch *Ira King Catches the Train Robbers,* or *Ira Falls in Love in the Congo.*"

James said, "Don't you feel bad about leaving? About Melissa? Romeo's Juliet was Italian, you know. It's hard for a thinking man to say that Italians are inferior—it seems."

"Yeah," Stanley interrupted, "I was trying to figure it out, just which one of them girls is Melissa, Ira? Is it the young one, or the old one we used to tease and call Palmolive?"

"She's the in-between one."

"What do you mean, in-between? They ain't but two, went to the same school with them all my life—'til they dropped out."

"There are three, Stanley. A little girl six hasn't started school yet. Melissa is seventeen. She's Palmolive."

"Seventeen?" James looked intently at Ira's face. "Are you bitter, Ira?"

"No. Not bitter. It's like a grain of popcorn that exploded."

Stanley shifted on his hams. "You ought to of told your best friends, Ira. It's kind of like you don't trust us."

"There wasn't anything to tell, until this happened."

"Come on, Ira! That ain't what old Natale told me!"

"Oh, Stanley—that's *really* why I think I'll get the hell out of

Tongs. Right now, everybody in town's thinking, 'Fornication, fornication, in the barn and in the hay.' Like when anybody here gets married, everybody starts counting the months until the baby comes, just in case they slipped up."

Stanley giggled. "They's been some mighty big 'premature' babies born here. Eustace Miller was only married four months, and hers was borned big enough to plow! Anyway, Ira, I'd like to see you go out west and make something of yourself. The only one from our graduating class to do any good, so far, has been Paul Jacobs—he got a job last week driving the ambulance for the Beauville Funeral Home! Anyway, Ira, talking about premature babies, what was it like, huh boy?"

"What was what like?"

"You know, nookie."

"Hell, Stanley. You know as much about *that* as I do. You've been courtin' Midge Farley, haven't you?"

"That don't mean nothin', Ira. Midge Farley don't put out."

"Hush, Stanley. He can no more tell you that than the pines can tell you why they don't get tired standing out in the rain all night, or a fish tell you how it feels to be wet, or the grass tell you how it feels to be green."

"I *can* tell you, Stanley, but I have to start at the beginning. That was two months ago, just after graduation. I was feeling kind of superior to everything. Jake's Bess had seven pups, and he promised me one. The sun was shining every day, and Delaney told me not to call him mister anymore. He drove me to County Line—we walked right in a joint, stood at the bar, ordered a beer—just as big as you please. He kidded the waitress about her shaker, she was real pretty, and Delaney had everybody in there laughing."

"That sumbitch is cool, he's plain cool."

"That's when it really started, in a way, because the waitress looked at me and winked to Delaney. She said, 'Tom, maybe your cousin would like to visit Madame Pow Wow. She's camped her trailer out back—she tells some sexy fortunes. Told me one I still can't believe! Can't wait for it to come true.'"

"I've heard about her, Ira."

"Well—Delaney fairly chug-a-lugged his beer and had me drinking mine as fast as I could. His eyes were popping and flashing like the

Fourth of July fireworks show, and he said, 'Drink up, boy!' Let's get your young fortune told!' I drank as fast as I could, and by the time you could say Jack Robinson we were out back, standing at the steps of a white trailer with red trim, and Delaney was pounding on the door, saying, 'Open up here, quick!' The girl opened the door and old Delaney whipped a five-spot on her and pushed me inside. He followed me and sat on a chair right by the door while she took my hand and led me through some silk draperies toward the far end of the trailer. The beer had me going, and everything in there seemed too bright. There were a lot of red and yellow and blue silk kerchiefs hanging from the ceiling, and there was a little baby sleeping in a crib. At the back of the trailer there were two cane-bottomed chairs facing a small table. She pushed me toward a chair and sat me down. I couldn't see Delaney, but I could feel that he was watching me. She sat in the other chair and spread her thin hands on the table. She had long black hair and black eyes and bright red lipstick. She wore a leather band around her head with a red feather sticking up Indian style in the back, and she had a white blouse, like that new civics teacher wore last year, that was cut so low in front I could see down between her tits when she leaned forward. 'Give me your hands.' She took my hands, pressed them together in prayer position, and then cupped them between her hands. She said, 'Let's see what is in here,' hooked her dark little thumbs around my knuckles, and pulled my hands apart, like you would open a book. I was looking at her tits, man, because she was really leaning forward. 'I see your future in here. You are a young man and you must listen carefully and remember your future. It is your true future. There are three black women in your future. Not Negroes, rather, black as I am black—black hair, dark skin. The first is younger than you, and you already know her—she will be your lover.' I didn't know it then, but I found out she was talking about Melissa."

"Wowee—" Stanley opened more cans of beer.

"Madame Pow Wow closed her eyes for a minute, resting. 'And the second one is living in the West, she is a nurse, I think. And the third one is younger, and she is prettier than any of the others.' She put her hands on the table and straightened her back, looking at something over my head. I looked at her small waist, clinched tight with a black elastic belt. I wanted to just put my hands around her waist. 'But you will not be happy with her,' she said. Then she took my hands separately and touched my hands to the tips of her breasts. 'But you must look at her nipples, here, and see that they are white, for if they are dark, she has had a baby and is not the right woman for you. If she doesn't let you see the nipples when you ask, she's not the right woman for you.' I pressed with my fingers but she pulled back. 'No, I am not one of your black women. I am your fortune-teller, and I have told your true future. Now, go away with your friend.' "

Stanley interrupted, "Ira—you shoulda just grabbed onto her, that's what she wanted you to do, I bet. Old Delaney wanted to watch you get it with her—I've heard tales about that Indian fortune-teller!"

"No." Ira ignored, or didn't hear, Stanley's remark. He pursued his thoughts as if he was learning for himself what happened that graduation summer. He drank beer and continued, "My Aunt Essie said that since I was the only King left in the world, she was going to will her farm to me. Not that I expected her to die, not that I thought it was my land, I just walked up Mill Creek the day after graduation.

"I guess I walked about a mile in the creek, then got out to let my feet dry. I put on my lace-boots and started to come home. I'd always been afraid to go any further up the creek, where it gets darker and tall trees close over it, like a tunnel. I knew that some Kings had been killed up there—a long time ago. It felt spooky, kind of fun. I decided to go on, but I wished I'd brought my .22 rifle."

He paused to drink beer. "The creek got so narrow I could jump it in places. Then, slowly, I noticed a low roar. It got louder as I went on. I thought it might be a swarm of wild bees, but soon it was too loud for bees. The sound never changed in tone, and I felt that it was very close, then very distant. Sometimes the wind carried it out of hearing, and as I stood still it came back again, louder than before, more of a hum, picking up the sound of my heartbeat. It was like the sound of The Falls—when I thought of The Falls it scared the hell out of me, because I realized that it was the sound of water. I ran from the creek bed to higher ground, then I walked toward the sound, parallel to the creek. It was louder when I entered a pine thicket. Trees tangled overhead and cut off the sun. I broke through into a clearing and looked down a slight hill at the creek. There was a great rush of white water over a pile of sticks in the stream. They seemed to be tossed in the creek at random, but they held the water back. They looked as if they were axe-cut. I realized that it was a beaver dam.

"Water flowed through the dam as well as over it. I tested it with my foot and it was steady. I walked out onto it, bending over to balance with my hands. Then I tried to pull out one of the sticks. It was wedged in tight, so I tried another. The second one slipped a bit and broke free. I threw it on the bank, thinking I'd take it home to show Pa and Delaney. I was pulling on another stick when I heard Melissa scream, 'You bastard!' It echoed in the trees. I looked all around but couldn't see her because of the trees. I stared into the thick bushes and canes. I yelled, 'What do you mean?' and she yelled, 'You're tearing down the beavers' dam—they'll have to work all night to build it back!'

"Then I saw her over on the far bank. She was reflected in the pool of still water above the dam, and I remembered her from school, the girl we used to call Palmolive because she was so dark. We joked she needed soap. I could tell by the way she was breathing that she was really mad. I stumbled across the pile of willow sticks, my weight pressing them down in places so that the cold water came in the tops of my lace-boots, knowing that I hadn't come up the creek looking for her, but knowing at the same time that she was the black woman the fortune-teller was talking about. As soon as I could, I grabbed a tree limb and pulled myself up on the bank. She hadn't moved an inch. I dried my hands on my trousers and told her that I wasn't tearing down the beavers' dam. I saw that her hair is long and pretty—she's got a nice shape, kind of thin, but still she's got curves—she's filled out since she quit school. I said all I wanted was to see the beavers, and I asked if she'd ever seen them. She answered me, 'Oh, yes. Lots of times. But you'll never see them. They're not meant to be seen by you. Not even if you set a steel trap, because a beaver would rather chew off his leg to get out of a steel trap than let you see him!'

"I made three trips back to the beaver dam, hoping to see her again. I took my hand axe and cut a clearing through the canes, between a shady knoll and the pool. On the sandy knoll I used the canes to weave a hideout, a beaver blind, making a lot of noise so she'd hear me. The fourth time I went up there I could feel that Melissa had been there. Her presence was strong in the beaver blind."

Stanley cleared his throat. "Very cozy, Ira. Just like a motel. Cozy little playhouse."

"Yes. Well, to make a long story longer, she was right about the beavers. I never saw one. But I saw lots of her."

"I'll bet you saw *all* of her!"

"She reminded me of that special rabbit old Bess treed in a cat-face gum and we smoked it out and skinned it and roasted it over our campfire, Stanley. I can always remember when we pulled it from the scorched hole in the dry wood. It was singed and wild-eyed afraid, soft and scared. And I often felt bad about killing it, ashamed."

Stanley made a face. "You left out the best part. What happened the first time. What was it like?"

"It happened. But it's ended now."

"Ended?" Thoughtful James asked.

"It was like killing a rabbit. You want to do it real bad, and it feels good for a few minutes, but then when it's over you feel bad about it and wish you'd left it alone. But the next day, or a couple of days later, you're wanting to do it again. You feel dirty, but you keep on doing it."

"Well, if that's all there is to it, I do believe I'll just go up the Mill Creek and lay around that beaver blind myself. When are you leaving town, Night Rider? Me and James just might go together. We might try it. They's two gals out there."

Ira didn't seem to mind. He said, "There're really three, if you count the baby. Just don't mention my name. Don't say *I* sent you. I was up there today and told her good-bye. I hate it that this secret got out. I wish somebody nice would marry her and have a happy life. I can't."

CHAPTER 5

THE NEXT MORNING, FOLLOWING HIS COUNCIL WITH JAMES AND Stanley, Ira told his parents that he was leaving Tongs. His mother cried. His father gave him twenty dollars, saying that in a year's time the world would have changed, "More than you can imagine, Son." He told Ira that if he wanted to work in the store he could. He said, "But this is my trade, Son. It's all I can help you with. It's all I know. We can make a living at it, in a year or so. Sales are down, but times will change."

Ira called for Nathan's faded blue Chevrolet with TAXI hand-lettered on its doors to come and take him to the Trailways Bus Station in Beauville. He was sad, yet he was at the same time excited.

* * *

On the afternoon of that same day, Stanley and his cousin from Mize were both killed on the Okatoma River bridge.

Stanley was working at Pittman's station that noon, when his cousin rode up on his new, second-hand, fifth-generation Indian motorcycle. The Mize people were glad to be rid of him. For a week after he bought it from a widow woman, his brother had pulled him through Mize with his pickup while he popped the clutch and blew out smoke and kicked up gravel, for a few heart-stopping beats until the old Indian gasped and died. Then his brother would pull him again and he would pop the clutch again and kick up more gravel. Finally, he got the carburetor adjusted and learned the gearshift well enough to ride the Indian. With a paintbrush and a can of dime store enamel he painted the motorcycle Chinese red. He painted the handlebars, the tires, and the seat. After drying overnight, parts of it were still tacky when he rode it to Tongs.

Stanley loved the machine. He checked the gas and kicked the tires. He took to it like a duck to water. When Mr. Pittman came to relieve Stanley for lunch they rode away with Stanley on the buddy seat. They purred across the bridge and up the steep hill into Tongs, stopping at the Elite Cafe where Stanley tried to impress his girl, Midge Farley, the waitress. Later, by rote, like a witness in a trial, she said they each ate two hamburgers.

Then they made a quick run back across the Tongs Bridge at Shiloh Crossing. The red Indian flashed onto the bridge, urged on by Stanley's cousin's wrist grown strong with pride, confidence, and speed. The silver-painted iron girders vibrated with the roar as they screamed across the bridge and down the hot asphalt road to the Beauville Highway intersection, where they stopped and turned around. They were heading back to Tongs, running flat out, hugging the center line. Again they flashed onto the bridge, and the silver girders barked an echo when the front tire blew. The oil-hot machine slammed into the wooden bridge railing, flipped, and catapulted them both over the railing, onto the gravel shoals of Shiloh Crossing, eighty feet below.

❂   ❂   ❂

Ira travelled light, living on milk shakes and hamburgers. From Beauville he rode the bus by the authority of an accordion-folded ticket that he kept snugly buttoned in his back pocket, behind his billfold. It took him to Memphis, Fort Smith, and then Oklahoma City. When he got to Oklahoma City he had twelve dollars in his billfold, and he wondered what Delaney would do in his situation, for Delaney was Odysseus to the boys of Tongs, Mississippi, but none of the Delaney things worked for Ira. He was wearing a cotton shirt and Levis, not a fine suit, and he could imagine how ridiculous he would have looked, smoking a cigar or strutting into a barbershop for a shampoo.

The hamburgers agreed with him, for he lived on hamburgers. He sent his mother a postcard saying that he was looking for a job, and a place to stay. He mailed the card from the bus station and then walked the streets, looking for a rooming house. Eight blocks from the bus station he found a white two-story frame house with a big ROOM-AND-BOARD sign in front. Mrs. Parsons owned the house, and she let Ira move in for just two dollars. She gave him a close visual examination, the newspaper classified pages, and she showed him the hall telephone. He found a job that first evening, after supper.

Ira answered the ad of Mr. Willard Ford who owned and operated the Willard Ford Carpet Service, which consisted of Willard's panel truck with SAVE! SAVE! SAVE! painted on the back and Willard's garage that was filled with scraps of carpet bought from railway salvage and factory close-outs. He installed and cleaned carpets, and his specialty was a roach and flea treatment that he mixed from Gulf Spray and denatured alcohol. He put the spray down before the new carpet was installed.

He told every prospective customer about that special. Then, on an excuse, he'd go out to his truck and Ira was supposed to say, "Boy, I sure hope you take the bug-proofing, because that's my job and I do it real good. I put it down double-thick and let it dry before we lay the pad. That way, no bug can stand to be on the fine new carpet, never. Over the years the floor just keeps on fighting bugs."

"How much does it cost?" was the usual question.

"Fifteen dollars, but sometimes Mr. Ford will do it for ten."

Willard Ford always did it for ten dollars, and Ira's spiel got most of the jobs. Willard Ford was so pleased with Ira that he took him to get his driver's license, gave him a raise, and let him drive the panel truck. Business was good. Ira always had money. He didn't know much about banks, so he changed his extra money into larger bills that wouldn't make a big wad, putting them in the zippered compartment in the back of his billfold.

A letter came for Ira on the fifth day that he lived in Oklahoma

City. James Goff wrote him about the motorcycle wreck. He included a poem that he'd written for Stanley Rawls. The last four lines were:

> *Motorcycle meteor screamed*
> *an end to double dreams—*
> *Mill Creek beavers are left,*
> *alone, all alone.*

Ira's room at Mrs. Parsons' was upstairs, and on the wide stairs he often met a nurse who lived at the end of the upstairs hallway in the room nearest the bath. Mrs. Parsons told Ira that although it was against the fire code, she allowed the nurse to keep a hot plate in her room. She told him that when the nurse came to live there she didn't even have two dollars, winking, because she could see that he'd bought himself new shoes and a sports coat. She told him about the Friday night dances at the YWCA.

The nurse worked irregular hours. Ira smiled and spoke to her when they met on the stairs, or in the hallway. Some mornings she would be leaving for work when he went down to the dining room for breakfast. One morning he met her walking to the bath, her dark hair caught up in a shower cap, her long neck tilting her chin up, and her shoulder soft against the red bathrobe. She looked at his eyes and closed the flap of her robe. He avoided her eyes, and they passed in the narrow hallway.

Although Mrs. Parsons was a good cook, the nurse always ate out, or in her room. Then there was a stretch of several days when Ira didn't see her in uniform. She wore street clothes, and then she came to meals in the dining room.

One afternoon, three days after she started coming to meals, she waited for him at the top of the stairs, after supper. She smiled and asked him if he'd like a cup of coffee.

Nurse Sarah was twenty-eight. She wore a black hairpiece and flattered herself that you couldn't tell it. She wore it in a tight knot, and under that knot, in her imagination, she kept a tin fruit-cake box filled with loose beads. When she put a strand of beads in the tin box, she would fasten the clasp, hold the strand over the box with the clasp pinched between the thumb and forefinger of her left hand, and snip the thread with scissors so that the free beads cascaded, if they were graduated, from large to small into the tin box. Then, when she was sitting beside a signal bell or buzzer in some dark hallway or anteroom or just off in a corner listening for the rustle of sheets and death rattle, she would pass her time mentally restringing those beads. She kept the threads and clasps in the bead box also, wound around an old theatre program of Chekhov's *Seagull*. Sometimes she would get a whole strand selected from the box and restrung, even if they were graduated, only to find that there was no slack in the string to tie the knot. Sometimes she strung the costume beads as an exercise for reading people's thoughts, and if anyone happened upon her when she was stringing beads she could easily get the loose beads, the theatre program, and even the scissors all back in the tin box and close the round lid and hide it away under the hair knot without being observed.

Her room was decorated with Mexican souvenirs. She had a bull-fighting poster and a tourists' sombrero tacked on one wall and a loop of red peppers around a pair of painted gourd maracas tied from a nail on another wall. The bedspread was bright red—it matched her bathrobe—and the small goat-hair rug beside her bed was rainbow striped. Sure enough, there was an electric hot plate on the bureau. She had a coffeepot on the hot plate.

"Well sit down, there, at the table. My name is Sarah."

"I'm glad to meet you. My name is Ira King."

"Ira King, no kidding? Do you like my room, Mr. King?"

"Sure. It's fine. Are you Mexican?"

"Oh, heavens no. This is just my collection." She turned up the hot plate to heat the coffee and took cups from the top bureau drawer. She set the table with paper napkins, putting a small jelly glass beside each cup. Telling Ira that in Spanish countries the people drink wine with their coffee, she filled the glasses from a Thunderbird bottle that she also kept in the top bureau drawer.

"Mexico is the closest I even got to Spain. At one time in my life I was more ambitious. I thought of myself as a scholar, taught myself Spanish. Now I buy the Mexican newspapers and read them for practice. Do you read much?"

"Oh, yes, I read a lot."

"Good. It's nice to read. I can read while I work. Doesn't that sound like a dandy job? It may seem strange to someone young like you, but I take jobs with the very sick. Constant care, they call it. Sometimes it's grim, but there is, especially at night, a peaceful time to read. When it's dark and quiet outside and one is waiting, oh, say! Don't let's talk about that. Do you like the wine?"

"Sure. I haven't seen you in uniform lately. He paused, awkwardly. "Sarah, did you change jobs?"

"No. My patient moved. I'm taking a short vacation. I can get another job as soon as I inquire at the hospital, but I want to rest awhile. I go to movies quite a lot. Tell me something about yourself. Where do you come from?"

"I'm from Mississippi, been here about three months. I'm saving up a bankroll to go to college."

"That's exciting! What will you study?"

"I'm not sure. History or something, anything but be a clothing store owner."

"Anything but?"

"Yes, my father owns the King's Store in Tongs. A dry goods store. I'd hate to be a clothing merchant or a doctor."

"Well, there are many other professions." She refilled the jelly glasses. "I've taken up this profession late, after botching several others."

"Somebody has to do it, I guess."

"No. Nobody does a particular job because 'somebody has to do it.' Don't make that mistake. People work in medicine because something about it fascinates them. Perhaps it's their own fear of death, or the ritual of self-denial, or the opulence of the big money they expect to get when they finally make it. Perhaps it's a depravity. I even worked in the insane asylum and enjoyed that."

"Where? Here in Oklahoma?" he asked too quickly.

"Yes, why?"

"Because I have a friend, my cousin, in one of them. In Mississippi."

"Oh, I'm sorry."

"Don't be. He's been there several times for treatment. The last time they just said they'd have to keep him for good. He probably doesn't mind." Ira looked down at his wineglass.

"Did you miss him?"

"Sure, he was my cousin. He was big and old and crazy."

"Tell me about him." The nurse brought the Thunderbird and an ashtray from her bureau. She got a package of cigarettes from her purse and graciously offered one to Ira, but he didn't smoke. He watched her take one from the pack, selecting it as if it were very important that she get exactly the right cigarette. He watched her strike the match and bring the flaming match to meet the tip of the cigarette just as the mouthpiece filter met her dark lips which pursed as she inhaled. The blue twist of smoke from the dying match curled over the brim of her little tin sombrero ashtray. He told her that Cassfield had epileptic fits, and that when he had a fit he would fall down and hit his head, and he told her how Cass liked to smoke his pipe and stare into the fireplace, and how sometimes he fell forward into the fireplace, hitting his head on the hearth. He told her that his Aunt Essie cut Cassfield's hair with hand clippers; she kept it so short you could see the bumps all over his head which matched the scars on his face and chin. Sarah refilled the jelly wineglasses, and Ira warmed to the memory of a snake hunt, talking with his wine-thick tongue the dialect of Chambers County.

"They said that he was thirty years old, but he was the only grown folks that I liked to play with. Cass knew how to have fun. The best thing about him was the way he could cuss. Now, I've heard some pretty good cussin', but I never heard anybody cuss as good as Cassfield. The reason he could cuss so good was that he didn't know what it was that he was saying. I think he knew words by the sound that people talked with. Sometimes he would cuss his dog when he was petting it. He would pet the dog hard, or stick out one finger like he was pointing at something and just poke the dog. But the dog understood. It would just lay there with its mouth open and its tongue lolled out. Cassfield would grin at the dog and the dog would grin at Cassfield. When he cussed like that he would talk low and easy. He always used the same words, but they came out all jumbled up, so that they didn't make good sense."

Nurse Sarah smiled at Ira.

"You never heard anybody could cuss like Cassfield. He would cuss anything under the sun. His pocket knife, the preacher, the mules—he'd cuss anything. If somebody drove down the road in front of his house, and my Aunt Essie said, 'There goes Son Barlow,' he would grin and say, 'There goes Son Barlow sumbitch, goddamn!'

"We played together all the time. He showed me how to do all kinds of good things that most people don't ever think about doing, like sometimes we would go down to the creek and catch snakes. We'd catch anything that moved. We'd trap fish, birds—anything."

Sarah listened, interested.

"But I just taught him one trick. Most things, like climbing trees, or swimming, Cassfield couldn't do. He couldn't skip a rock on the water. At school I learned how to jerk the rings off pop bottles. You know, you can take two bottles and put them together and pull them apart real sharp and the top ring, right where the cap fits on, will snap off one. When I showed Cassfield the trick, he could do it better than you ever saw. He had real strong hands and wrists. One day we pulled the rings off all the bottles at his house so we went to get some more. There were some wooden cases of empty bottles stacked behind Dale Pittman's service station near Cassfield's house.

"It was hot and the man in the station couldn't see out back, he was listening to baseball on the radio. I could carry one case of Coke bottles, which are the best because you can hold them tight in your hand. Cass didn't know, so he got all different kinds. He got RCs and Big Oranges and Pepsi-Colas, mostly. He got three cases. We took them down under the Okatoma River Bridge and pulled rings for hours. We strung the glass rings on haywire and hung them in pine tops. I wanted to burn the wooden cases and throw the bottles in the Okatoma, but Cass took them all back to the station. He didn't know that the bottles weren't any good with the rings pulled off.

"It was almost dark when we got to the store and Mr. Pittman heard us stacking the cases. He hadn't owned the station long, and he didn't know who we were. He came out of the station and hollered at us, 'You tramps put those bottles back!' He thought we were *taking* them. 'I know you. You'll steal empties tonight and try to sell them back to me in the morning!' He kept on hollering so loud that he scared Cassfield, me too. Cass just started cussin' him. He cussed him real good. Real crazy. Then Mr. Pittman picked up a stick of stovewood from a stacked pile of stovewood that he had there by the station and hit Cass a glancing blow on the head. It split one of the old scars on Cass's eyebrow and blood ran down his eye and alongside his nose. Cass grabbed him a stick off that pile of stovewood and started yelling and swinging it around his head like a wild Comanche. He ran at Mr. Pittman and knocked him down. Knocked him cold.

"The next day two men came and took Cass to the state hospital at Whitfield. He didn't care. He just cussed the sumbitch car they took him in, the sumbitch damn porch, and the sumbitch stump in the yard and his sumbitch dog, and everything."

Ira didn't look at the nurse while he told about his cousin.

When he finished the story he glanced at her face. She was tense, concentrating, her eyes fixed on the smoke rising from the tin sombrero. Ira stared at it also. Then she grabbed her purse and fumbled the latch. She took two dollar bills from it and crushed them into Ira's hand, saying, "We have finished our coffee and our wine. There is a liquor store on Napp Street. Do you know where it is?"

"Yes."

"While I fix some more coffee, would you skip over there and buy another bottle of wine? Will they sell it to you?"

"Sure. I have an ID."

"You aren't twenty-one?"

"No. But Willard Ford, my boss, fixed it for me. It says I'm twenty-one."

"Good. Let's finish this glass before you leave. I have something to tell you. I like to think of you as a college boy. I'd like to help you get started in college, soon, get you started reading something good, instead of those dreadful magazines I see you sneaking into your room. You could read good novels. A college boy taught me to read good books, and I can teach you." She drank from her glass. "I was married to a nice fellow, a big fellow, Pill, who drove a cattle truck to Kansas. He used to buy cows here and pay for them with hot checks, then haul them up to Kansas and sell them in time to cover his checks. He liked to tease me about dipping his wick in KC— that's probably what caused it. The college boy was working a summer in the hospital and he asked me if I'd like a book, or else I asked him if he had anything to read, I don't remember. Anyway, he gave me a book and after I finished it we talked about it. That week

Pill was in KC, and I phoned the college boy to bring me some new books. Sauterne was mentioned in the book I'd just finished, so I got a bottle of Sauterne and read about it in the encyclopedia. When he got to my house, I had a fancy picnic basket packed with fruit and cheese and olive-and-anchovy sandwiches. I showed him the basket and the bottle of Sauterne, pointing to a page in the novel. He laughed. He took some cold 7-UPs from the refrigerator, dumped them in the sink, and refilled the chilled bottles with Sauterne. He snapped the caps back on and put them in the basket so that they couldn't turn over. I smiled, and he laughed again. We took the basket to a city park and sat on the grass, between the goldfish pool and two gay sales clerks.

"Pill kept running to KC, and I kept reading that college boy's books, and you, Jackie Horner, you sat in a corner, and you're waiting for me to tell you something spicy, but I shan't. Let's go now, you and I, no, you go, I'll wait here."

As he closed the door Nurse Sarah turned to the hot plate. She hefted the aluminum coffeepot and knew that it was half full. Then she started to string the beads. She did a string to find out what Ira was thinking just then, and, smiling at his lust, she did another string of black plastic octangular beads which represented the big fellow, Pill. Then she stripped them all back into her bead box.

It took Ira fifteen minutes to get back with the wine. He was surprised when he returned to find the nurse almost asleep in her chair, a lighted cigarette in the ashtray. She raised her face when he entered and said, "Well, Little Jackie Horner, just pour us another cup of coffee and another sip of wine."

"If it's all the same to you. I'll have mine without coffee."

"Sure, Jackie Horner, sure." He poured her a cup of coffee and filled her glass from the new bottle, watching the coffee steam.

She smiled at him. "Have you ever had a girl, Jackie Horner?"

"Well, sure. Back home."

She closed her eyes and he watched the coffee get cold, and he watched a miniature oil slick form on top of the cold coffee, remembering that he'd read how Ben Franklin kept oil in his screw-top walking cane, remembering that he'd read how, before the storm, they pour oil on the coastal bay to keep down the waves.

"Tell me about it."

"There's not much to tell."

"Oh, Jackie Horner, there is. There always is something to tell. Don't be embarrassed, I'm a nurse."

"Well . . . she was a nice girl. She was Italian—they didn't have much money. My folks didn't want me to marry her. I didn't want to marry her. I wanted to go to the university."

"Was she your age?"

"I guess I was two years older—I remember her first from the third grade."

"Did she know how to make love?"

"Yes, I guess she did."

"Was she pretty?"

"Yes. She had dark hair and brown eyes."

"Did she have a nice figure?"

"Average, I guess. Tell me some more about Pill."

"Screw him! I'll tell you about life." She lit a fresh cigarette and refilled her wineglass. She started stringing beads, watching the smoke curl up from her cigarette, and she didn't speak for ten minutes.

Ira sat still with his empty glass. His eyes were burning, and he knew that it was very late. The nurse sat still. She started a new string of beads, and that activity put a childlike smile on her lips. Because of the wine, she did a baroque pattern, spacing the larger beads with seed pearls. When she had finished she pinched the tips of the string together, but they were too short to tie off. Ira, red-eyed and stiff, mumbled his appreciation for the coffee and wine, but she seemed to be sleeping with her eyes open. He poured part of her cold coffee into the smouldering sombrero, thinking that it resembled a volcano.

He turned off the hot plate, then unplugged it, for he knew that to unplug it without turning it off would cause an unpleasant flash and snap of electricity, and he didn't want that. He stepped lightly toward the door.

She said softly, without looking up, "Ira, keep to the right in the hallway. There's a loose board on the left side, and if anyone hears it squeak, they'll talk about me at breakfast."

"OK. Good-night." He turned the doorknob softly.

"Good-night. Don't lock your door, Ira. It's dangerous—in case of fire. Women have to lock their doors, but a young man is safe."

"I guess you're right. I'll leave my door open."

"And watch out for the loose board."

It was late and quiet. No cars or trucks passed. A slight wind brushed the outstretched fingertips of a dry oak limb against his window screen. He sat on his bed and watched the reflected glow of the city through the bare oak tree and listened for her door to close softly, the click of the bolt, and her dark feet to come gliding softly, like pictures, down the hallway.

❀   ❀   ❀

That December Ira sought out the Federal Post Office and followed the signs to the army recruiter's office. He and Willard Ford had talked about it often, and they decided that it was just a matter of time until he'd be drafted, for Korea was in the headlines every day, over five thousand men had been killed in the war. He wrote a letter to his mother while he waited to see the recruiting sergeant, and he smiled at a hand-lettered sign on the sergeant's desk which read, "HAD DIARREA? GONOREA? TRY KOREA."

Then he was riding in a green army bus to take his induction physical. He looked at the young men on the bus who were all his age, and Ira wondered if he would like the army. He wondered if they'd ever make him a sergeant, if there were still WACs in the army, if the food was really so bad—he turned the pages of the handful of bright pamphlets that the recruiting sergeant had given him. Cook or baker, no. Radar school—electronics, no. Ira overheard a fellow across the aisle tell his companion that the combat arms were the most interesting; they were: infantry, "just walk your ass off," armor, "tanks—hot in the summer, cold in winter," and artillery, "the big guns, you don't have to walk, lots of excitement." So Ira King, moved by the overheard comments of a stranger, put down "artillery" for his choice.

CHAPTER 6

THE BOYS WHO STOPPED AT PITTMAN'S STATION FOR GAS ON SEPTEMBER first, Melissa's birthday, got from Stanley the gossip about Ira King and Mr. Natale's girl, but they got the first-edition error. When they learned that Ira King, who'd been voted "most likely to succeed," had been caught fooling around with a Natale girl, an Italian, they assumed that it was Natale's oldest daughter, Anna. Therefore, in the weeks following Ira's departure from Tongs, Anna Natale started receiving callers. But the callers didn't go directly to the house and ask for her. They prowled the farm, like foxes, looking for a sight of her. Mike found three of them, Fred Farley, T. J. Pittman, and Paul Jacobs, behind the barn, smoking cigarettes and hoping that Anna would chance their way. He asked them what they wanted, and they, shamefaced and mumbling, said they'd come to see Anna. Mike thought he understood. Remembering how hard it is for a young man to walk up to a girl's house and knock on the door, he gathered the three boys together and headed them up to the house and into the big living room, telling his wife to make coffee.

While the coffee gurgled in the pot the boys and Mike Natale smoked cigarettes. They talked about the cotton and they talked about the corn of the season past, and they remarked that there had been an unusual number of snakes that year. Then Anna came into the living room to meet them. She was the plainest of Natale's daughters, but she wasn't homely. Her dark hair and skin made her teeth white, and she was breasty, a feature which appealed to the boys, but she didn't have Melissa's fine features and quiet certitude. Those boys didn't even see Melissa, for she stayed in the back room, knowing the reason they'd come to the Natale farm. Boys had never come before, except Ira King, who walked up the creek, following the water, not consciously looking for a Natale girl. She listened, through the pine wall, to their awkward conversations about farming and snakes, for she knew that Ira King had left Tongs, and she knew that his leaving Tongs had made her notorious, but she didn't dislike Ira for that. She resolved to wait. She believed that he would return to Tongs. It might take a month, two months, a year even, but she believed he would return. She thought about his having other girls, but that didn't trouble her mind.

Ira had made her no promises, but she had his chrome-clipped leather purse filled with two-dollar bills and a jumble of quarters, dimes, and halves. She thought he'd come back for that, and she thought he'd come back for her.

Since none of the boys were willing to quitclaim, their competition made Anna prettier, and it followed that in three months she married one of them, Paul Jacobs, who drove the ambulance for the Beauville Funeral Home. Paul Jacobs and Ira King weren't friends when they were in school. They both remembered their fathers' tales of old-time knife fights between Kings and Jacobses. One time a Jacobs boy had been cut—one time a King.

After his marriage to Anna Natale, Paul continued to believe, as they all had, that it was Anna whom Ira had been seeing, and after his marriage he couldn't forget the notion that Ira had slept with his wife. Sometimes he could go three days without thinking about it, but always, at least by the fourth day, the thought came into his head, and it made him hate Ira King. He was glad that Ira had left Tongs. He hoped that he never came back.

When Paul married Anna he went into a farming partnership with Mike Natale. It was a Wednesday afternoon that he'd stopped at the Natale farm and parked his ambulance by the field with the radio turned up loud so he could hear any calls and was watching Mike burn a pile of brush when Mike Natale fell dead. Paul wasn't helping Mike, for he was on duty. He wore a clean white short-sleeved shirt, black slacks, a black belt, black socks, and black loafers. They both watched the brush pile catch slowly and then get hot and smoke until flames licked up, three feet high. Then Mike Natale turned to face Paul. He looked surprised. He took one step, and then he fell.

Mike's death settled one mystery around Tongs, for when Paul helped Mrs. Natale read the family papers he found four old term-life insurance policies that Mike had bought since he came to Tongs. They paid off over thirty thousand dollars, and everybody figured that Mr. Natale (they all called him mister after he died) had been unable to buy any land, or even a pickup truck, because of his high insurance premiums, and Gappy said that it wasn't such a bad way to do after all, since what everybody wanted land for was to have something to pass on to their kids, and money was just as good as land, for most kids would sell the land, anyway. They buried Mike Natale in his green suit.

Everyone said that Paul was set for life. He bought the Nathan Edwards farm with its big brick house, and he bought a new car. Mrs. Natale stayed out in the old house by Mill Creek with Melissa and Shirley. Paul explained to her that she and the girls would always be provided for. He promised to bring them three hundred dollars every month just to buy food or dresses, or anything they wanted, and he quit driving the ambulance.

The three remaining Natale women got along well. Melissa stayed pretty and quiet. She helped the baby girl learn to read, and she and her mother taught her to sew. Anna learned to drive the car so that she could take the three of them to Tongs for groceries. She took them to the movies in Beauville on the nights when Paul played poker, and she took them up to her house every week so they could use the new Bendix washer. They enjoyed riding in Paul's nice car and seeing new roads, towns they'd never expected to see, and the fresh, green countryside around Tongs.

Anna joined a home-making club, and she went to a doctor, a dressmaker, and a beauty parlor in Jackson, trying to lose a few pounds and be prettier than Melissa, who wore a man's shirt and jeans, or simple cotton one-piece dresses—often without underwear —kept her own counsel, and grew into a graceful, beautiful woman.

She never seemed to regret Anna's good fortune, nor did she regret being brought back to the unpainted tenant house and let out by the mailbox to walk up the dirt path with her mother and little sister.

Paul speculated in timberland with the Natale money until he owned all of the river bottoms from Tongs south to The Falls. He made money. He bought farmland at "forced sale," craftily, by influencing an heir, so that the other heirs accused him of "splitting the family." Each year he bought a bigger car. People began to say, after a while of his parlaying Natale's insurance money, that he was bright enough to be a state representative, or maybe even lieutenant governor. Perhaps they got that idea from his frequent trips to Jackson, where he claimed to know "big people," where he kept up with state politics, and where he bought all of his clothes in the store that dressed the governor.

In one of his Tongs business deals, Paul suggested to Chuck and Mike Winslow that they buy a new GMC log truck. He told them he'd give them steady work hauling logs out of his newly acquired bottomland. They had no credit, so he signed the note at the National Bank of Beauville so that they could pay for it. They agreed to work for him at thirty dollars a day, them and the truck. It was less money than they could have made with the truck if they'd worked independently, but if they were independent they wouldn't have the truck. At least that's the way they figured it, and they figured and refigured it several times every day. Of course, if they didn't work, they got no money, and when it rained enough to make the bottoms swampy, they couldn't work.

It was cold, unseasonably cold for April. A steady rain had been falling for two weeks, off and on. The log roads in the bottoms were so soggy that the crews couldn't get in to start cutting until a week after the rain stopped. Chuck and Mike waited, making no money, talking about how much water would be on the river after all that rain, thinking about setting out trotlines. Mike wanted a boat so badly that after a few days he managed to convince Chuck they really needed one, couldn't live without one for Sunday fishing later in the spring, when the river calmed down.

"If it warn't for the money I'd of had a boat last year," he mused. "But that seven hundred dollars we got from Mr. Jacobs petered out to two hundred and fifty, plus we don't know when the bottoms will dry up, lately, and we've still got truck payments. Maybe we could make a boat—naw, I seen the one them Lowry boys made. They tarred it and everything, but it still leaked. It was so heavy it took four men to put it on their truck, and when they got it in the water it went where *it* wanted to go instead of where *they* wanted it to go."

"You know how much a boat costs, Chuck? You know how much a blacksmith would charge to run a welding seam four feet long?"

"Oh, about a dollar six bits, two dollars."

"That's what a fishing boat would cost. I saw one last year when I was logging with Bert, in a lake over in Odell County. It was made out of two Ford hoods welded together. They looked like they come off about, uh, about a forty-six Ford; and somebody evened them off at the hinges and welded them together. It made a fine boat."

"A iron boat wouldn't float."

"Sure it'd float. I seen it, tied up at a little fishing dock, floating like a feather. Hell, uh iron skillet will float in a dishpan. Uh iron washpot would float in still water."

"Once it got some water sloshed in it it'd go down like a damn rock."

"If it goes down we ain't lost but two dollars. If it floats we have a boat that won't rot, won't waterlog, and ain't too heavy to get on the truck. Let's drive around the hardtop roads and look at the junkyards for us two Ford hoods."

And they did. One of the hoods that they found was dark blue; the other was black. They had to pay a dollar each for the hoods and three dollars for getting them welded. The blacksmith welded a U-bolt to each end, so they'd have something to "tote it by, or tie a rope to." They intended to paint it, but they were too impatient for the christening to bother with paint. Two hand-carved paddles and a six-foot sash cord completed the rig. They talked about putting in wooden seat boards but decided to just sit on the bottom of the boat. Since the Okatoma was level with its banks, they hauled their boat to a pond north of Tongs for the launching. Of course their family and friends came along.

They lifted it from the truck and ran, one holding the U-bolt handle of each end, to the edge of the pond where they launched it sideways. Mike held the rope while Chuck foot-shoved his end out into the water. The boat floated high and pretty, "like frosting on a cake," their father said.

"Look at it, Mike! Just like a Jersey heifer on that little lead rope. Ain't it purty?"

Chuck cautiously tried the stability of the boat with one foot, then he stepped in.

"Keep to the middle and it won't tip, Son."

He crouched low, holding to the side with his hands, and inched his way to the far end. Then he sat down. Mike pitched him a paddle and stepped more confidently into the shore end of the boat. He sat cross-legged, like a movie Indian, and pushed his paddle against the bank.

A hush fell over the shore-bound folks when the boys flashed their paddles and skimmed to the middle of that little pond. They made a clumsy turn, knocking and scraping the paddles against the metal hull, then they flashed back to the bank, panting.

"Paddle on opposite sides, boys, and dip your paddle in clean and sharp, like an axe hits a stump, then pull straight back and flip it out of the water, clean. Don't let it drag against the side of the boat, and use your forearms and wrists. Boy! I've sure got some smart boys, haven't I! A little practice and they can't be beat."

"That's right, Mr. Winslow, they're sure smart. I'll bet the price of Ford hoods goes sky-high in Chambers County. Everybody'll be making these boats!"

The two took back to the pond, like ducks, turning figure eights. They practiced until it was too dark to see. Then they beached the boat and lifted it up on the back of their log truck. They handled it like a sack of eggs.

"No heavier than a horse collar, is it Chuck?"

"Naw. It's a purty, ain't it? I reckon it don't weigh over thirty pounds."

CHAPTER 7

Tongs's new doctor, Stephen Forsythe, liked his new Ford. He privately called it Influenza, because of the flu epidemic from which he made the money to pay for it. It snuggled into the ruts of dirt roads, or hummed straight as an arrow down the black asphalt highways. He was daydreaming, thinking of ways to expand his practice, thinking about his wife's wanting to get pregnant, thinking about his little hideaway cabin he'd bought from Paul Jacobs. He tuned the radio to a Jackson station, unconsciously caught a moth that fluttered on the dashboard and put it, softly, out the small vent window. He drove across the Tongs Bridge and pulled up at Pittman's station for gasoline.

"Hi, Doc," the gold-toothed attendant said.

"Hello. How about five gallons of ethyl?"

"Sure thing. How's she running?" The attendant patted the hood. "Right at two hundred horses."

"Fine. It runs fine. I don't drive too fast, but I like good, steady power."

"But a doctor has to have a fast car. Has to have a dependable car."

"That's right."

"It's quite a machine," he said, overspilling a teacup of gasoline, returning the hose to the pump. "Wish I had one just like it, only I'd get a red one. You on a call, Doc? I understand you brought another one into the world. Mrs. Funderburk's boy?"

"Yes. Eight-pounder, fine boy. Thanks, Mr. Pittman."

"Sure. Sure thing. Eight-pounder, huh? Nice size for catfish."

The doctor turned in a big, dusty circle and recrossed the Tongs Bridge. Past the bridge he slowed and turned left onto the sandy road which led to his property. He'd told his wife that he was on a call. He felt mean and sneaky, and it was exhilarating. The unpainted, shotgun-style bungalow was built with its axis parallel to sandy Mill Creek. He pulled up close to the east side of the bungalow, between it and the big chinaberry tree. He'd hired two women to clean the house, and they took part of Essie King's things, for he'd told them to leave nothing, and they'd burned what they didn't want. He liked the feel of his new key going into the new lock, and as he turned the key his mind flashed an X ray of the individual tumbler pins, each poised on its own individual spring, machined and polished, engine turned, waiting to be forced up, compressed, so that the locking cylinder could turn and withdraw the bolt. Then, closing the door slowly, he heard the brass locking bolt slam into its niche in the doorframe, and underneath that slam he heard the individual ping of each tumbler spring vibrating from the shock.

The tight, antique house had been almost that quiet when Essie had lived here. She was Ira King's aunt, the tight-lipped widow of a quiet man who kept no chickens because they were "dirty and noisy." Even the pinch of Garrett's Snuff that she dipped was taken in quiet, almost hiding, behind the kitchen door. She'd been a beautiful girl. Her cousin, Delaney, had ached for her, but her pinnacle was never high. There was some noise and laughter when Cassfield was around; for she, more than anybody else, could laugh at him, scold him, tease and puzzle him. And Ira King had been noisy, breaking limbs off the chinaberry tree or baiting Cass into a footrace to the creek.

It was dark inside, because the locking shutters were closed. The doctor's eyes adjusted to the darkness as he stood for a moment with his back to the door. Then he walked toward what had been Essie's kitchen. He passed through the big fireplace room with the scrubbed hearth and black Hessian andirons where Cassfield had smoked his pipe. He didn't know about Cassfield. The ashes had been swept away, and Fred Farley had tacked a piece of screen wire over the chimney top to keep out the bats and swifts.

He found the handle and opened the new door. It turned on smooth, new hinges. He'd painted and decorated the old kitchen to be his study, patterning it after the surgeons' lounge at the hospital in Blueridge where he'd been an intern. There were two brown leather overstuffed chairs, a magazine rack, and a rubber plant. A narrow, well-proportioned shelf above the magazine rack offered pencils, a desk calendar, a magnifying mirror, cigarettes, cigars, and a table lighter. A bright reading lamp hung by its gold cord from the ceiling. He switched it on. There was no open window, because the room simulated one that was nestled deep inside a big-city hospital. It represented that room where he'd first watched a doctor with hairy arms and bloodshot eyes sit back with an unlit cigar and contemplate his red-spotted Oxfords.

The doctor settled into his overstuffed chair and selected a cigar from the shelf. He lit the cigar with the table lighter, scanned a magazine, and took deep puffs. He thought of his wife. She was blonde, blue-eyed, wide-mouthed, full and round. Like many other expectant fathers, he would take his wife to her doctor in Beauville for a prenatal examination. He assured himself that she was having a normal pregnancy. Then his mind wandered. Wouldn't it have been nice to stay at the hospital and specialize? Wouldn't it be interesting to study one specific, instead of every single ailment or accident that could kill or discomfort the human body? Wouldn't it be pleasant to publish articles in the journals, join a country club, and associate with other doctors—instead of being a hermit in Tongs, Mississippi? She was going to have a healthy baby, probably it would be a girl and look like her. He scanned the table of contents for an article to read. He looked at the authors to see if he recognized a name. His name wasn't there, but he imagined that it was, following an article titled, "Can a GP Be Happy in a Small Country Town on Twenty Thousand Per?"

He should have a phone out here for emergencies, he thought, as he got out of his chair to take his walk. He tried to walk a mile or two every day. This day he turned west from the bungalow and followed the clear creek down to where it ran into the Okatoma. He walked under his pecan trees. The crows had their glossy-backed lookout in a nearby pine top where they seesawed on the topmost branch, the apex of the pine tree, and started their raspy caws when the doctor entered the pecan grove. Then, with indolent calmness, they flew north over the doctor's head. He watched them closely, not caring that the crows would steal pecans. When he emerged from the pecan grove he could see the slow S curve of the Okatoma and the mouth of Mill Creek. He stood under a pine, a perpetual Christmas tree, its topmost branches decorated with a loop of glass rings strung on haywire.

He walked out onto the sandbar in the V of his creek and the Okatoma, thinking that it was his property line. The Okatoma was clear, yet when he compared the mass of it to the small flow of the creek it proved to be a shade darker than Mill Creek. He remembered that Gappy had asked him if the river water was safe for the boys to swim in. Gappy had said something about Beauville contaminating the river, something about the funeral home putting blood in the river.

He reckoned that he was about a mile above the Tongs Bridge. He looked into the Okatoma again and saw small fish that he didn't know. They were holding themselves in formation, like fighter planes, against the slow but steady current. They were all about eight inches long and shaped like gars, yet each was a different pastel color. They were blue, green, pink, yellow, and orange. The formation held its position as if it were a set of stringed marionettes, with each toy fish balanced, suspended from a single control bar. He wondered if they were young gars and, if so, why they were different colors. He watched them, noting that they had little snoutlike noses and long powerful streamlined bodies. Then with a single relaxed swift impulse they banked to the left like a squadron of fighter planes, sank, and disappeared into deeper water. He remembered the school chant that the Muncey girls had practiced behind his office while he moved in, while he and the hired truck driver had struggled with his X-ray machine: "Alligator, alligator, alligator gar! Who in the heck do you think we are? Tongs, Tongs, Yea! Yea! YEA! Go! GO! Rah! RAH! RAH!"

He walked back to the bungalow, thinking about the fish, thinking it didn't make sense that they'd be of different colors, then remembering that sheep were sometimes black—most often white, but sometimes black. And thinking, isn't there something in the Bible about a herdsman showing peeled wands to the pregnant cows so that they would have multicolored calves, for the multicolored calves had been promised to him? Then he thought about his wife who was round and pink and happy to be pregnant. Thinking, "Even I, the modern medicine man, can't predict the sex of my child." Speaking softly to himself, "It's a trite thing to say, but I really don't care if it's male or female, just so long as it's intelligent and healthy." Thinking, "Do men with pretty daughters regret their sexuality when bumpy-faced boys in old cars come to take them on dates? Did her father resent me? Are fathers disappointed when their sons copulate with the raw-boned country girls and refuse to stay in school, refuse to join the family business, or whatever?"

Back at his cabin he crossed the porch to unlock the door and check everything inside before going to his office. He switched off the lights and slammed the front door hard, feeling the bolt seat firmly into its hole in the doorframe. From force of habit he pushed against the door to be sure that it was really locked. He got in his new Ford and turned the ignition key. It started smoothly. The motor was tight and well muffled. The springs were stiff and quiet, and the upholstery had a new car smell, slightly tinged by the antiseptic smell of his black bag.

CHAPTER 8

THREE MONTHS BEFORE HE FINISHED HIS HITCH IN THE ARMY, IRA MET Janet Martens. He met her in a bar, and he thought when Ralph brought her to their table that she was the most beautiful girl he'd ever seen. He looked at her, without talking, and drank his beer and told himself that she was the woman, or one of the women, the fortune-teller had told him about, one of the black women before the white woman who was to be his true love. Janet told him that although she had lived on a reservation and had gone to the reservation school, she was not a full-blood Indian. But she chose to be Indian.

Janet became his steady, and then she told him of her plans to buy a new mobile home. She worked in Lawton, in a loan company, and she saved her money. During those last three months in Oklahoma, Ira got a week's leave. They took a bus trip to Dallas, where they stayed, as Mr. and Mrs. Parmer, in a twenty-seven-dollar room on the twenty-first floor of the Hotel Adolphus. In the afternoons they went to first-run movies, and they found the public library. Ira read books about Indians. In the evenings, they ate at restaurants that they both thought were unbelievably elegant. After dinner they drank in a nice bar on Elm Street. It was plush and quiet. It had a big, clear television set mounted on the wall.

Ira spent a lot of money on that trip, and they argued about that on the way back to Oklahoma City—after the money was spent.

When they got to Fort Sill, he gave Janet five hundred dollars to help with the down payment on her mobile home.

She bought an Evening Glow mobile home that was twelve feet wide and sixty feet long. It was carpeted and fully furnished, with three bedrooms. But she refused to marry Ira when he asked her, four days before his discharge from the army.

* * *

On the day of his discharge, Ira cleared the supply room and picked up his medical records. Then he walked to the PX Center to buy, before he surrendered his ID card, two bottles of tax-free Scotch for himself and two cartons of tax-free cigarettes for Janet.

Back in the orderly room, the company clerk, a new draftee, a college man, looked at Ira admiringly. "God! I envy you. What are you going to do now, Ira?"

"I guess I might go to college, somewhere. You went to college, didn't you?"

"Yeah. A hell of a lot of good it did me."

"You got a soft job, behind that typewriter. Besides, you won't be in the army forever," Ira replied.

"No. Just twenty months, three weeks, two days, and six hours. Plus or minus a few minutes. I can't keep up with the minutes."

"Yeah," Ira said. He walked away from the clerk's desk. "It's sweet," he mused, "no more uniforms, no more reveille at five-thirty A.M., no more inspections, no more physical training drills." He thought that he'd probably not miss the army.

After the first sergeant signed him out, Ira went to his barracks and packed his Scotch, his G.I. underwear, and black army low-quarter socks, twenty pairs of them, in his new civilian suitcase. He wrapped Janet's cigarettes in brown paper and put his civilian shirts and slacks and white underwear in the old suitcase that had belonged to her. It was the one she'd taken to Dallas.

At the finance office they paid him for his unused leave time and travel pay to Oklahoma City, his point of induction. It made a comfortable bulge of twenties that he folded and pinned inside his sports jacket. He pinned the money with a big safety pin from the post laundry. Then Ira carried his own bags to the PX Center, where the taxi drivers could tell from his looks, from his bearing, that he was leaving the army. One of them grabbed his suitcases and threw them in his open trunk.

"Downtown?"

"I wanted to get a sandwich first, in the snack shop."

"Yeah, sure. I'll wait."

It was a slack time of day for taxis.

Ira started into the snack shop, thinking he'd better get something on his stomach before he met her, because he was light-headed, and he knew that talking with her would make him nervous, but he remembered, then, the little sign on the cash register in the snack shop, PATRONS NOT IN UNIFORM MUST PRESENT MILITARY IDENTIFICATION FOR EACH PURCHASE, so he turned back to the taxi. "What the hell, no need in waiting. Take me to the bus station. Downtown."

When Janet met him in the grill across from the bus station, Ira had no appetite. He smiled at her and told himself that he should have eaten something back at the post, because he was nervous and knew that his stomach would growl, but he also knew that he couldn't eat, so he ordered a beer and watched her watch the people who passed behind the reversed ꟻꟼIꓤ⅁ sign painted on the front window.

"You think you want to leave Oklahoma, OK. Why you going to Fort Worth?" she asked.

"Let's say, I wouldn't pick Oklahoma for my all-time favorite spot on earth. And because I don't want to go back to Mississippi. Because I might go to college on the GI Bill."

"Well, I won't leave Oklahoma. I'd never leave my home. The Indian-fighting army made my people leave the green country of the east, Alabama, Mississippi, Arkansas. Indian names. But I wouldn't leave Oklahoma for ten armies. Send me your address. I'll pay back your five hundred."

"It's not a debt. Will you come to Fort Worth to see me?"

"Sure, I'll come see you. Dallas was fun."

"Will you marry me?"

"Let's don't start it again."

He looked at the microscopic grains of powder on her face and the little dark pores around the sides of her nose. She thought she was being nice, but he could tell that she was anxious for twelve o'clock to come, so that his bus would leave. She hadn't begged him to stay, but she did ask him to send his Fort Worth address when he got settled. She wiped the corners of her mouth on a napkin and said, "Ira, I can't drink a beer. I have to go to work in an hour."

He was thinking, part Indian, dark and pretty, bad habits—I suppose she's more than part Indian, she won't cry when I leave, I suppose. He finished his beer and they crossed the street to the bus station. While he stood in line to buy his ticket she looked at the magazines on the rack. She didn't say anything while they stood in line beside the bus, and when the driver opened the big silver door she just stood there and craned up at him, for he was much taller than she. He wanted to kiss her mouth, but turned instead to the growling flank of the silver bus. He gave the driver his ticket and got on the bus, taking a window seat so that he could look down at her, for she hadn't moved. He knew that she wouldn't cry.

He stretched his legs toward the aisle and told himself that he enjoyed the feeling of leaving her, for he wanted to be apart from her and miss her and think about her. He knew that in his imagination he could make her do the things that were easy and logical and relaxing, for she was impulsive and illogical in the manner of handsome women who know that men admire them. He pushed the idea out of his mind of her staying near the army post and near the soldiers. While he looked down at her, she lit a cigarette. It was one that she had in her purse, for he saw the two unopened cartons still folded in the brown paper, tucked under her arm. Her hand didn't shake when she lit the cigarette, and then he knew she wouldn't cry. He visualized her flat stomach, her small sharp breasts, and her dark nipples. He thought that she was doing a ritual by coming to the bus station with him. She was serious about saying good-bye to him, but she preferred to stay, and she didn't want a husband.

Then a redcap pulled his two suitcases from the dolly and slid them into the baggage compartment. She recognized her old suitcase. She looked up at him, blowing a polite puff of smoke through her small, pursed lips. He looked at his hands and his fingernails, flexing his trigger finger as if he had a .45 in his hand. She waved when the bus revved up, holding both elbows close to her sides, like a fashion model, or a hostage bound by Indians, he thought. Then she started walking toward the terminal door, not waiting for the bus to leave. She stopped at the big glass door and looked back, then she turned her back to the door and leaned against it. It slowly opened from the pressure of her shoulders and hips. She kept watching the bus while she backed out the door. Ira gave her a Jack Benny—with his hand under his chin—it was one of their secret signals, and she smiled.

Then two girls got on the bus and he tried to think about them and look at them and think they were pretty, because he knew that if he didn't think about something besides Janet, he would just keep seeing her crawfish through the glass door.

An old man carried their bags and boxes. He was the father of one of the girls, it seemed, and apparently they weren't sisters, for he helped one and let the other take care of herself. They must have been cousins, or just friends. The old man got off. The blonde had a pretty nose, the profile of her nose and upper lip was clear against the green tinted window across the aisle, for she was standing in the aisle, stuffing a pasteboard box behind the rubber retaining cord of the overhead rack. She had to stand on tiptoes, and that made her figure nice, but her nose and lips, to Ira, were her best points.

A soldier on leave sat in the seat in front of him. He crunched his seat back so that Ira had to move his legs to save his knees. Some other soldiers got on and he was glad that Janet didn't wait. He was glad she didn't cry.

The girls giggled. He decided that since the blonde was pretty the other one would be more possible, and he wished that he had a .45, or better yet, a .38 revolver. It would be hard and smooth and heavy, and the cylinder release would click softly like the lock on an antique jewel box. When the bus pulled away from the station, he picked people on the sidewalk that he could have hit, if the window had been open—if he'd had a pistol. He only picked a few, but he could have hit almost anyone, even with the bus moving, for he was a good shot.

The girls left their seats and started toward the back of the bus. He frowned at them, then he stared at the blonde's face, not caring whether she saw him or not. She blushed and asked the soldier in front of Ira to move so that she and her friend could sit together. The soldier was glad to, and Ira wished she'd asked him, so that he could've refused. They straightened the seat, giving him room to cross his legs again. He looked out the window. The bus passed through the outskirts of town to where the country was flat and ugly, good land for Indians, he thought. There were no pines like in Mississippi, just stunted oaks and knee-high wispy grass. Then the blonde asked the soldier, who had moved across the aisle, to lend her a cigarette until the next stop. She and the other girl then searched their purses for a match and, having none, they asked the boy for a light. He handed them a Zippo, and Ira wished they'd asked him so that he could have told them he didn't smoke, for he didn't like to see them testing their feminine prowess, he resented having to smell their perfume. Real women weren't like them, he thought, Janet didn't play games, she talked with her eyes, and you always knew what she said. Nurse Sarah didn't play games either, even Melissa was more of a woman than these girls, and she was from the backwoods.

They smoked and talked until the next stop, where the soldier got off. He left his pack of cigarettes with them, free, and would have given them the lighter too, if they'd had enough sense to ask for it. The bus started again, and the brunette said she was tired and went up to the front of the bus to their double seat where she curled up, covering her legs with her coat.

It got dark and Ira turned on his reading lamp to see if the blonde was asleep. Her eyes were closed, but he could tell by her mouth that she was awake. After a few minutes she stretched and pressed the button so that the chair would lean back a notch, and he saw her full face. He turned the reading lamp off and sat in the dark, thinking that he could feel the girl watching him through her closed eyelids. He thought about putting his hand over the seat and pinching her neck, or her full cheek, but he decided that she would probably scream, for he would have pinched her hard. He turned his lamp on again, and he could see the pink membrane between her nostrils and the bulge of her eyeballs darting left and right under her closed eyelids as she continued to pretend that she was asleep. He whispered, "bitch," just loud enough for her to hear it, and moved up to the front of the bus, beside the driver, where he watched the oncoming headlights and the dashed white line of the highway, thinking about Janet, remembering the night Delaney took him to that beer joint at County Line and got his fortune told, then remembering Melissa, remembering the olive green in Melissa's cheek, in the corner of her mouth, a mouth fresher and more friendly than Janet's, a mouth that didn't smoke cigarettes, a country girl.

He told himself that he should try to find a job, or else enroll in college—or maybe do both——maybe get a part-time job. He closed his eyes, remembering Janet, again, telling himself that he'd have to check on the procedure for getting the GI Bill. He fell asleep.

Janet took her coffee break with a man, a clerk-teller of her loan office, while Ira slept, somewhere between Oklahoma and Dallas. He paid for their coffee and jelly doughnuts. She chewed slowly, holding the doughnut with two fingers, her little finger crooked, oblivious of her companion, staring past him at the tall chrome coffee urn. Her inattention angered him, for he was an official of the company—a minor official, and he'd interviewed and hired her. He blew the steam from his coffee, and Janet, still looking past him, resolved to repay Ira his five-hundred-dollar loan by visiting him on weekends, if he sent her his address in Fort Worth. She wouldn't tell him, she thought, but she'd clear her debt to Ira King with visits. She figured she was worth a hundred dollars a weekend.

CHAPTER 9

IT WAS TEN-THIRTY, AND BRIGHT LIGHTS WERE FLASHING AROUND THE bus station when Ira arrived in Fort Worth. He put the suitcases in a locker in the bus terminal and hit the streets to find a nice beer joint and a reasonable hotel. It was a good city, it appeared to Ira, the kind of place where Delaney would fit right in. All the streets were paved, some men wore cowboy hats. Nobody looked at him like he was a freak, and they were rather friendly and would speak to him, if he spoke to them first—it was not that much different from Oklahoma City.

Ira got his first job in Fort Worth with a newspaper, in the circulation department. He was impressed with the variety of the men he worked with: three or four were students at the big Baptist seminary in Fort Worth, one was a semiprofessional gangster who made book, one was the mayor of the nearby village of Blue Mound. The City Circulation Manager was reputed to have been, in the thirties, the "advance man" for three whales that were shipped across the country for exhibition on flatcars—he liked to smoke Cuban cigars and say, "I beat it across the country, staying a day ahead of them big sardines. Every day they got a little riper until I had to drop the act in Kansas."

Ira went back to Mississippi in 1953 when his Aunt Essie died, and while he was there, his mother died. There were two Tongs funerals within a week, and dreary Tongs saddened Ira. After the funerals, he got drunk with his father and Delaney. Joe's face was puffy.

Stanley was dead, killed on a motorcycle the same day Ira left Tongs, and James Goff was away teaching school in Gulfport, or Biloxi. Ira asked Midge Farley about Melissa. She told him that Melissa never hardly came to town—that she lived with her mother since her father died.

Delaney had quit working some months before. He spent all his time hanging around Joe, drinking, spending Joe's savings. After a week of indolence, Ira could stomach no more. One evening Joe and Delaney were drinking with Jerry Bradley, an old down-and-out guitar player who was somewhat famous in the local counties. He wore the greasy top of a pair of long-handled underwear for a shirt, blue overalls with one gallus strap hanging loose down his back, and a skinny, Mississippi dress hat. He'd written some songs that had been recorded, but that evening he sang "The WAWbash Can-Un Ball" repeatedly, as well as his poor imitations of Meridian's Jimmie Rodgers: "Why Should I Be Lonely?" and "Yodelin' My Way Back Home." He'd given his famous name to his daughter. She, Jerri Bradley, he proclaimed, crying proud whiskey tears, was in college. She was going to be a schoolteacher. Ira watched the three of them and drank along with them, and there, with his father and Delaney, he decided, smiling quietly to himself, that it was time for him to get back to Fort Worth, back to his job. He reminded himself that he'd been saving money in Fort Worth. If he worked another year he'd have three thousand dollars, enough to quit work and start college. He couldn't, morally, sell his Aunt Essie's farm—he was the last of the Kings—and he didn't want to stay in Tongs for it, so then, drinking with the men, he decided to right a wrong. The following morning he made the arrangements, secretly, for Melissa Natale to get title to his aunt's place, surprised when he'd actually done it, feeling better about Melissa then, telling himself that with the farm and the house she could get a husband and have a family of her own.

He left his father in the dusty, disorganized King Store, living off the sale of socks, underwear, white "dress" shirts, cotton "work" shirts, and perhaps ten suits a month. The old house-store combination, the big two-story shell that was built entirely of fat-heart long-leaf pine lumber, the store that had represented his social stature and his fortune and inheritance when he was ten, was drying up, bankrupt, when he was twenty-two.

So Ira went back to his newspaper job in Fort Worth. When he was fired from there, he got a night job at Swift and Company on the loading dock, where he worked for eight months without starting college, even though he had enough money to pay tuition, more than enough—but he told himself, when the registration deadline slipped by, that if Janet were to marry him he would have to drop out, anyway.

Several afternoons he went to the campus and drank coffee in the new student center. He looked at pretty girls and read magazines in the library, listening to conversations, trying to guess how hard it really was, being a college student. Remembering what Nurse Sarah had told him about her college man who read novels for an English course, he went to the bookstore and bought all the texts for "The American Novel." After reading those books, he decided, or realized, that Janet wasn't ever going to marry him, that she would visit him, perhaps, but wouldn't marry him. He enrolled for nine hours the following semester, and he kept his night job at Swift and Company.

Occasionally Janet did visit him, and Ira finally got used to the moist, rancid slaughterhouse stink, and eventually he came to think that it was clean work, for it was cool in the meat lockers, and it was clean, too, except for the stink.

The only person whose job Ira envied at Swift's was the rat shooter, who also worked nights. The rat shooter was a loner who worked with a five-cell flashlight taped to the barrel of a .22 rifle with which he shot them in the dark, when he made his rounds dropping ratbane and checking his steel traps. He was a small man, thin like Ira, and he moved through the stink and noise and steam with grace, for even at night the packinghouse was noisy. There were Diesel switch engines jerking boxcars back and forth, steel-on-steel brakes squealed, electric generators whined and groaned, pumps forced thick liquids through giant pipes, and there was always steam escaping from somewhere, covering the rat shooter with noise and darkness.

Ira gave him coffee from his thermos one night, asking him what he did with the rats he shot. "They don't leave this place alive," the rat shooter replied. "Well, I know that you kill them," Ira said. The man screwed up his face in an attempt to appear mysterious. "The only thing they don't use in this packin'house is the hogs' squeal—you heard of calf fries, pickled pigs feet, paunch, chittlins—." "Well, yes, but that's not rats." "Canned sausages—everything that don't go anywhere else goes in canned sausages. Only thing I'll eat out of this place is roundsteak and goddamn bacon, you can see what you're eating with roundsteak and bacon." "Can you hit anything with that rifle?" Ira asked, to change the subject. "Shit—" "If you'd like to come over to my place some afternoon, we'll have a shooting match. I'm pretty good." "Shit. Where do you live?" Ira told him the address, and he replied, "Shit. I'll come see you, see if you can shoot."

The heavy work was good for Ira. When he hefted the beef halves and carried them into the trucks to hang them on their hooks, it made him breathe hard and feel alive. The fresh veal was well bled and wrapped in cheesecloth. He liked the smell of it.

Ira's little rented house in Fort Worth was on the back of a trashy lot; his window overlooked the city reservoir. He had few visitors at his place.

The mailman seldom brought him letters, but he had a shortcut path through to the next street, right by Ira's house, and since Ira was usually just getting up from working the previous night, he would ask the mailman to stop for coffee. The area around the reservoir was hobo jungles, and hobos had ransacked the house several times while Ira was away at work, especially in the winter. He kept a .22 rifle on the wall, but he didn't shoot the rabbits and squirrels and quail that passed outside the big window. A roadrunner lived on the rocky slope and Ira tried to feed it, but he could never find anything that it would eat.

The rat shooter brought his rifle when he visited Ira. He wore brown coveralls and a red plaid cap with a long bill and convertible earmuffs. The earmuffs were folded up so that they looked like tufts of gray hair sticking out on each side of his head. His brown shoes were leather low-quarters with crepe rubber soles. His hands were thin and wrinkled. He left his rifle beside the front door and knocked his feet on the cement block that served Ira as a front step. Ira sat him at the kitchen table. The guest didn't remove his red plaid cap. He seemed to see everything in the little house without looking at anything directly. Ira asked him if he'd like coffee.

"I certainly would, I surely would."

Ira filled his coffeepot. "I enlarged this back window so I can have a good view of the reservoir," he said.

"Uh huh."

"This place has been broken into twice. Bums."

"Uh huh." He eyed Ira's .22 on the wall. "You shoot purty good, huh?"

"Sure, I'm pretty good."

"I'm the only one, besides the police, that can take a gun in at Swift's. Do you believe that?"

"Of course. I've seen you. That's why I wanted to have a shooting match. I've got plenty of tin cans."

"Your shells or mine?"

"Mine. I've got a fresh box."

"Longs?"

"Yes, matter of fact, they are. What do you use?"

"At work, rat shot. They eat hell out of my bore. I've had to buy two new rifles since I had that job."

"I see." When the coffee was hot Ira poured two cups. They drank it without talking. There was a bit of cool wind leaking around the bay window, a haphazard affair made of three standard house windows nailed together. Ira mentioned that he had to get some weather stripping up before winter and paint the outsides of the window frames where they showed naked wood. Some sort of folding shutter would be ideal, he said, and he'd need to nail down the two windows in the other room to keep the tramps out.

"What's your name?" the rat shooter asked.

"King. Ira King."

"They don't hardly nobody know my name out at Swift's. You know what they call me?"

"No, I can't think of ever hearing anybody call your name out there."

"If somebody on the loading dock wanted to talk about me, who would they say I was?"

"Well, let me think—"

"That's right! You thought of it! They'd call me the Rat Man. I don't 'preciate that. Clyde Ponder is my name."

"I wouldn't either, Clyde. Who calls you that?"

"Very few people—to my face, but I can tell when I walk past people that they don't know my name. They don't say, 'Hello, Clyde,' or 'How you doin', Clyde,' because they don't know my name. One time the gate guard said to me, 'Hello, Mr. Rat Man,' and he grinned like a possum eating shit. Well, I tell you, I give him a cold stare that taken that grin right off his face. I just shifted my gun over to the crook of my left arm, pointing at him, and looked him cold in the face. He never said another word about rats to me!"

"I guess the reason they don't know your name is that you work nights and don't ever get to talk to people, very much."

They reflected on that while they finished their coffee. Clyde gestured for Ira to hand down the rifle for his examination. He went over it carefully, sighting down the barrel and snapping the trigger. He put the rifle butt on the floor, between his feet, and used his thumbnail to reflect light up through the barrel from the open breech. He squinted into the barrel.

"Don't clean her much, do you?"

"Enough," Ira answered.

"Dime a shot? Or is that too steep?"

"That's fine."

Although the vacant lot was cluttered with empty cans, they prowled through Ira's trash box and picked out four new ones. Ira scoured his dresser drawers for the small box of .22 shells.

Clyde, professional that he was, shot from a forward-leaning crouch. Although it was daylight he kept the flashlight taped under the barrel of his rifle. Ira soon learned that it was no contest. Even overconfidence couldn't beat Clyde. He shot like he could hit two hundred cans straight and still be tense, apprehensive, concentrating, and serious. After his third turn Ira said, "All right, Clyde, I quit. I can't afford to lose all my money today."

Clyde grinned. "Just a dollar 'n' sixty cents, so far."

"That much you're welcome to, but not my whole bankroll. Come on in the house and let's have another cup."

Clyde politely knocked his shoes on the cement block as he had before. He checked his rifle for safety and put it beside the door frame. He seemed more relaxed then, because he went straight to his chair at the kitchen table. "Mr. King, do you live alone, here?"

"Yep, just me."

"No wife or nothing? No lady friends?"

"No wife—why?"

"Oh, I was just noticing the place. It don't look much like no woman lives here."

"You're right. I guess it looks like a pigpen."

"But then"—Clyde was looking at something Janet had left—"there's some rolled-up nylon stockings there, under the edge of the bed."

"So? What of it, Clyde? What difference does it make?"

"Oh, none, none. I just got in the habit of noticing around the walls and baseboards and under tables and things. I thought there for a minute it was a big old rat."

"No, Clyde. That's not a rat, not even a mouse. It's just a pair of stockings I keep to shine my boots with. I learned that trick in the army."

"No kiddin'?"

"Sure. It's better than a spit shine."

"Well, it sure fooled me!" He blew the steam from his hot coffee. Ira saw that his face was clean shaven, but he had a wonderful growth of gray nose hair that looked as if it had never been trimmed. "King—how would you like to have a kid?"

Ira stared at Clyde Ponder. "Just what the hell would I do with a kid?"

"Could clean house for you, that wouldn't hurt. You know, wash dishes, wash clothes, cut the grass, wash your car."

"That grass? My car? My car is old. That's not dirt on my car, that's where the paint wore off."

"A kid could do whatever you need. I know. I've got a houseful of kids, and we manage to keep them all busy, what with one thing and another. They're awful handy."

"Is it your kid you're trying to get rid of?"

"No. Belongs to my sister that died." He looked at Ira's expression intently. "She's a love-child, don't know her daddy." He waited, but there was no response from Ira. "I've got six kids of my own to worry with, and my wife's poorly."

"Well, that's the *last* thing I need, a girl. In fact, I don't need anything less than that."

"Sure, don't blame you. Got too many myself. Just thought I'd ask before I put her on the welfare. That goes hard with kids, makes them lose their pride, makes people look down on 'um— that's not so bad, if a person has pride. She's a pretty girl."

"I'm sorry about your problem, but—"

"Oh, that's OK. I just happent to think you might not have no chilren and might need someone to help around the place. She's real quick to learn, but that's not here or there."

"No. Thanks for thinking of me, but I couldn't."

"I'll see you," Clyde said, as he left without thanking Ira for the coffee, or the shooting match. He just mumbled that he was leaving and picked up his rifle at the door. He'd parked on the front street, not knowing the alley entrance that Ira used. Ira stood at the door watching him pick his loose-jointed way through the knee-high weeds and clumps of prickly pear cactus, walking along, dragging his legs after him. Ira watched his back, the proud slope of his shoulders, the bending backs of his knees, the flopping upturned earmuffs of his cap, and the easy swinging pendulum of his right arm and the rifle.

❀   ❀   ❀

When Ira got home, early the next morning, he found the girl under his floodlight, sitting on his cement-block step. She was small-boned, sitting with her knees hugged up under her chin. She had short, straight blonde hair and she wore beltless Levis with a white blouse and brown loafers. The white blouse had round pearl buttons and frilly cuffs and collar. Except for her hair and the feminine blouse, she could have been mistaken for a boy. Her features were regular, but her face could have been that of a handsome boy. She had thin lashes and green eyes.

The girl looked down, thinking that Ira would be mad at her. She had sensed from the Ponders that she was leaving their family for good, and she was afraid to believe what they'd told her about this man—that they were returning her to her father. Pauline, the oldest daughter of Clyde Ponder, and the best writer, wrote the note as Clyde dictated. The girl held it folded in the palm of her hand. When Ira reached the door she handed him the note, asking, "Are you Mr. King?"

"Yes," he said, taking the note.

"This note's for you."

Ira took the note and stepped past her to unlock the door. He went inside the house and turned on the lights and the butane burner. He unfolded the note and read it, then wished he hadn't, because he had guessed the contents as it passed from her hand to his, he guessed the whole note, except for the last line—"We told her you are her father." Then he turned it over and saw another sentence, an afterthought. It read, "Her name is Jean Harlow Davis." Ira reread that sentence. Then he turned the note over and read it all through again. He folded it slowly and put it in the back part of his billfold.

"Come in, Jean. As soon as we get warmed up we'll take a ride back over to the Ponders." The girl came inside the lighted house, but she didn't look up. She didn't look while Ira cooked the eggs and link sausages, and she wouldn't eat any supper.

"Where does Clyde Ponder live? Have you been living with them?"

There was no response.

"Come on now, you know the Ponders. Where do they live?"

"I don't know how to get there," she replied.

"Well, what's the name of the street?"

"I don't know."

"How old are you?"

"Eleven."

"You're eleven years old and you don't know the name of the street?"

"It's a long word on the sign. I couldn't read it."

"And you don't know the way to get there from here?"

"No."

"Well—it's a couple of hours 'til daylight," Ira said, as he set his

Westclox. "You sleep on that mat, if you want to. I'll find Clyde Ponder for you in the morning." He turned out the light.

At eight o'clock the alarm went off. Ira didn't shave or cook breakfast. He hustled the girl into his car and drove three blocks to the pay phone. He called Swift's and asked for Personnel. He asked the thin voice of Personnel for Clyde Ponder's home address, explaining that he was Ira King and he worked nights with Mr. Ponder. After a few minutes the voice gave him a Carlisle Street address. Ira and the girl drove to Carlisle Street and found the house locked. "Where are they, Jean?"

"I don't know."

Ira kicked the door and waited several minutes. There was no sign of life in the house, which had the look of a greasy abandoned boat. Ira started back to his car, and the girl fell in step behind him. They picked their way through the weed-choked yard and down to the curbless, dusty, graveled street, drove back to Ira's house, and Ira napped until work time. He left her in the house and went to work, leaving in plenty of time to get there early. He asked the gate guard when the rat shooter came to work.

"About nine P.M. But we're going to be eaten up with rats for the next two weeks. He's on vacation. Dirty little bastard!"

CHAPTER 10

THE WELFARE WOMAN TOLD JEAN TO GO OUTSIDE AND PLAY. SHE looked around the little house slowly, as Clyde Ponder had, as if she were trying to memorize every detail. She was slow to take the chair that Ira offered. Then, immediately after she sat down, she brusquely stood up, as if she had forgotten something, and took off her coat, revealing her magnificent figure. Holding the lightweight coat in her lap, she sat down again. Ira started telling the story. She smiled at him, and occasionally she smiled at the reservoir that she could see through his enlarged back window.

"Have you got a light?" she asked as she took a pack of Chesterfields from her coat pocket. She struck the kitchen match that he gave her across the bottom of the ashtray that she'd found, conspicuously clean, on the table. She lit her cigarette and inhaled. Ira kept talking. She had no pencil or notebook. Then he finished, out of breath. She asked, "Do you live alone?"

"Yes."

Her eyes fell to Janet's rolled-up nylon on the floor by the bed. She pursed her lips. "Do you drink?"

"Yes."

"A lot?"

"No."

"How long have you had your present job?"

"What damned business is it of yours! I'm not adopting the kid!

I don't even know her! I told you what happened, it's your job to straighten it out."

"I'll do my very best, Mr. King. I don't mean to be nosy." She crossed her legs. "Are you quite sure that she's not a relative, not even a *distant* relative of yours?"

"I'm positive."

"But you see, there's the question of her name. I can't even report, for sure, who she is. You wouldn't happen to have a copy of her birth certificate, would you?"

"No."

"What was your friend's name, the man who brought her?"

"I'm not sure he's my friend. Clyde Ponder. You can check Swift's if you want to."

"Did you see Mr. Ponder leave the girl?"

"No. I told you, I was at work. I work nights."

"Did you ever see Mr. Ponder *with* the girl?"

"No. But the day before he left on vacation he offered to give me a kid."

"And you accepted?"

"Hell, no! Don't you try to Sergeant Friday me! Take the kid and get the hell out of here!"

She smiled, snuffed her cigarette in the ashtray, and rose, putting on her coat. "You'll be hearing from us, Mr. King. There is no evidence of maltreatment, no proof of kinship, so all I can tell you now is that you'll hear from us. Do you have a phone?"

"No. Do you mean you're not taking her?"

"No, Mr. King." She smoothed the hem of her skirt. "Thank you for your hospitality. I'm sorry, but we just don't have any place for her."

Ira sat still as she closed the door. He was so mad that his face burned. Then he opened the door to let out her cigarette smoke. He didn't see the girl outside. He cleaned his rifle, and when he'd finished he was still mad. He started to curse the welfare woman and realized that he'd forgotten her name. He knew that it was her sexuality that angered him, the way she took off her coat, the way that she smoked the cigarette, the way she crossed her legs—she'd told him her name slowly, carefully, so that he could remember it, so that he could call her—but anger had swept it from his mind.

He was walking around the corner of the house, looking for Jean, when he heard her quick steps scamper behind the rear wall. He realized that she'd been just outside the window, listening to his interview with the welfare woman, hearing him say, "Take the kid and get the hell out of here!"

Ira went back inside the house, madder still, embarrassed. He felt that he should be hungry, but he'd lost track of his meal schedule. He put several eggs in the skillet with the last of his link sausages and scoured out the dirty dishes and the stale coffeepot. The smell of sausage and eggs filled the kitchen. Then the girl quietly entered the door. She crossed the room to sit on the mat, where she'd slept the previous night. Ira fixed a plate and put it on the floor beside her. "Here," he said. "You hungry?"

She looked up at him, expressionless, then she looked at the plate of food and started eating.

Ira fixed a plate for himself, and ate at the table. While he was eating he heard a knock at the end of the house. "It's the mailman," he thought. He ate the last bite of sausage and went outside to the mailbox that was nailed on the south wall. It could be a letter from Janet saying that she'd be down for the weekend—but he hadn't heard from her in over three months. He didn't expect a letter from Janet. He saw the mailman waiting. Since he often had the mailman in for coffee, Ira realized that the mailman was waiting for an invitation, tightening the leather strap that girthed a bundle of letters. He looked up. "Morning, Mr. King. Nice day, ain't it?"

"Sure, Mr. Mailman, I guess it is." Ira took his letter from the mailbox.

"Sure smells like coffee around here, Mr. King."

Ira read the envelope. It was from Delaney, in Mississippi, from the Belle Arms Hotel in Beauville.

"Oh, hell. I'm sorry, Mr. Mailman. Come on in." Ira stuffed the letter into his jacket pocket. "That's the pot you smell. I forgot it yesterday and left it full of old grounds. Just washed it in hot water, so it smells pretty strong. Come on in, though. I can boil up some instant coffee in about two minutes. I need some too."

They rounded the corner of the house, mounted the cement-block step, and entered. The mailman unslung his leather bag with a practiced, easy sweep, propping it against the doorframe—where it looked like a cowboy's saddlebag. It was natural leather with fancy lacing around the seams and floral carvings on the front and sides. The mailman had taken his chair at the kitchen table before he saw the girl.

He spoke to her, "Well, hello there, Young Feller. Puttin' on the feed bag, I see. Mr. King, I didn't know you had no girl. Bring her out to my place sometime. Hey! I've got six horses out at my place you could ride, if you come see me sometime. Six! She sure does favor you, Mr. King."

The girl looked at the mailman, then she returned her eyes to her plate.

"So far, Mr. Mailman, she and I haven't talked very much. A fellow who works with me left her here, then ran off on vacation. I tried to get her placed with the welfare people, but they won't take care of her because she doesn't have a birth certificate. I don't suppose you'd have a place for her, for a few days until her uncle gets back from vacation?"

"No, Mr. King, I don't. I've got three boys myself." He gave Ira a wink, meaning that boys and girls don't mix, not at that age. "Wonder who they think they are, not taking in a fine girl like her? Surely lots of children don't have birth certificates. That's like saying a dead tramp out by the reservoir ain't dead lessen he has a death certificate! That's plumb silly. What else did they say?"

"It wasn't a *they*. It was a she. She just sat here, smoking up the house, no pen or pencil, didn't write down a damned thing I told her, asked me questions like a damned detective, and then she left. She said there was no evidence of maltreatment, so they'd have to leave the girl till I heard from them."

"That means next year. You can claim her as a tax deduction. Did you sign anything?"

"No. I don't think that woman could even write."

"I see what it means. They're playing you coy, Mr. King. They figger they'd rather leave a kid with somebody who has a job and a warm house, rather than put her in their orphanage. They're right, too. Once a kid is inside, it's hard to get anybody to adopt her, especially an older kid—"

"I guess you're right," Ira said.

The mailman gulped his half cup of coffee and swept up his fancy bag. Saying that he was going to be late, he thanked Ira for the coffee and tossed a friendly " 'Bye, now" to the girl as he left.

Ira pulled a chair to the big window and opened his letter from Delaney. He read it through, slowly. Then he read it again. It started, "Dear Ira, Things have gone from bad to worse. Joe would kill me if he knew I was writing this letter. You gave your Aunt Essie's farm to that Natale girl and she turned right around and gave it to your 'old friend' Paul Jacobs. That's all Joe talks about now. Now lightning has struck. The store is burned. I'm staying at Beauville with Joe. Don't send him any money. If you want to see your father alive, I don't want to scare you, but losing the store has really got him low, maybe you'd better come back. Delaney."

Ira put the letter back in his jacket pocket. He left the girl sitting on her mat and walked down to the bank of the reservoir. Following the limestone goat trail around the little beach, he kicked loose stones into the rippling water. Deep in thought, he walked completely around the reservoir, five miles. He passed the boat club on North Shore and then detoured around the frame houses that hunched beside the water on East Front. He flushed jittery killdee near the water, and by the time he crossed the iron NO TRESPASSING catwalk over the spillway he'd decided to go back to Tongs. He walked quickly, then, sweating, back to the cabin, got a handful of dimes from his bureau drawer, and walked out to the pay phone where he called Swift's and told them that he quit, to send his salary and his W-2 forms to him at General Delivery, Tongs, Mississippi. He then called the bank and asked them to close out his account, saying that he'd be downtown soon to buy travelers' checks with the balance. He called City Offices and got the number of the welfare agency. Three different voices from the welfare agency responded to his question, and his repetition of that question, but they all claimed ignorance of his problem, and ignorance of any way of solving it. He wet his lips and silently cursed himself for not remembering the welfare woman's name. Then a fourth voice came through the telephone. It was a man's voice. He sounded like he was late to lunch and impatient. He said, "We're full-up with lost and abandoned children. We try, but we can't assume every parent's responsibility!"

Ira swore at him a long, well-founded oath that started with that man's ancestry, three generations back, and continued through him to his children and any children that they, miserable species that they were, might generate. It included the Fort Worth welfare agency and all its employees, the police force, and the school board; but most of it was wasted, for the man had hung up.

Then Ira called his father in Beauville. The clerk at Belle Arms answered quickly, with his Chambers County accent, telling the operator that Mr. King was out. He seemed to be reluctant to say when Mr. King would return, so Ira left a short message that he was coming back to Mississippi.

It took a day for him to pay the utility bills, his rent, pack, and service the old car. He had the radiator reverse-flushed, bought two new recapped tires, and put a new fan belt in the toolbox. He bought a case of cheap motor oil at the railway salvage. The girl had a big appetite that day. For lunch Ira cooked all of the eggs, scrambling them with ketchup and tabasco. For supper he brought hamburgers from the cafe near Swift's.

It was almost dark when Ira left in the loaded car to get the hamburgers. The old car was packed full, and the house lights were out. The girl thought he was leaving for good. She sat on the cement-block step while he started the car and turned around. Then she ran to the car and grabbed the door handle on the passengers' side, but the old door was stuck. Ira had been backing in reverse. He stopped the car and shifted to first gear, not seeing her. When he released the clutch and slowly rolled forward, she jerked at the door handle. Ira eased down the sandy trail toward the alley, with her trotting beside the car. He stopped at the big bump where his trail intersected the alley and saw her. He rolled down the window, surprised, asking, "Do you want to go with me?"

She nodded up and down in great, serious movements. He reached across and opened the jammed door with the inside handle. She got in and pulled the door shut. Ira turned into the alley.

"I'm just going a mile to get supper—hamburgers. You could've waited at the house," he said, ashamed that he'd neglected to tell her where he was going.

"I didn't think you were coming back."

"Of course I was coming back."

"I couldn't stay here by myself, with no food. You put everything in the car."

"That's a fact. I've got to go to Mississippi."

"I'll go to Mississippi with you. I sort of don't have anyplace else to go."

"You'll get plenty tired of riding this car before we ever get to Mississippi."

"I like to ride," she said, looking over the dashboard at the traffic, noticing every cafe that they passed. "What can I call you?" she asked, looking away from him, down the Fort Worth street.

"That's not true," he answered abruptly, "what Clyde Ponder told you about me."

"I know. I knew it wasn't true when I saw you."

"Then—you can call me anything you like. Call me Ira."

"OK."

"You knew it wasn't true?" he asked curiously.

"Yes. My father wasn't skinny, and he had a red moustache."

"Oh."

"Well . . . you're not *skinny,* but you're not as big as my father. He was a rigger."

"A rigger?"

"Yes. Because of his work he had to travel a lot."

"I see," Ira said, as he parked the car. He got hamburgers to go, and they returned to the cabin for supper. Ira rechecked everything in the car, including his savings, five thousand dollars in travelers' checks. They spent their last night in the cabin. Ira set the alarm for six-thirty—he planned to drive straight through to Mississippi.

But they didn't make it in one day, straight through. It was a hot Saturday in the middle of July. The old car held up well, the radiator and water pump survived, but it seemed to take Ira hours to work his way even to Dallas. It was just like city driving, all the way from Fort Worth, then it was stop-and-go all through Dallas. They were wilted by the time they arrived at the outskirts of Dallas, headed east on Highway 80. Ira selected a drive-in cafe and stopped for an early lunch.

"Hamburger?" he asked the girl.

She nodded, while the carhop held her stubby pencil close to the lime-green pad of tickets, each with *Thank You* printed on the back.

". . . and to drink?"

"Coffee," Ira said, recalling the folklore that it's best when you're hot not to drink something cold. He asked the girl, "What do you want to drink?"

"A Coke," she replied.

While they waited for the order, Ira looked at the people in the other parked cars. There were boys with dates, solitary salesmen, plain-clothes inspectors. Some cars were filled with families. He stole a glance at Jean. She could have been his daughter, he thought. He remembered the mailman's saying that she looked like his daughter. Then his mind flashed ahead, east on Highway 80, a way he'd been before, and he imagined getting to Louisiana, then crossing the high, narrow, frightening bridge over the Mississippi River at Vicksburg.

The hamburgers came, and they ate them in silence. Ira could remember something about its being illegal to take a minor girl across a state line. He'd heard that, he thought, on a radio show called "Law Enforcement." He wondered what he'd say if the police stopped him.

He tipped, paid, and then the carhop took the tray from their window. The old car started easily and ran quietly, as they joined the flow eastward.

It was pleasanter on the open highway. The air was fresher, but it was still hot. Before they got to Terrell, however, Jean got carsick, or hamburger-sick. So they limped along, stopping when necessary at roadside parks and gas stations. It seemed to Ira that she did just as well riding as she did sitting in the hot tree shade of the roadside parks, for they'd tried some of each. By midafternoon they got to Mineola, Texas, and he took her into a cafe to eat a bowl of tomato soup. He drank two cups of coffee and asked her how she felt.

"I feel pretty good. That soup was a good idea."

"Darned hamburgers—we had hamburgers for supper and hamburgers for breakfast. Too much grease, I suppose. It's a wonder I didn't get sick, too." But he didn't believe what he said. He told himself that she'd probably gotten sick from the anxiety of being dumped on a stranger who didn't want to take her in, and who then suddenly said he had to go to Mississippi, two states away, a place that she might have never heard of before. He decided that he'd do better to work on her stomach psychologically.

"Well, Jean, if you feel better, we might as well get on the road. I'm going to buy a bottle of Pepto-Bismol for you to sip on. Do you know what that is?"

"No."

"It's a pink medicine. It tastes good, like Spearmint gum. It settles your stomach. Then, for supper, we'll have some boiled potatoes and beef stew, or vegetables. I've got to watch out for you. Can't have you sick."

"I'll make you late getting home."

"No. Don't worry about that. We'll get there tomorrow."

He got Pepto-Bismol at a drugstore in Mineola. They drove on. They smelled pines. The smell of pines pleased Ira. At seven-thirty they had supper. At ten they were well into Louisiana. Ira stopped at a cheap motel that had a big VACANCY sign glowing in neon red. He signed the register for himself and his daughter, getting a room with twin beds. He told her that he'd check the car and lock it while she got ready for bed. He locked the car, stood on the gravel court—staring at pinecones, drank a complimentary cup of coffee with the motel manager, and then went in the room. She stood there, where he'd left her, dressed exactly as she'd been dressed since the first time he saw her. "I didn't know which bed you wanted," she said.

"I'll take this one," Ira said, walking to the far bed. He pulled the pillow from under the bedspread, fluffed it, took off his shoes, and lay down. He rolled on his side, away from her, facing the wall. "Good-night, Jean," he said. He heard cars passing on the highway. She quietly turned out the light. He guessed that she, too, slept in her clothes. He fell asleep quickly. Sometime during the night he dreamed about crossing the high, narrow bridge over the Mississippi.

CHAPTER 11

THE CLERK AT THE BELLE ARMS TOLD IRA THAT JOE KING HAD BEEN buried three or four hours, that Mr. Delaney arranged the funeral—they'd been sharing a room for several weeks and, the clerk said, "had a lot to drink. Last Friday morning, about nine o'clock, Mr. Delaney, your father's cousin, came down and asked me to send for a doctor. It was too late, of course. Mr. Delaney had the funeral this morning. Just at lunchtime I discovered your note under the counter. Whoever took your message must've slipped it into Mr. King's box. I guess the wind blew it out. I'm sorry Mr. King didn't get it before he died. I'm truly sorry.

"Mr. Delaney changed to room three-one-six. I showed him your note Sunday evening—"

"But you said you just found it at noon today?"

"Oh, of course, that's what I meant to say. Anyway, Mr. Delaney's up in his room. You understand, we kept it as quiet as we could. It's bad publicity for a hotel, you know. Makes people reluctant to stay there. You and the girl just take the elevator to the third floor. Room three-one-six, he'll be there, I'm sure."

Ira got boozy Delaney and his suitcase in the car, paid a big hotel bill, and drove across town to the Johnson Tourist Court which had been rebuilt, he saw, with a swimming pool and a new sign proclaiming, "Johnson's Midtown Motel." Delaney stirred in the back seat, looking perplexedly at the girl who sat beside Ira. "I sent all my samples back to Houston House, Ira. I've even retired. I'm not a high-roller anymore." Ira parked under the neon sign, got out, and walked to the office, where he asked the price of a room for two men and a girl. The woman said it would be twelve-fifty. He thanked her and returned to the car.

"Twelve-fifty," he told Delaney.

"This damn town is getting too expensive, too rich for my blood, Ira. There's a fishing camp at Shiloh Crossing. Costs twelve bucks a week, with a screened-in porch. Me and Joe stayed there a week after the store burned. Screens on all the windows, keep the mosquitoes out. Private, too. We'll have warm nights for another month."

"Sure," Ira replied. He eased the old car onto the new cloverleaf intersection and found his way to Tongs on the new highway. His six-year absence seemed to have shrunk all the distances, and he was surprised to get to Shiloh Crossing in fifteen minutes. The fishing camp was dark. Delaney stumbled from the car, and took his bearings. Standing in the glare of the headlights, with his right hand on the ram's-head hood ornament, he slowly led the old Dodge down a deep-rutted gravel road to a berth beside the third cabin. The screen door to the porch stood open, but the cabin door was locked. Delaney staggered to it and kicked it open. They moved in. Ira put his Coleman lantern on a shelf, seeing by its light that there were four cots in the big room. He put Delaney's suitcase on one, his own blanket and pillow on another, and told Jean that she could choose for herself from the remaining cots. Delaney carried two chairs from the kitchen to the front porch, then went back to get a bottle from his suitcase.

Jean fell asleep on her cot while Ira and Delaney sat on the front porch in the dark. They drank from the bottle and talked about Joe and Essie. Delaney was surprised to find that Ira didn't care about regaining possession of Essie's farm. He then said, "Too bad about your friend Stanley."

Ira replied, "Yes. I remember getting that letter just a few days after I left, telling about the motorcycle wreck."

"It happened the day you left, Ira, the same day."

"What about James?"

"I wasn't here when it happened, but from what I heard, that poor kid just went to pieces. He was anemic anyway, but they said that he quit eating for about two weeks. When he felt a little better, he started in at that college in Feston. He's in Gulfport now, or Biloxi, teaching in a new high school they just built. I tell you, just about everybody you knew is gone from Tongs."

"Yeah."

"Paul Jacobs married Anna Natale right after you left, in just a month or so, then Old Man Natale died and was worth thirty-four thousand dollars in life insurance. Paul got all of that. When you gave the farm to Melissa, it didn't take him five days to get that, too. He must have guessed you or Joe would try to get it back sometime, because he got the title cleared in Beauville and then turned right around and sold it to the new doctor, Forsythe. I checked for Joe, he kept after me to try to do something—it's a good title. Airtight. Joe wouldn't believe it, but it really is."

"What about the store?"

"It went up in black smoke. Even if they'd been a fire department, they couldn't of saved it. You know, it was solid heart-pine. Joe left a bank account of about six hundred bucks, that's all. You didn't inherit much, Son."

"Well, I'll work. Always have."

"You told me before, something about working in a packing-house?"

"Yes. Loading trucks."

"Then, Ira, you don't have a wife?"

"No. I never got married."

"Oh. I see." Delaney raised the bottle and took a long but quiet and delicate sip. Then he passed the bottleneck across his sleeve and handed it back to Ira. Ira held it, balanced in the palm of his hand. He hefted it to gauge its weight, like a butcher would heft a pound of hamburger. He took a drink.

Delaney looked closely at Ira's face, peering through the darkness and the whiskey he'd drunk. He said, "Ira, hell—it don't figger. What about the girl?"

Ira tasted the strong perfume of sour mash. "A man left her, abandoned her, at my place in Fort Worth. I tried for two days to get the welfare people to take her, but they wouldn't."

"How long ago was this happened?"

"Four days."

"What you going to do with her?"

"Hell, I don't know. I've found that it's damned hard, impossible, to give a kid away. Besides, I sort of like her."

"Maybe so—but it's asking for trouble, since you don't have a wife." Delaney cleared his throat and lit a fresh cigarette. "At her age girls can change—almost overnight."

"I guess so," Ira replied.

"If she starts looking womanish to you, it's asking for trouble."

"Well, don't worry about that."

"Ira, damn it, I'd like to see you living on Essie's old place. You know, for a long time I was in love with Essie. This was back when your grandfather was alive, when he had the millpond—flooded all that Mill Creek Hollow, worked six men at the mill when Joe and Essie and I were kids, younger than you, and we all fished together in the millpond, hunted ducks on it in the wintertime. I hunted and fished with Joe so I could eat supper over at their place. I was really stuck on Essie, but she never'd have anything to do with me—her pa refused to let her court with a first cousin. Joe was courting your mother at the time." He drank from the bottle. "Now he was a cutter, though, old Joe King. Your ma didn't seem to mind. She knew he was good stock, would settle down and make good. Essie married old shit-head Matt. He was twice her age, and he wore his teeth out chewing on a pipe. He wore 'em clean down to the gums, flat across the top, smooth. Son-of-a-bitch. The only thing that made him better than me was that he wasn't her cousin. She didn't love him. I always thought it served her pa right. Matt gave her one kid —Cassfield. I held it against her pa—he said us being first cousins would make our children idiots—and Matt gave her Cassfield!"

"I didn't know that, Delaney."

"It was a long time ago, Ira. Anyway, I'd still like to see you get her farm back."

"I know *now* it was a mistake, giving it away."

"Sure it was. Maybe we can scrape up some money, together, and get that doctor to sell it back to us. Live on it."

Ira drank from the bottle. "I thought if she had the farm—Melissa —somebody would marry her."

"Oh, she's too dumb. Too simpleminded for that."

"I never thought of her as simple. I always admired her, except when we were children."

"I don't think she's got anything you'd want, Ira. She's fat."

Ira didn't reply to that. They stayed on the porch for another hour, quiet. Their silhouettes were darker than the night, and when Delaney struck matches the flash lit his face, and the red glow of his cigarette reflected off the chrome ram on the hood of the old Dodge.

After breakfast the three of them got in the car and drove up past the service station to the asphalt road, turned right, crossed the bridge, and drove up the steep hill into Tongs. Ira stopped the car in the street in front of the King Store.

"Of course the lot's worth something," Delaney said, "if you could find anybody in Tongs that would build another store. Want to take a closer look? The sheriff's been keeping everybody out of there."

"No. I want to get cleaned up and find a job. Is there anything in Beauville?" Ira spoke, unable to look at the ruin.

"Sure, let's drive on, people are rubbernecking. There's a chicken-packing plant, and a new regional office of the REA."

"I don't want to fool with electricity."

"They have all kinds of jobs—surveyors, land agents, service sales-men, complaint men, office workers."

"Oh, really? Well, maybe I'll try, this afternoon."

They drove on through Tongs and turned around at the depot.

"Stop a minute, Ira, let me run in this Jiffy Mart and get a few things."

"What things?"

"Some bread and cheese."

"Have you got money?"

"Sure."

Ira switched off the ignition key and turned around in the front seat so that he could see the girl. She smiled. "This is where I lived when I was your age," he said. "I used to go to school here, and I used to watch movies in that little out-of-business theatre we passed. Did you see the theatre?"

"Yes. Was that big house that burned yours?"

"I lived there. It was a store."

"It was bigger than the theatre?"

"Yeah."

"I like movies better than school."

"I'll bet you do."

Delaney came out of the store with a brown paper bag. "I got some rat cheese, off a block. Damn stuff's high as a cat's back!" Ira started the car. When he drove back through town he avoided looking at the store. He looked at the other buildings, remembering that September morning when he put his suitcase in Nathan's taxi there at the curb in front of Gappy's barbershop, leaving Tongs.

"Beauville got everything, Ira. Interstate highway, more cotton gins, chicken-packing plant, REA, everything. All Tongs got was a bus stop and a new doctor, but he's prospering. He's got Essie's place, like I told you, and a new brick house and new car—expecting a baby, I understand."

"He doesn't live on Essie's place?"

"Lord, no. You know how doctors are, he just bought it for fun. I hear he goes out there every afternoon to relax, plays poker there at night. Have you got a suit to wear to Beauville?"

"Sure. Always trying to make a sale, aren't you?"

"Never hurts to try. Now you go on and get yourself a nice job. The kid and I'll wet a hook down around The Falls this afternoon."

While Ira washed in the Okatoma, Delaney drove up the bumpy trail to Pittman's station. He filled the car with gasoline and borrowed two cane poles from the attendant. "Dry as a bone," the attendant said when he checked the oil. Delaney fished two cans of oil from a pasteboard box in the back seat.

"Fill her up to the *add* mark and quench her, Sonny. Nothing wrong with an old girl who likes to drink, is there?"

"It's wrong if she drinks oil," the boy grinned.

"You'll find, young man, as you grow older, that it's all the same. It all comes in quarts, like an elephant. Now don't dribble it, what are you doing, playing basketball?"

"It's to the *add* mark and I've got half a quart left."

"Dump it in, Son. It ain't gold. Next time I'm in town I'll—here, Son, have a cigar—drive you over to County Line, drink a beer, pinch the waitress on her round ass, you know. Thanks for the poles. Oh, you still sell worms?"

"Naw. We don't bother with them anymore. If you want to catch catfish, we got some of that new blood bait."

"Blood bait?"

"Yeah." The attendant went inside the store and brought out a cellophane package. "It's dried chicken blood. Little cubes. They make it in Beauville at the chicken-packing plant. It's tough, see?" He tore the package open and twisted one of the cubes in his fingers. "Just put it on your hook and drop it in, pretty soon the water makes it soft and the flavor oozes out. Along comes a catfish and swallers it, wham, there you go!"

'Chicken blood, huh?"

"Sure thing. They pull out some big ones with it. Two-bits a bag."

"One bag, please. Rather have worms, I believe."

"Here you are. It's perfectly dry. Cut in squares. Much neater to handle than worms. Just put it on your hook and away you go."

"Thanks, thanks a lot."

Delaney drove back to the cabin and found Ira waiting on the front porch. "Where's the kid?"

"Inside."

"I got some poles and bait. Now don't go sparking up no old romances. We'll be down at The Falls, if we're not here, when you get back."

"OK," Ira said, getting in the car.

"I filled her up, Ira. Good luck with the job."

"You too. Be careful at The Falls—it's a dangerous place." Ira loosened his black necktie for the trip. He eased the old car into reverse, turned around, lined her up with the dirt road, and rattled off toward Beauville.

Delaney was in a cheerful mood. He started talking to the girl, not even thinking that he was being heard, while he changed into a pair of old trousers. "Hell with the shoes," he thought—he would wash them in the river if they got muddy. "Let's see, we drank all of that bottle last night. I'll get some more when Ira gets back, I guess." He grabbed half of the loaf of bread and sliced off a big hunk of the yellow cheese, wrapping it in the paper with the package of blood bait. He looped the strap of his old binoculars case over his arm, gathered up the poles, and asked the girl directly, "Are you in the market for some fishing, kid?" Not waiting for a reply, he stepped off briskly. She ran to follow. "The place we're going to is lousy with catfish. It's where I used to go with Ira's father, my cousin, back before Essie—Joe was courting his wife then. Now *he* was a cutter, then."

They followed a smooth winding footpath along the riverbank. Delaney paused to slap a bunch of fox grapes with the poles. "Wait until frost and those will sure be good," he said, high rolling. Then he walked so fast that the girl had to trot to keep up, and he kept talking. "Essie, my cousin, married an old slow-type of a fellow. He broke a new ground for her up above Shiloh Crossing, the last man that I ever saw plow an ox. One of his fields used to be an Indian camp. After a rain you can always find flints and arrowheads there. I'll show you. Listen! Hear that? Dry, wooden click, click, click, listen. That's what Tongs people call a rain crow—it's a yellow-billed cuckoo." She listened, and while she listened he quietly took the binoculars from their case and searched a magnolia tree for warblers. The cuckoo refused to call again, perhaps it had flown, so they continued their walk.

They walked in silence until they heard the cataract roar. Delaney led her past the crash of white water down the west bank to the foot of the big pool where the water eddied and the roar of the falls wasn't unpleasant, but constantly present. He unwound their lines and baited both hooks. The attendant had given him real catfish poles with heavy sinkers and no floats. The lines were long, almost as long as the poles, and the hooks were heavy, an inch wide from point to shank.

Delaney put both lines out, separated, so that the current wouldn't tangle them. Then he rammed the butts of the poles into the clay bank. "That one's yours, kid. Did you ever fish before?"

' No."

"Then, watch how tight the line runs down into the water, and watch how the tip of the pole quivers from the strain. Just watch the tip of that pole, and if it starts jerking, watch it, now, be ready—but don't pull it up. Let him swallow it. When he feels the hook he'll let you know that it's time to pull it in. Maybe I'll catch the first one and you'll see how it's done. There now." He watched the tips of both poles intently. "What! No customers? Well in that case just relax and wait."

He looked at the girl's green eyes, thinking that she looked enough like Ira to be his daughter. "Ira King is shackled to Chambers County. He may not *know* it, girl, but he is. Six years ago I'd of told any fellow from Tongs to get the hell out, go west, see something of the world. That's what I told Ira. Now I'd never tell one to leave, for fear he'd not live to get back, or not have *sense* enough to come back."

She listened, but she didn't reply. Delaney's hand swept a smooth sitting-place in the sand. He looked past the tips of the poles and across the pool of The Falls.

"One time I was down here with Joe. We heard a mourning dove, and we thought it was an owl. We got in a big argument about why owls hoot during the daytime. Then Joe started telling me a tale about some mermaids he once saw here. He said they were three feet long, with fishtails and scales on their bottom half and bare bosoms on top."

Jean smiled at the notion of mermaids.

"He said they had long yellow hair and haircombs grew in the palms of their hands. It was a clear day, like today, but quite a bit warmer. He pointed across this wide part here, to where he'd seen them. As I remember it, there were some drift logs washed up on that sandbar, there, where that boulder sits out in the water. The hot sun was making little squiggley steam waves off in the distance, and when I squinted my eyes and looked over at those drift logs it seemed I could almost see them. Joe was just dreaming and yarning, but he went on and on about those little mermaids, said they were even prettier than Clara."

"Who was Clara?"

"Well, she was the woman he married. She was Ira's mother. Sometimes the wind changed and we could hear them singing. I couldn't even see them without squinting and looking real hard, but Joe didn't have any trouble seeing them. He just laid back, wide-eyed against the bank, and kept time with their singing by patting his foot. I couldn't daydream and yarn as well as he could, but it turned out for the best, I reckon. He got the prettiest girl in Chambers County. She was beautiful."

Jean Harlow looked hard across the pool, then she smiled again at Delaney.

"No kiddin', girl. And don't think it won't happen to you. One spring day, two or three years from now, you'll be sitting down here, and the Okatoma will be running clear, and you'll look across there and see those Mississippi mermaids singing, and you'll wish you could see them closer, for they're all colors. They have red lips and yellow hair and green eyes, like you, and they'll make you wish you were out there singing with them. You've got green eyes, you might be part fish."

She smiled at the idea.

"For now, watch these lines, and remember how I set them out, while I take a short nap. Don't jerk the pole too soon if you get a bite, either, just meet his pull. You'll have to know a lot about fishing if you're going to get along with Ira King. He cut his baby teeth on catfish, and setting rabbit gums and quail traps and shooting any bird that had bright feathers—you picked a good one to grub onto, you could have done lots worse, honey. Now shut up and let me rest, catch us some supper." Delaney folded his arms behind his head, closed his eyes, and reclined on the sandy clay bank.

CHAPTER **12**

IRA HAD BEEN SITTING IN MR. REAMS'S OFFICE FOR TEN MINUTES. It was a glass-paneled cubicle in one corner of a large room. In the large room there were five desks. For each desk there was a type-writer. metal wastepaper basket, and file cabinet. All the desks were stacked with letter files and each desk had a note pad calendar and a telephone.

The only privacy offered by Mr. Reams's office was the privacy of conversation, for anyone in the large room could look through the glass panels. The glass was there so that Mr. Reams, the office man-ager, could look out, but it worked both ways. Ira uncrossed his legs and smoothed the trouser seams at his knees. There was something about his feet, the feeling that his shoes weren't shined, or the feeling that there were holes in his black army socks, that made him tuck them far up under his chair. He read the sign on Mr. Reams's wall, THE BUCK STOPS HERE. His four-page application form that he'd completed was neatly centered on the glass top of Mr. Reams's desk. It contained the answers to questions about his life, his military experience, his education.

Mr. Reams entered the large room. He walked over to his secre-tary, leaned on his knuckles against her file cabinet, like an army sergeant might do, Ira thought, and he wrinkled his brow impor-tantly as he talked to her. Ira watched him talking, but heard noth-ing through the glass. He felt the total darkness between his toes.

Nervous prickles stung his neck and the hairline of his temples. He was acutely aware of his black army tie which matched his suit in color. Nevertheless, it looked like a leftover, salvage army tie.

Then Mr. Reams came into his office. He smiled and sat in his big chair with casters on the legs. He quickly read the first two pages of the application that Ira had printed in black ink. On the third page he shifted in the big chair, and without looking up from the paper, took a cigarette from the package on his desk. Ira knew that he would speak and that he would keep his eyes on the application form while he spoke. He opened his mouth. "You left item twenty-seven blank. The one about, 'Have you ever been discharged from a previous position.'" Ira took his feet from under the chair and stretched them toward the desk, thinking of how to phrase his answer.

"Yes, sir. I can't answer that 'yes' or 'no.' It was an involved situation."

"It's a simple question. Have you or haven't you?"

"No, sir, I wasn't fired."

Mr. Reams continued to look at the application form. Ira felt his backbone tighten, and he saw it clearly, like the backbone in a veal carcass at Swift's, where he brought veal from the cooler to the loading docks on overhead rollers. Where he wore nice white coveralls and a clean paper cap, liking the fresh smell of the veal. It was bled, skinned, gutted, and chilled. The carcasses were sawed in half, right down the backbone; it was those carcasses that, wrapped in cheesecloth, Ira had pulled onto the truck dock, lifted against the pull of gravity to release the rolling hook from the hamstring, and carried into the trucks.

"Do you mean that you were politely asked to leave, or something like that?"

"No," Ira said—his mind flashed back to the newspaper job. "It wasn't a very polite place."

Beyond Mr. Reams, Ira could see the shoulders of his secretary who sat typing at one of the identical desks, like the one that Ira might have. Mr. Reams looked up, closed the application form to its original position, and brought it down flat on the desk.

"Which of the jobs was it?" he asked.

Ira answered slowly, as if it pained him to remember. "It was the newspaper job. I was a district manager in circulation. I had twenty-three boys with newspaper routes."

Mr. Reams smiled. "So you were a district man? Shit! I had a district myself for two years in New Orleans, *Times Picayune*. It's a tough business."

"Yes, it is," Ira admitted, surprised to learn that this man knew the circulation business. It relaxed him somewhat.

Mr. Reams said, "I guess you know what a down route is?"

Ira nodded and smiled across the desk. Mr. Reams settled into his big chair to talk. "One Sunday morning when I was on the *Picayune* I loaded up my papers about two o'clock, made my bundle drops, and stopped at an all-night cafe to drink coffee. It was our policy to have the boys on their bundles and folding papers by four o'clock. About three-thirty I backtracked, checking the bundles. I drank another coffee. At four-thirty I checked the bundles again, and found seven of them exactly where I'd dropped them. I went to the boys' houses, bad part of town, and I couldn't find a single one of those boys. They all decided to quit their routes on the very same Sunday morning. By then it was daylight, so I just picked up the seven bundles and dropped them in the middle of Canal Street."

"It was convenient to have Canal Street in your district."

"Hell, it wasn't! I had to drive two miles to get to it. But I wasn't going to let the city manager find out that I had eight hundred papers undelivered!"

"How many complaints did you get?"

"I got exactly fourteen complaints out of all those papers, and I want to *tell* you, I spent the rest of that Sunday and part of the night looking me up some replacement boys. I was desperate! I even thought about going in the cathouses asking, 'Anybody in here want a real good paper route? You can make a hundred fifty a month, if you work at it!"

Ira grinned at Mr. Reams's joke.

"Let me get us some coffee in here." He pressed the buzzer on his desk. "Miss Wright!"

The head secretary kicked her roller-bottomed chair from under the typewriter and advanced to the glass door.

"Will you bring the thermos and tray, Miss Wright?"

She turned, an automated boob on ball bearings, and coasted into the big room. She rolled over to a table by the door, picked up a tray, put a thermos pitcher, cups, saucers, spoons, sugar cubes, and a tin of Pet Milk on it. Then smoothly she reversed, turned, and rolled back into Mr. Reams's office.

"Did you manage your district well?" His question caught Ira with the hot coffee at his lips. Ira hesitated a moment to consider his answer before lowering the cup.

"Yes. That is, it looked good. I was always up papers on total circulation. I guess I had about the average number of complaints, and no down routes."

"That doesn't sound at all bad."

"It sounds good, but the district was rotten inside. It was in bad shape when I took it over. Most of the boys had lingering debts from the previous manager. He absorbed the loss, but they'd been ruined. They learned they could owe money and not pay it. I extended money to them, paying the bills out of my own pocket, thirty or fifty cents or a dollar each week. It kept the heat off me, but soon the boys got so far behind that it was easier for them to quit the routes than catch up. Some of them owed more than they could have made in two weeks. Then, it seemed sudden, the roof fell in, half my routes went down. I couldn't find replacements fast enough to cover them. I was throwing ten routes myself. The next week the boss took me off the district, put me to running city-wide complaints, so I drew my pay and left."

Mr. Reams exhaled and said, "That could have happened to just about anybody. Doesn't matter, really." He picked up the application form again. "Company policy won't let us hire anyone with 'yes' on item twenty-seven. Why don't you mark it 'no.' I'd like to have you on our team."

Ira glanced through the glass at the ball-bearing secretary who had resumed typing. Beyond her he saw a line of desks, each desk with its own telephone and calendar pad. He looked at his scuffed shoes, his black army tie, and thought again about the darkness between his toes.

"No, sir. Thanks, Mr. Reams, but I couldn't do it. I'd like to work for you, but in a way I really was fired."

Mr. Reams straightened in his chair and extended his hand for a farewell handshake with what Ira took to be genuine warmth. "Thanks for stopping in, Mr. King. I hope you find something to your liking."

"Thank you, Mr. Reams. Thanks a lot."

Ira looked at the mechanical secretary as he passed her desk. She had good posture. Her face was well painted, and every one of her hairs was in place, but she didn't look up when he thanked her for her trouble.

The sun was bright outside, but not too hot. Ira threw his coat and tie in the back seat and rolled up the sleeves of his white shirt. Since he was on the north edge of Beauville, he had to drive back through town to get on the Tongs highway. He passed the Belle Arms Hotel where his father died. Stopping for a red light in front of Beauville's new theatre, he stared at the marquee, remembering Stanley's saying that he ought to go out west and become a movie star. He remembered, "You ain't so bad looking, Ira. At least I know *somebody* that don't think so!"

"That *somebody* was Melissa," he thought, remembering Delaney'd said she was fat. "But Paul Jacobs must have given her *something* for the farm," he thought. "He must have given her some money or something. Putty-faced Stanley. I should have told him all the details about sleeping with Melissa. It's a hard thing to describe, though. But I could have exaggerated it—made a good story for Stanley. I could have told him how she took off her clothes—which she never did—we were afraid we'd get caught naked. If I'd told him the way it really was, it would've been a disappointment. And old up-in-the-clouds James said that I couldn't tell about it. No more than the grass can tell how it feels to be green. The hell I couldn't. I should have told Stanley a good yarn for his hot curiosity. I should have kept that farm, too. But who'd ever expect a woman to just give a farm to a man who was already married to her sister?"

❁   ❁   ❁

Jean watched. There wasn't a crossing at The Falls and no road came to the west side, where they were. A dirt road came in from Tongs to the east side of The Falls. Alongside that road and throughout the pasture on the whole east side, picnickers and fishermen had preened the grass, gathering up all the deadwood for their fires. They even burned the dried cow chips at night to keep the mosquitoes away. The meadow was as pretty as a golf course, for cows kept the grass cropped short, and boys on holiday kicked or threw stones and tin cans and dead fish into the maw of the pool. The west bank shouldered clay bluffs, deep gullies, and pine trees choked with underbrush. Most of the town boys could swim the pool, but they all were told from childhood that the current was dangerous.

While Delaney slept, they didn't get any bites. Jean cautiously took his binoculars from their frayed case and looked through them. She turned the focusing knob as she'd seen him do, and she surveyed The Falls, the trees, the clouds, and she watched an old panel truck drive up and park on the east side. The Muncey family got out of the truck and started unpacking their folding stools and fishing poles. The twin girls ran up into the pasture and their little brother helped his mother put out their cane poles. They set out twelve poles. After a while the twin girls came back and took a lunchbox from the truck, unpacked the lunch on the sandbar near their poles, and started eating.

Jean saw them clearly. She saw that they had no soda pop, but drank from the Okatoma. With the binoculars she watched a big fish, maybe five feet long, arch up from the water and expose its silvery, dirty-brown scaled back to the sun. Its long head tapered to a sharp snout, the mouth of which was lined with rows of interlocking, pointed teeth. Although it was a long fish, paradoxically its body was thick and heavy. Jean didn't know, but the Muncey family would call that fish "alligator gar. Trash fish. The meanest, ugliest, most no-account fish in the river. Feeds off dead things and runs off all the good fish." It submerged. And if that man, Mr. Muncey, who was just finishing his lunch, had a .22 rifle in his truck, he'd take it out on the tip of his sandbar and stand tense, poised, waiting to shoot into that fish's coarse prehistoric head, or the ganoid scales of its back, when next it surfaced.

Then the bootlegger drove up in his low-slung, sporty Mercury with mud flaps and a great, long radio aerial. He stepped out and looked east, up the road he'd just travelled, watching his dust settle. Then he put on his baggy hunting coat that was stuffed with half pints, locked his car (even though it was empty) and walked south into the trees to hide his bottles.

Delaney awoke with a bad taste in his mouth and a terrible thirst. He coughed and cleared his throat, spat, got up, yawned, and stretched. He looked at the poles and saw that they were unmoved. He started to scoop up and drink a handful of river water but stopped, remembering the funeral home blood, deciding he'd rather be thirsty than drink Okatoma water. He saw that Jean had his binoculars. "Hey kid, you see any birds while I was napping?"

"No," she replied.

"You want some food?" he asked, checking the poles again, pressing them deep in the clay bank. "Let's leave these set out and go up here to a clear-water spring. I know one that's only a hundred yards up this gully."

She looked at him, smiled, and followed him up the red clay gully until he stopped in a wide shaded place, a natural grotto. The dry banks of the gully were clean and sharp, like terra-cotta walls surrounding a patio. The warpaint-red clay contrasted with green-velvet leaves of the kudzu vines. On the floor of the gully the carpet of fallen pine needles was ash gray and brown. Spring freshets had left pebbles, white sand, and conglomerate stones in the spring where Delaney knelt. He wet his handkerchief and wiped his face. Then he sat down with his back against the red clay wall. Jean sat at his feet, right beside the spring, watching Delaney open his package of cheese and bread. Dividing the portions, he gave half to her. She folded her bread, crumbled the cheese inside, and ate it from the end, like a hot dog.

Delaney reckoned they weren't far from the old Shiloh Church. Because of the breeze he imagined he could hear the church singing, Sacred Harp singing. He thought, "It was a day like this, and a place near here, the one time I got Essie King out in the woods. I could talk then. Especially to women. I could always talk good, but I went all out for her. I dressed up nice, but then, she was dressed nice too. That's why God made Sundays, and the pine-needle mattress, they say. We were getting our shoes damp in this gully and I was saying to walk up the bank and take off our shoes 'n' socks and dry them and Essie said it was her best dress and they were singing

98

over at the old church and I said up on the bank the pine needles were thick and soft and clean and dry and I had my pretty cousin all to myself. She said they'd miss us and wonder where we were, but we took our shoes off and I made a little twig fire and put the socks on forked sticks over the fire to cook dry and Essie was giggling and laughing and said they'd burn. Then I was laying her back on the pine needles and kissing her good and I thought I'd better take it slow so I stopped kissing her and took a flask from my inside coat pocket and had a nip. Her mouth fell open. I guess she was shocked, her pa didn't drink. I gave her a quick swig and she coughed, red-faced as a panther. It ran out her nose and down her cheek in her ear. That's when I learned that girls have to have lemon or sugar or Coke in their whiskey. She sat up crying, scratched my face. Her curls were down and the wind changed so we got the church-singing good and loud, like it was right behind us. She flew out of there barefooted, but she never told Joe or her father. How could she? She was just about ready to go all the way, her blood was hot, and we could hear the church-singing, ever so soft, and that wasn't a sin. But I put one thimbleful of sour mash on her breath, and you'd think we was all going to hell in a handcart. I wouldn't want to have her back up here, today, but I would like to have that half pint she spilled. That bootlegger's car is down at The Falls right now, they ought to build a footbridge over The Falls so that people could get from one side to the other."

"Come on, girl." Delaney's mind left the memories of Essie King and Joe King and the church singing. He was talking, "Let's you and me get back to The Falls, see if we caught anything. There'll be lots more people coming this afternoon, on the east side, since it's just a week till school starts. This weather can't hold forever. It'll be like a county fair over there." She followed Delaney down the red clay gully toward the deepening roar of The Falls. They walked on dry ribs of white sand which covered the bed of the gully, beckoning to the soft green tendrils of the rich kudzu vines which waved down the sides of the gully.

There was something on one of the poles. The pole arched as Delaney horsed in the squirming catfish. It bucked and twisted and pulled, trying to stay in the water. The thrill of it made Delaney sweat, and he felt a tinge of pride, colored by shame. It was a four-teen-inch channel cat. He put it on land. Its small hard eye looked up unseeing, its other unseeing eye was pressed into the riverbank clay, its limp feeler whiskers waved when its mouth closed and opened as its gills tried to draw oxygen from the air, its sharp rigid spine fin was locked in the defensive position, and Delaney mashed its head with a rock. He put some green leaves and wet mud over the fish to keep it cool and rebaited his hook. After setting it out again, he pulled in Jean's line to see if the bait was still on it. The neat square of bloodbait had degenerated to a tear-shaped blob. He put fresh bait on that hook and reset it while she hunched down close to her pole, watching the taut line make ever so many small vibrations against the strong current.

The bootlegger sat on a dry boulder, out ankle-deep in the water of the east side. He'd folded his heavy coat for a cushion and had his trousers rolled up past his knees. In his mind he sketched a map of his walk in the woods. Like a young father who'd just put out the Easter eggs, he could remember every spot where he'd hidden a half pint. Some were in stump holes, some were buried under leaves or pine needles, one was in the catface of a gum tree. If he got a buyer in the afternoon he could shake hands, taking the buyer's three dollars, and the two of them could go "for a little walk in the woods" where he'd pause beside one of his hidden bottles, scratch at the leaves with the toe of his shoe, and say, "Hot damn, I believe they's a little turtle or something under them leaves," and his cus-tomer would then quickly scoop up the uncovered half pint, pocket it, and be gone. It would be hard for any laws to catch this boot-legger with booze. He'd never been caught. He just hid his Easter eggs and then sold the clues for finding them.

Delaney watched the bootlegger shift his leg to take a cigarette pack from the pocket of his folded coat and strike a match against the dry-topped boulder. Delaney thought, "I'll bet he's thinking all about his half pints, remembering right where each one is hid. Thinking how he won't touch a drop until he's sold fifteen bottles, then he'll take the forty-five bucks back and give twenty-five of it to his wife. Then he'll take twenty and drive over to Red's Place at County Line and drink beer with that gypsy woman who used to tell fortunes. Little whore. I gave her five dollars to lay Ira—all she did was tell his damn fortune. Drink beer and play the juke box and play with her knee under the table, he will, and still have ten bucks left for her at closing time. That's what the little man's mind is thinking, but he ain't sold those fifteen bottles, yet."

Then the Winslow boys drove up in their new GMC. They parked behind the bootlegger's car and walked down to the sandbar, leaving their two-Ford-hoods boat on the truck. They were a little puffed up because the beautiful Muncey girls were cheerleaders at the high school. They talked with the Munceys and looked at the string of four catfish they'd caught. The twins blushed and smiled. They were identical blondes with blue eyes. Mr. Muncey asked, "You boys figgering to trotline? I see you got your boat on the truck?"

"Naw, Mr. Muncey. We been hauling logs, just got caught up with the cutters. Thought we might paddle around a little for the fun of it."

"I see. Pretty nice water today, except right up in the mouth of The Falls."

"We were thinking about coming over them Falls in our boat. It's not much of a drop-off."

"Yeah. Could be done. But if I was doing it, I'd want a boat with a motor waiting just below The Falls, in case anything happened."

The boys squatted on their heels, like Mr. Muncey, and looked across the pool at the smooth dimple that hung perpetually above the cataract and at the blurred, curved crash of water sliding over the lip of The Falls.

At the foot of The Falls the churning water turned upon itself with foam and spume like white manes flying from a close-penned and rearing herd of frightened mares. The water backed upon itself and eddied up, then down. It was a Tongs mystery that sometimes when a fishing line was cast into the foot of The Falls it was grabbed up by the current and pulled, deliberate and slow, as if it had a great dead fish on it, while other times the whirlpool would reject a line and spit it lifelessly back to the fisherman.

Chuck Winslow said, "Let's just paddle around down here in the pool a little bit. I think Mr. Muncey's right. It wouldn't be safe to come over The Falls, 'less you had a good motorboat standing by. A wooden boat might slosh full of water and still float, but them Ford hoods are going to the bottom when they fill up."

Mike concurred. The admiring girls watched them carry the boat by its end handles. They waded out into the deepening water and launched it off the underwater ledge, near the bootlegger's perch, and a strange thing happened. Although the bootlegger knew them well, they were his customers, he didn't speak to the Winslow boys when they walked right past him. He was thinking that they wouldn't want Mr. Muncey to see them on friendly terms with the town bootlegger, for Mr. Muncey didn't drink, and he wouldn't be apt to let his girls go to the movies with boys who knew the bootlegger.

Delaney saw all that, and he knew why the bootlegger didn't speak to the Winslows, but he knew also that he wasn't interested in the Muncey girls, and he knew that he didn't give a fig preserve for what Mr. Muncey thought of him. If he could just get across this body of water he'd hug that bootlegger's neck and walk him up to the bank and shake hands and give him three dollars for a little clue that would uncover an Easter egg.

Delaney stood up. He waved to the Winslow boys. They saw his waving and flashed across the pool to the west bank where they rammed the prow of their iron boat against the damp clay bank, right beside Jean, who stared at them and the boat with wide-eyed admiration. Chuck threw her the painter and she held it with a fierce, white-knuckled grip while they scrambled ashore and tied it to a rock.

"Hello, lads. Are you going to fish? Or frolic?"

"Hey, Mr. Delaney! Whatcha caught?"

"Just one nice channel cat. Nothing to speak of. I was wondering if you two would give me a ride over to the vicinity of that rock, where the bootlegger is drying his feet? It'd be worth four-bits to me."

"Well, I dunno, Mr. Delaney," Chuck answered. "We never had but us two in the boat before. She rides kind of low in the water with just us two, and you're a full-grown man. Why don't you send this little girl?"

"She ain't my girl to send. She's Ira King's girl. Besides, bootleggin's against the law. It'd be something to send a child up to the bootlegger. Come on, lads. I'll sit real still."

The boys were like Siamese twins with the boat, and it never occurred to them that one could wait on the west bank with the girl while Delaney and the other one paddled across. They mulled it over and decided that the water at the south end of the pool wasn't too rough for three. They untied the painter and got in the boat, holding it against the clay bank with their paddles while Delaney cautiously stepped amidships. He slowly sat down, tucking his knees up under his chin. The boat settled. There was only an inch of freeboard on either side when they pushed off from the clay bank and dipped their paddles carefully, working against the steady current that swept clockwise around the bowl-shaped pool back into the foot of The Falls. When they neared the middle of the pool they felt the sickening pull of powerful water—their faces were blood-drained and white with fear. Although they didn't say anything, they all felt it, knew it. They felt the current grow stronger, warping the boat upstream, while every stroke that they made tipped one side of the boat so that a cupful of water lapped over and slipped into the bottom of the boat. Seeing the water, they paddled stronger and rocked more from side to side, but made no headway. The boat got heavier and heavier, and then, just as Chuck had imagined it, one side went down and lapped a great gulp of river water and just didn't come up. The boat slipped completely underwater without sending up a single air bubble. Delaney straightened his legs and stood up against the sinking shell. In fact, he stood straight up when it was about three feet underwater and it looked to Jean like he was standing on a sandbar. But then he settled back in the water between the Winslows and they all started swimming toward the east bank. Still, the current was against them, and in the two or three minutes that it took the boat to sink they'd drifted even closer to the foot of The Falls. Water there lapped and sloshed, kicking up bubbles and foam. The strength of the current panicked all three, it sucked them under. They knew to hold their breath and wait for it to cough them free and toss them up to the surface. They were separated. When their lungs were bursting, when they'd held their breath forever, the young boys kicked and clawed and struggled for the surface. They broke free and gulped the air. Exhausted, they kept their heads above water while they drifted toward the sandbar on the east bank.

The bootlegger had watched Delaney get into the boat and he'd seen them start across the pool, but his mind was on his bottles and he looked south, to where the Okatoma left the big, round pool and continued as a river to the Gulf. He heard a muffled, throat-rattling sob and looked to the Muncey family. The girls were holding hands. Wide-eyed, their eyelashes flashed and tears came to their blue eyes, for they'd never seen anybody drown before. It was such a bright afternoon that it seemed unreal to Mrs. Muncey. The instant the boat sank, even before the men were sucked under, she started gathering their fishing poles, for something told her that she could no longer fish in water where men had drowned. She jerked the poles and lines from the water and flung them on the dry sand behind her.

When the people on the bank saw the boys' heads and gasping mouths, they all started talking at once. That was the first real sound of the sinking. Then they yelled and screamed to the boys, and Mr. Muncey ran frantically around his truck, looking for a rope or a pole or a log or something, and when he found nothing he waded out hip deep against the incoming current and held out his hands encouraging the boys. He saw that they were treading water, he used his strong voice to stroke them, like the coxswain of a racing shell. "Steady! Pull! Watch your STROKE! Don't fight it! RELAX and steady KICK and PULL! Come on, boys! You can make it!"

When the boys got to him he didn't try to lift them, but grabbed each by his collar and let the water support their weight as he towed them to the bank. He said, "Hey, you! On the rock there. I suspect you've got a fast car. There's still one man in the river. Get up to town as fast as you can and bring the sheriff and the doctor! We'll need a motorboat too, tell the sheriff that!"

Nobody, especially the bootlegger, could have denied Mr. Muncey then, for he was a big man, wet and heroic. There was no room to quibble or ask why. The bootlegger bolted from his perch. He splashed to the bank in his socks and dashed through the loose sand to his car. When his left foot kicked the clutch pedal to the floorboard it curled around the rubber-topped pedal like a rooster's claw. Then he urged the fast car forward and it took the spur. He flipped the switch of his shortwave receiver. It was tuned to the sheriff's broadcast band and he could hear the sheriff's calls, but he normally had no need to call the sheriff—he had no transmitter. He hit eighty on the dirt road. There was no radio traffic; all he got was a static roar. When he gunned by the schoolyard he leaned on his horn and didn't stop blowing it until he slid to a stop in front of the sheriff's office. The sheriff had come out to the sidewalk. He recognized the bootlegger's car. "Sheriff! Git down to The Falls, git a motorboat if you can, they's been a drownding!"

Then, driving around the corner, the bootlegger saw that the doctor's office was closed. He thought immediately that he could look for him at his little cabin near the Tongs Bridge, and if he wasn't there he would be at home. He was speeding when he passed the sheriff's office, and he hit eighty-five down the steep hill to the bridge. He'd made many deliveries along the doctor's narrow dirt road. He knew it well. He slowed almost to a stop and turned right. Settling into the ruts, he gunned her up into the yard and stopped beside the doctor's Ford.

The doctor drove well, but not as well as the bootlegger he followed. Strange, he thought, that he'd been in Tongs three years and didn't know about a place called The Falls.

Jean watched everything. She saw the sheriff's car slide up right to the edge of the bank with its red light flashing. She saw the crowd start to gather. She saw the bootlegger return and then she saw the doctor drive up.

There was little for the doctor to do. The Winslow boys were standing up, walking around. He looked into the pupils of their eyes and asked them if they needed a tranquilizer. They declined, shaking him off. The doctor walked around in his shirt-sleeves. The sheriff was the same kind of man as Mr. Muncey. He deputized Mr. Muncey and showed him a line along the bank that the people couldn't cross. They weren't supposed to cross it. Mr. Muncey marked it with his discarded fishing poles and defended it. Then the sheriff radioed the sheriff in Laurel to contact a skin diver who worked for the butane company and send him over. He told his regular deputy to strip to his shorts and swim south, with the clockwise current, until he was opposite the far bank and then cut for it. "When you make your cut, Tommy, swim like hell. You'll be going crossgrain to the main current, but it won't be too hard. Don't look back or to either side. When you get to the bank, climb up the cliff as high as you can and look for some sign of him. I'll keep an eye on you, so if you see anything just wave and point."

The bootlegger saw that the sheriff was too busy to care, so he trotted down into the pines and scratched up his hidden bottles. Since he'd left his big coat on the rock, he stuffed them inside his shirt, tightening his belt as far as he could stand it, to keep them from falling through. Then he went back and mingled with the growing crowd. Word had spread, as it does, and a flow of new people came down the dirt road toward The Falls. He sold whiskey openly, slipping the little bottles from his shirt until he'd sold out in half an hour, and then he went home to scratch up his reserve, a whole case of half pints, from under the loose corn shucks in his pine-pole crib.

CHAPTER 13

ALTHOUGH HE HADN'T GOTTEN A JOB, IRA FELT GOOD WHEN HE RE-
turned to the fishing cabin, changed clothes, and hung up the
suit. Quickly, he made a cheese sandwich and slipped the folding
knife into his trousers pocket. He ate on the way, for he was anxious
to join their fishing. He followed the winding trail down the west
bank, passing by the fox grapes and the place where Delaney had
heard the rain crow. He could then hear the faint roar of The Falls;
it reminded him of the sickening army sound of artillery shells
moaning overhead—not the bang of the guns which fired them, or
the explosion of their detonation, but the scream of their passage.

When he got to The Falls, he saw a hundred people standing on
the east bank and Tommy Ethling standing up on the highest part
of the west bank. He knew that Tommy had been swimming, for
his hair was wet and his wet undershorts had picked up a stain from
the red clay. Tommy didn't recognize Ira and glanced away from
him, then saw him again and knew him and stumbled down to meet
him. He didn't know how to tell him about Delaney. Ira looked
across to the east shore at the crowd which stood just above the
rocks where Joe had always told him to watch for mermaids.

"Ira, Mr. Delaney's in The Falls." Ira looked at Tommy's face. He
stared at the embarrassed shock in Tommy's eyes, realizing instantly
why the crowd was there and why the sheriff's car was parked by
The Falls. He looked at the white spume of the leaping river. Then
he saw the girl sitting on the bank downstream.

He fetched her, carefully winding the lines about the poles so that they wouldn't get tangled in the kudzu vines, while she uncovered the channel cat that Delaney had caught. She carried Delaney's binoculars. They walked back up the trail along the west bank toward the cabin, and when they got there Ira heated her a can of beef stew. He skinned and gutted the catfish, cut its head off, and put it in a pan of cool water, setting the pan by the window.

He left Jean staring at her bowl of stew and drove up from the fishing camp, turning right onto the asphalt road. He crossed the Tongs Bridge and passed the turnoff to Essie's place. Then he urged the old car up the steep hill and past the Baptist Church. When he got to the corner of the school grounds he turned right and followed the town street to where it was unpaved and became no more than a dirt trail through the pasture and down to the picnickers' side of The Falls.

When he'd parked his car he started for the river, pushing through the crowd, sensing that the crowd was neither shocked nor sad. Nobody recognized him. He overheard people talking about many different things. A voice said, "He was drunk. He made a bet he could swim The Falls. Mr. Muncey tried to stop him, but he stripped off nekkid and jumped off that big rock."

At the river bank he ran against stern-faced Mr. Muncey. "Have you found him?" Ira appealed.

"No. You can't come past this line."

"Don't you know me, Mr. Muncey? I'm Ira King. He was my father's cousin. He was my cousin, my friend. He buried my mother and my father and my aunt."

"Nobody can pass this line. I'm a deputy, Son."

"Don't you remember me, Mr. Muncey? You came in my father's store lots of times. You knew my mother and my aunt. I remember when your little girls, twins, started school. They always dressed alike, like twins. He was my friend. We were going to buy a farm and settle down together and have a place. Don't you remember me?"

Mr. Muncey was drunk from the glory of pulling the boys out of the river, and the way the bootlegger had run at his command, and the way the sheriff had deputized him, and from enforcing the line. His eyeballs were glazed. They'd never focused on Ira's face until then, when he squinted and looked into the young man's eyes.

"Sure. Sure, Ira. Come on through. Watch your step here. I've been holding the line. We've sent for the skin diver from Laurel. We'll find him for you, Ira King."

"How did it happen?"

"It shouldn't have happened. They should've known better. They all three tried to cross the river in that little Ford-hoods boat. It was too much weight." Ira stood with his shoes in the water, staring at the white water of The Falls.

Then, after a while, Paul Jacobs arrived. Although it was a week-day, he wore a suit with a white shirt and necktie. He stayed high up on the bank and got the story from several different people. He talked to the Winslow boys to see if they were all right. Then he quietly climbed up on the back of their GMC. Many of the people knew that he owned the land they were standing on, and many of them knew that it was his money that had secured the loan for the truck he was standing on. He removed his hat, a brown Mississippi felt hat with a short snap brim and a thin outside hatband. It was of the sort that Tongs men called "dress hat." He looked through the open bed of his truck into the dirt of his land, and he curled his hatbrim in his palms while the people began to gather around the big truck in a moist half-moon. He wet his lips. "Since there isn't a preacher here, and since we've had such a tragic thing to happen here, I think a few words are in order."

The people were hushed. Some mumbled "Amen."

"Lord, we appreciate the way you looked after these two boys and delivered them to us. Look after Mr. Delaney and deliver him also, we ask in Jesus' name."

"Amen."

"And now, further, I want to announce to all of you gathered here that I'm going to have a steel gate put straight across the road up there by town. I'm going to fence off The Falls. There's never been anything good to happen here. Tom Delaney wasn't the first person to be lost in The Falls." Then he climbed down from the truck and most of the people were thinking that he'd do it, too. And they were also thinking that he would get their vote if he ever ran for public office, as it was rumored that he might.

Ira's sweaty palm turned the folded pocketknife over and over in the secrecy of his pocket while he looked at Paul Jacobs's well-shined shoes and sharp cuffs and listened to him talk. The bootlegger had gotten his wares to the Winslow boys and they were alive and drinking and responsible, telling and retelling their story, and they'd been just as close to it as Delaney had, maybe even could have saved him, at least should have known more about the capacity of their strange boat than he did, but they came through it OK, because they were young, and because they worked for Paul Jacobs, and Paul Jacobs owned their truck, and Paul Jacobs owned this land and even the west bank and The Falls and clear up to the Tongs Bridge and even beyond to Essie's house and up Mill Creek to the beaver pond. They were young and healthy and had had a good breakfast and a good dinner and good exercise and now were having a happy notorious drink and even with all that, white-skinned and well-brushed Paul Jacobs felt that they should be mentioned first in his speech, he felt that they were more important than Delaney, who was old and didn't eat regular meals and bathed in the river and, although he had represented the finest, Houston House, could no longer brag that he owned a clean set of underwear. He was down in the maw of the black pool with the trash, rocks, mermaids, tin cans, dead fish, lost hooks, and alligator gars. Ira turned the hard knife in his palm and wondered why Paul Jacobs deserved his good fortune and why one of the Winslows couldn't have taken Delaney's place in the river.

"They found him. They found him!" The word passed from mouth to mouth like a fat, crazy-spinning moth. The crowd was a limpid cheese when it scooted down to the riverbank. No part of the crowd was in a hurry or wanted to be first, but they all wanted to see the dead man. Their spokesman, the bootlegger, said, "Old Delaney just decided to come up for a drink. You know him! He heard they was a party going on!"

A titter of a nervous giggle rippled the porkchopping crowd, and they didn't notice the thin man who stayed back at the truck, the man who was sick, who crawled on his knees in the cow-cropped grass. He got up and looked at his face in the stiff-armed eye of the rearview mirror of the idle log truck. He wiped his wet face with his shirt-sleeves and walked east up the dusty road to where he'd left his car.

❄   ❄   ❄

Delaney's sister came from Jackson for the funeral, bringing her new husband who'd never met Delaney and looked, himself, to be more dead than alive. That morning Ira unpacked Delaney's suitcase, inspecting it to insure that there were no grisly surprises for her to uncover in it later, when she got back to Jackson. There was a safety razor, a comb and brush set, several bottles of hair tonic, eleven pairs of rolled socks, a bundle of letters, a lightweight jacket, and a fur cap. There was also a bundle of worn notebooks and frayed bird guides tied with rawhide thongs. Ira decided to keep them, not give them to Delaney's sister. He lifted the jacket and found it heavy. From the right side pocket he took out a pistol. It was an old but clean Smith & Wesson revolver. He swung open the cylinder and saw that it was empty, then he closed the cylinder thinking, "She won't need this, either." He slipped it under the mattress of his cot, closed the suitcase, and wrapped it in a sheet of heavy paper, tying it around the middle with the line from one of the fishing poles. He dressed again in his dark suit and black army tie, leaving the girl in the cabin, while he arranged for the funeral. Delaney's sister had stayed overnight with the Muncey's, and Ira took the wrapped suitcase to her there.

At the church Ira saw Melissa. She was with her mother, her sister Anna, and Paul Jacobs. Gappy was there, and so were Mr. Pittman and the Muncey family. Ira didn't recognize anybody else, but guessed that a young, well-dressed man was the new doctor whom Delaney had told him about. Then the Winslow boys came in and sat near the front. Ira didn't recognize them. While the preacher was talking, he wondered if the girl was OK, back at the cabin. He tried to remember if Melissa had gotten darker, thinking, "No. It must be the shadow she's sitting in, but Paul is right beside her, and he doesn't look dark. He looks fair-haired. The old woman just looks older, and I guess the baby girl, Shirley, didn't come. God, what's happened to Anna? She's bleached her hair. No hairdresser this side of Jackson could have fixed it that way. So that's what money will do for a plain girl. Melissa's got money too, but she sits still, like she always did, meditating, like the world is too common-place for her full attention, like she might just up and fly away at any moment. We used to tease her, called her Palmolive because we thought she needed soap, because she was so much darker than the rest of the kids. She's like she was the last time I saw her. I'll bet that she and the old woman talk Italian all the time. It's queer. James would have come up from the Gulf Coast for Delaney's funeral, but nobody in Tongs knew how to get in touch with him."

Melissa was thinking, "Ira's behind me and he can see me. Why didn't you write like you said you would, Ira? I kept your six dollars for you, and I'd still go into the loft with you—but now we're older —I'd go into the house with you, or to the motels in Beauville, or Jackson. Baby. I tore down the little cane house you built—where we found the snake that one time. Could you believe I did a thing like that? Ira, they're both dead now, Ira. Nobody could tell you no, now. It's a good thing I came to this funeral, unless maybe you're married. Would you be married? I did my part. I kept your six dollars and it's grown now because my family is wealthy now. Paul divided up the money, to save on income tax. Paul knows all the tricks. Your father couldn't stop you now, and just look at Paul, he married an Italian and everybody likes him, and I could give you just about everything you would want, if you aren't already married, or you could leave her, you left me, you could leave her for me, where are you staying, how long will you be in Tongs, you are beautiful, you are beautiful, I can't see if you have a ring on your finger I'll ask Paul to find out for me if you're married and where you live."

The preacher was a big man, big enough to work for a living, some infidels said, some pool-hall idlers. He had a square, hard face and his hard lips slammed together straight and clean when he talked, like the pages of his heavy Bible. He talked fast, it was his style. He talked almost as fast as his thoughts went, faster than most people could follow. When it came time to pray, however, he'd shift into low gear and slow down, lowering his voice and talking slow, like he was just talking to God and nobody else. He was talking fast about Delaney, not taking time to clear his throat or wet his lips. Ira watched his lips clapping shut, saw a little white froth of spit form in the right corner of the preacher's mouth. The preacher kept banging his lips and the spot moved around to the middle of his lips. He didn't know that he had spit on his lips. He was really wound up. He kept talking fast until the spot dissolved or fell off. He was in a frenzy, drunk with his own King James words, and his mind raced ahead of his words. He couldn't talk fast enough to keep up with his thoughts.

The preacher knew Delaney, and he did a good job of talking around his vices. He remembered the weekends when Delaney had stayed in Tongs with the Kings, sleeping up in the loft of their store. He remembered some of the Sunday mornings when Delaney had gotten up before the sun and met the scout troop out there, beside the church, to take them on long nature walks. The preacher's son had been a scout, and at one time he could identify forty-one different birds. The preacher said that Delaney was generous and kind. He didn't say that his boy was in that crowd Delaney took to County Line on the night of their graduation and left there, drunk, to find their own way home. He didn't say that Delaney thought it was a big joke, an initiation into manhood.

Delaney's sister's husband seemed to have fallen asleep. His head nodded and his slack jaw tried to pull his mouth open, but he kept his back straight and occasionally peeped out from under his heavy eyelids.

The preacher talked until he knew that it was time to stop, and then his powers of invention failed him, and he could think of no graceful way to end his eulogy. He opened the Book and started reading, fearing that it might not be appropriate; but it must have been, for the people all sensed the roundness and completeness of his sermon, just as well as if the lights had dimmed, or the thunder crashed. Then it was all over, and Delaney rode out, leading the procession to the cemetery northeast of Tongs, to be eased into a hole in a broom sage corner between two red clay fields.

On the way back to town Gappy asked Ira about his plans. Ira said he'd stay in the fishing camp until he could arrange the sale of his property, the burned-out store. For once Gappy wasn't very talkative. He was thinking about having to look at the hollow, black eyesore of King's Store every day. Ira thought about the store too, recalling that secret night he and James and Stanley drank warm, smuggled beer up in the loft and laid the plans for his leaving Melissa; Tongs, Mississippi; and going west to work on a ranch, to be in the movies, to be in the army, to have down routes—reality and visions blurred the picture on the movie screen of Ira's private imaginings.

Back in the cabin Ira told Jean to comb her hair and come with him to put Delaney's sister on the Jackson bus. That's when Ira realized that she had no comb, no toothbrush. He looked at her, thinking, "How could I eat in the same room with this child for ten days and not see how filthy she is. That one set of clothes, that same set of clothes is all she has. Delaney might have said something to me about it. Nobody else has seen her, not up close."

They drove to the Munceys' house in Tongs and parked behind Muncey's panel truck. They found Delaney's sister and her husband ready to go. Ira thanked the Munceys, and leaving his old car parked there, the four of them walked the two blocks to the bus depot. Ira carried the wrapped suitcase under his arm and eyed the old man, wondering if he'd make it. The girl followed with Delaney's sister, who looked not to the right nor to the left, glad that it was over, relieved that Delaney wouldn't be in Jackson next week or next month or next year asking for money, asking to stay in her back bedroom.

They waited on the sidewalk in front of the Elite Cafe while Ira went inside to check the bus schedule. The waitress, Midge Farley, told him that Mrs. Muncey had called just twenty minutes ago and that it hadn't changed since then, if they'd just be patient the bus would arrive in about four minutes. Ira asked for two tickets to Jackson. She said, as if she didn't remember Ira, or disliked him intensely, "Just like I told Mrs. Muncey, we don't sell tickets here. This here is a cafe, not a bus terminal. We have a schedule posted on the wall over there, and the bus stops in front, that is the extent of our responsibility. And I'll tell you one more thing, we don't get a penny for our trouble. You pay the driver for your ticket."

Ira retreated from her words and waited on the sidewalk with the others. He looked at the black gap in the row of buildings where King's Store had been.

The Trailways bus was coming, it had learned to stop at Tongs since the time Ira left. Then, he'd had to take Nathan's taxi to Beauville to catch the bus, he remembered. They couldn't see it, but it was passing the cutoff to Essie's place that the doctor owned. Then it climbed the steep hill leading to Tongs. It passed the church, the school grounds, and then they all looked up and saw it appear on the main street. It passed them and turned at the old train depot, coming back to stop in front of the Elite Cafe. Delaney's sister took Ira's hand and patted Jean on the head. Her husband looked at the girl and shook Ira's hand. They got on the bus as soon as the door opened. She fumbled in her purse for the fare and told the driver that they had a package too big for her to hold in the seat. He made change and flipped from his driver's seat like a cat. He leapt through the door, whipping a little chromium wrench from his hip pocket, walked down the side of the bus, jabbed his wrench into the locking hole, gave it three or four quick turns, and lifted the folding door to the baggage compartment. Ira handed him the Delaney box; he put it on the edge of the compartment. Then he braced his hands against the bus and used his foot to give it a quick hard shove into the dark recesses of the compartment. He strutted back to the passenger door. "All aboard!" He jumped up the steps to his seat, made a pencil note in his logbook, and closed the door. There was a hiss of compressed air when he released the brakes. The bus drove away, passing the school grounds, the church, down the hill, past Essie's place, across Tongs Bridge, past Pittman's station. It turned north at the highway intersection.

❋   ❋   ❋

At the same time the bus left Tongs, Paul and Anna Jacobs were returning Melissa and her mother to their little house on the WPA road. He pulled the big car halfway off the narrow road, near their mailbox that still had a dim MIKE NATALE stenciled on the side. All the doors opened on the big car, making it look like a great brooding hen getting ready to wallow in the dust. Mrs. Natale leaned across the seat to kiss Anna on the cheek, and Melissa told Paul again what she wanted him to find out about Ira King. At first he'd refused, so she made a stronger statement, "I want you to find out. I want to know where he is staying and how long he will be in Tongs." Her eyes flashed.

"But why, Sis? He's nothing to us."

"Find out. I swear if you don't find this out for me and come back here this afternoon to tell me, I'll go to a lawyer. Mama too, and Shirley. We're three. Anna and you only count for one. I'm good at arithmetic, Paul. I understand how you've divided up Papa's money."

"Sure, sure, Sis! No need to get excited. I was just thinking you could've said something to him at the funeral, if you'd wanted to. I'll ask the Winslows. They were talking to Delaney before he drowned. And I'll ask Gappy. He knows everybody's business. Don't worry, I'll be back in a couple of hours. 'Bye. 'Bye, Mama. See you."

Then, a mile later on the road to Tongs, Paul asked, "Anna, why the hell's she asking about Ira, anyway?"

"Because she loved him—she still does—didn't you know? Papa caught them together in the barn. He went to see Mr. King—Mr. King sent Ira away to keep him from marrying an Italian."

Paul Jacobs stared at the black-topped road. His mouth tightened. For six years he'd thought that Ira was his wife's lover. He took a cigarette from the package in his shirt pocket, pressing in the chrome cigarette lighter with his index finger. He stole a sideways glance at Anna to see if she was aware of his realization. She was relaxed, she too followed the road with her eyes. He tried to keep his voice soft, calm. "Didn't you have any boyfriends—back then?"

The notion amused her, she laughed. She said, "Not until the day you came, then I had lots of fellows, for five or six weeks, remember? Until I fell in love with you."

"Yeah." He lit his cigarette, believing her, knowing then that he was the first of that crowd to kiss her. Others kissed her in those five weeks of group courtship, but none claimed—and they certainly would have claimed—anything more than kissing. "So your father caught them—huh?"

"Yes. I've always understood Melissa's ways. In her mind she's married to Ira King."

Paul looked back at the black-topped road. In thirty seconds his mind had been cleared of the six-years' lingering bitterness that Ira King had slept with his wife; in the next thirty seconds his mind realized that Melissa thought she was married to Ira King—defiant, arithmetical Melissa thought she was married to burned-out, penniless Ira King.

"But there's no need you jumping when she says frog. She's my *younger* sister. She knows her place."

He was slow to reply. "I don't trust her—no, I don't trust any of the three women out there. They're all the same, your mother and Shirley are just like Melissa. Where would we be if she up and married Ira King?"

"He wouldn't have her before—why would he have her now?"

"Because he was rich then and she was poor. Now, it's just the opposite. There's *our* money involved, more than you're aware of. Didn't you hear what she just said about the property being divided up? She's crazy like a fox. I'll drop you off at the house and I'll go back to town, to see Gappy, and then I'll go out to see the Winslow boys. We've got to protect our interests."

         ✿   ✿   ✿

Ira and Jean got the car from Muncey's place and thanked Mrs. Muncey for putting up the couple. She said she was "Pure D glad to do it, but didn't that gentleman look old and sick!" Ira said that he did, adding that Delaney's sister was the last of the Delaney family.

"Well, Ira, that's one thing you have to be thankful for—this sure is a nice child you have. It's just a pity that Clara's not alive to see her granddaughter, and Mr. Joe."

"Oh, she's not my girl, Mrs. Muncey. She's an orphan I got in Fort Worth, and she doesn't have a stitch except what she's wearing. I'm on my way to Beauville now, to buy her some clothes. Thanks again for keeping Delaney's sister. Can't I pay you something for the trouble?"

"You know better than to ask. Don't make me mad—we were glad to do it. 'Bye, now."

By the time Ira and Jean got to Beauville, Gappy had heard about the girl's being an orphan, but Paul Jacobs changed his plans and went to the Winslow's first. They told him that, as they remembered it, Delaney said the girl he was fishing with wasn't his, she was Ira King's. But they added that they couldn't be sure, although it seemed that was what he said.

* * *

"We want to try them on," Ira told the woman in Beauville. "If you would, please, just pick out four or five pretty dresses that will fit her—some underwear—some shoes—" he felt the surge of generosity that characterized Delaney, the exhilaration of the high roller —"socks—shirts and jeans—a good belt. A good leather belt."

The woman realized that he didn't know, for sure, what he wanted. She put her tape measure around Jean's waist, squinting to read the measurement. "Let me write this down," she said. Four or five dresses, underwear, shoes, socks, shirts, jeans, and a belt. If you'll leave us ladies alone for about half an hour, I think I can fill the bill."

"Thank you," Ira said, starting toward the door, trying to avoid seeing the counters and merchandise. It wasn't the first dry goods store he'd been in since he left the King Store in Tongs, but it was the first Mississippi dry goods store he'd been in since then. He stopped for an afterthought. "What's your favorite color, Jean?"

"Blue."

"Then let us also have a nice blue robe—or housecoat—a long one."

"Yes, sir, we have some nice ones."

* * *

When Paul Jacobs stopped to talk to Gappy the shop was empty, and Gappy was idly swinging a barber chair on its greased pivot. There'd been added a sofa, a magazine rack, and a *Ladies Are Welcome* sign was painted on the front window. Gappy told Paul where Ira was staying. He said that Ira had a girl, an orphan, with

118

him, and some of the women in town thought it wasn't right for a man and a big girl, who weren't related, to be living together. Paul listened intently. He asked, "Gappy, do you reckon he's married?"

"No. Told me last week he wasn't."

"How long do you think he'll stay here?"

"Told me, long enough to sell that burned-out store. I hope he can, it runs down the looks of town. That might take some time, though, considering how slow things are going in Tongs, these days. I can't think why anybody would want to buy it. It'd be damn expensive, just to clear it off."

"Yeah," Paul said. His mind moved quickly, for he began to formulate a plan to get rid of Ira King. He flopped into Gappy's second chair and turned the handle that made it lean back. "But if somebody owned his own truck, and worked steady at it, it wouldn't take long to haul all that stuff off. That's a choice lot, if this town ever booms again. Make a good supermarket."

"Now, that *would* help my business," Gappy said, "if the men and boys got haircuts while the women did their shopping. It would help considerable. I'd be damn glad to see that mess cleared off. It makes the town look—messy."

"Thanks for your time, Gappy."

"Sure, Paul, anytime."

"And, if you hear anything else, anything, about Ira, give me a call."

"OK." Gappy nodded. Then he watched Paul straighten the chair, get up, and walk out of the shop. He watched Paul get in his new tan and brown Oldsmobile and back away from the curb. Paul made a big, lazy, illegal U turn in the middle of the main street and started back to the Winslows'.

The Winslows were still wondering about his earlier visit. It was Chuck's opinion that he was probably intending to make Ira King marry his wife's sister, like Ira should have done those six years ago when he left town, but Mike was arguing that Chuck was wrong, he said it wasn't that other girl Ira should have married, but Paul's own wife, the sister Paul married, when Paul drove up to their front yard.

They walked from the porch out to Paul's car and got in the back seat. He pressed a switch and the windows closed. He kept the motor running and the air conditioner on. The radio was tuned low to a Jackson station.

"You boys convinced me from the time you invented your Ford-hoods boat that you were more-than-average smart, and I like the way you've been keeping up on your truck payments. I really do. I happen to know that you've started a savings account at the bank in Beauville, maybe even thinking about getting married—that's good." The brothers exchanged glances, then Paul continued, "Now, what I have in mind for you is something for men who are more-than-average smart. It's something bigger than logging."

"Good. Good, Mr. Jacobs. What is it?"

"I want you to buy that burned-out lot in Tongs, where the King Store used to be, and start hauling that trash off and clean it up. The fall rains will be coming soon, there will be a lot of days when you can't get in the bottoms. If you think this little rainy spell we just had was something, just wait until November. The store is high and dry, right in the middle of town, make a good place for a super-market."

"Boy! That would be great! Chuck, buddy, how would you like to own a supermarket?"

"Just fine, Mike. I'd like that just fine!"

"That's the spirit, boys. Once you've got big money behind you, you can do anything you want to. I'll notify the bank in Beauville to let you have up to three thousand dollars to buy the lot—but be sure to keep my name out of the deal. I wouldn't want people to find out I was connected with it. You know, don't ever let your right hand know what your left hand is doing. People would start saying that I'm trying to buy up all of Tongs, and that's not true. Ira King is staying at Pittman's Camp, so get on down there and see what he'll sell that lot for."

"Sure, Mr. Jacobs. What's it worth? Wouldn't want to pay too much for it."

"Find out what he's asking. Get it as cheap as you can, but get it." Paul spoke softly, confidently—disliking Ira King for old, complex reasons—thinking that the burned store was Ira's only tie to Tongs.

Then Paul drove back out the WPA road to report to Melissa. He lied to her that Ira was leaving in a day or two, as soon as he'd sold his father's store, and that he was living with a girl. He said he'd asked Ira to come out and see Melissa, for old times' sake, and Ira had spat, then laughed in his face. He lied straight and hard, talking fast, overpowering her face until she dropped her eyes to the floor and was sorry that she had asked, was even sorry that she'd kept Ira's six dollars for him.

She left Paul on the front porch, where she'd eagerly met him, and walked around the house to the backyard. She passed the barn where she'd loved Ira, and followed her private path to the creek. She took a long walk in the tangled creek bottom, remembering Ira, and she decided, while she walked, that she'd lost him. She spent four hours pulling peeled willow sticks from the beaver dam, throwing them high on the bank—in deliberate sabotage.

CHAPTER 14

THE DOCTOR WASN'T AN EMISSARY OR CONFEDERATE OF PAUL JACOBS when he visited Ira and the girl. He'd seen Ira at the funeral, and he remembered Gappy's telling him about the events that led Ira to sell the farm to Melissa. He guessed that the dark, pretty girl who sat with Paul and Anna Jacobs was Anna's sister, Melissa. He'd spoken to Gappy before the funeral, and Gappy told him then that Ira had an orphan girl with him, down at Pittman's fishing camp. At least, Gappy had said, that's what Mrs. Muncey had told him. She said that the girl was wearing greasy clothes and had dirt around her face and up her neck into her hair. Gappy said that Ira King was "good folks," but he added, for he was a good, thorough gossip, and it was an intriguing notion, that there was a growing sense of apprehension among some Tongs folks that, somehow, it wasn't quite right for a man Ira's age to be living alone with a girl that age. It was reported that three ladies of the Baptist Church had visited Ira and the girl. That visit went well, reportedly, until one of the ladies lightheartedly remarked, "Well Ira, you can't be a heathen *all* your life." To which he had replied, with strong language, "Git, . . . Hell, . . . damn, and stay . . ."

The doctor's Ford squeaked over the deep, dry-caked mud ruts which led to Ira's cabin. He parked behind Ira's old car and got out, wondering where he got his strong compulsion to visit a man he didn't know, a man who had, reportedly, run off three clean ladies of the Baptist Church. Stepping onto the porch, he spoke to the house, checking to see that there were no dogs. There was no reply. He went inside. Remembering when he'd helped the county health officer in Blueridge inspect motels, he noted the essentials—no running water, no lavatory, no bathtub, no commode. There were no dirty dishes, however, and the portable stove in the kitchen was clean. The topmost item in the brown-paper trash sack was the whole skeleton of a fried catfish. The vertebra and ribs were picked clean, but a crust of browned cornmeal on the caudal fin showed that it had been fried in hot grease. Back in the living room he saw that the cots were made with the sheet corners tucked in like hospital beds, or army cots. Then he went outside to the front yard, for he was beginning to feel guilty for his snooping.

When towel-wrapped Ira and Jean came up from the Okatoma they were still wet. She ran into the cabin to put on a new dress, and Ira's hands made a soapy-clean squeak when he rubbed them through his hair. He wiped them dry on his trousers and shook hands with the doctor.

"I'm Doctor Forsythe. You're Mr. King, aren't you?"

"Yes. Ira King."

"We have something in common. I own some property that used to belong to you."

"Yes, I heard that you bought the farm. It belonged to my aunt."

"It's a pretty place. I'm really pleased with it."

"It's a good sandy-loam farm, and that clear creek, Mill Creek, is worth a thousand dollars."

"I have a practice here in Tongs."

"Good. I'll remember you, if I need a doctor."

"Will you be staying here?"

"A while, until I sell my father's store, the burned-out building across from the Elite Cafe."

"I see. Well, I just wanted to pay a courtesy call and welcome you to town, but then, you'll really more of a citizen here than I am. I mean, this is your hometown."

"Yes, it is, but thanks anyway for stopping."

"Oh. Will your girl need a preschool examination?"

"Well, Doctor, to tell you the truth, she's not my daughter. I don't know yet if we'll be here when school starts. I don't even know what grade she's in. She hasn't been taught to keep herself clean—she hadn't bathed for a week, until just now, when I took her down to the river."

"Where's her mother?"

"I never met her mother. The girl was abandoned at my house in Texas. Seeing that she doesn't bathe, I wonder if she knows about . . . you know?"

"Well, how old is she?"

"Eleven."

"Does she show secondary sex characteristics?"

"I don't know."

"But you helped her bathe?"

"But I didn't. I showed her a place and handed her some soap. I went upstream."

"Oh, yes. Of course." The doctor had embarrassed himself. "Well —well, bring her by my office tomorrow morning." He looked toward the house and lowered his voice to a hoarse whisper, "Tell her it's a preschool examination—which is true, of course. My wife works as my receptionist. I'll have her talk to the girl and make sure the child knows—what she should. What's her name?"

"Jean."

"She looks to be a bit shy."

"She is. I've only known her a week, though. She's beginning to trust me."

"Besides that," the doctor raised his voice, "with winter coming on, everybody should have a flu shot and a checkup. It'll be cold in this cabin."

"You're right, Doctor. I'll bring her in the morning. Thank you very much for stopping."

"Sure. Say, why don't you walk up to my cabin someday between two and three. I take my relaxation then, I'd like to show you how I've fixed it up."

"I'd like that. How about tomorrow?"

"That would be fine, but it's one-thirty now. If the girl can stay by herself, you could ride over with me now."

"Well, let me go in and ask her if she's afraid to stay alone. I'll just be a minute."

Jean came out of the cabin with Ira and she stood on the porch watching them get in the doctor's Ford and close the doors. The new motor started silently, she could only tell that it was running by a faint jet of blue smoke that came out the tail pipe as the doctor drove away. He went up the rutted road, turned right at the station, sleeked across Tongs Bridge, and slowed. Then he turned left at his private road and stopped beside his cabin. He unlocked the front door and showed Ira through the fireplace room into his new lounge room, formerly Essie's kitchen, saying, "Sit there, if you like. Isn't this quite a bit different from the way you last saw it?"

"Yes. It's very nice."

"I fixed it up with the idea in mind of the surgeons' lounge in the hospital where I interned."

"You were going to be a surgeon?"

"Not really. It was for all of the doctors—it just happened to be near surgery, I mean, I didn't intern as a surgeon, even though I admire them. Care for a drink?"

"Sure, why not?"

"Cigar?"

"No, thank you. You've really changed things here. This room was a kitchen. There was a dry safe there, where your magazine shelf is. One time my aunt's cat caught a copperhead snake and brought it in here. Ate the back half of it and hid the front half under the dry safe. It came to life and started striking at my aunt's feet, but it didn't have enough tail to get leverage, so it just flopped around while she stood on a chair, screaming. That was a favorite story in our family. This is damn good Scotch."

"Yes," the doctor mused, "I like that story—it's funny about snakes, the way people react to snakes. By the way, I know quite a bit about you. I've sort of been snooping."

"Oh? What have you found out?"

"Nothing serious. I just asked the town barber, Gappy, about the previous owners of this place, and he told me a story about your leaving."

"Yeah. I guess it was a scandal."

"And I treated your mother before she died, and your aunt, too. In fact, I made a call to your aunt in this very house."

"She died here, I believe. It's too bad you weren't in Tongs before they sent my cousin away. He lived in this house. Maybe you could have done something for him."

"What was his trouble?"

"Epilepsy. And brain damage caused by stroke."

"Then I guess I couldn't have helped him much—some types of damage just can't be repaired."

Ira, shifting in his chair, said, "I really like how you've fixed it up. Could I have another look at the fireplace room? It's the most interesting part of the house."

"Of course. Bring your drink." The doctor spoke as he led the way into the big fireplace room. It was empty of the cane-bottomed chairs and cast-iron bed with chenille cover that Ira remembered being there when Essie was alive. There was a poker set, a six-sided table covered with green felt, and six straight chairs at the far end of the room. A hang-down Tiffany lampshade was centered over the table, and there were three pedestal ashtrays snuggled between the chairs. The walls were painted off-white, and the floor had been sanded down to new wood and varnished. There were no pictures on the walls, the mantelpiece above the fireplace was painted and empty, the black mouth of the fireplace had been scoured out. Nothing of the Kings remained, except the two antique Hessians who stood like snag teeth from a bottom jaw.

"Card table?" Ira asked.

"Poker. Do you like to play? I have some fellows in a couple of nights a week for a friendly game, two-bit limit, mostly draw poker. The fellow who sells whiskey, Norm Funderburk, Gappy, sometimes Paul Jacobs."

Ira flinched when the doctor mentioned Paul's name. "No, thank you, I don't play. I see you put in new screens and windows."

"Yeah, and a paint job, patched the roof. It's an extravagance, I suppose. A doctor should be so busy with his work that he doesn't need a hobby to keep himself occupied. I was reading *Walden*. It set me off."

"*Walden?*"

"Yes. My best friend is Henry Thoreau. He said that most men lead lives of quiet desperation. I believe it. I've been quietly desperate, in a second-rate way, for the last eight years. I got through medical school, but I had to pay the price." As he spoke, the doctor wondered why he'd just told a stranger the thing that he considered to be most private. He wondered why he'd exposed himself. It wasn't his nature.

"What do you mean by that?"

"I guess I mean that I learned things I think I'd be happier not knowing—then I came to this dead town, thinking I wouldn't have to work my ass off."

"I know what you mean. No doubt there's not enough around here to keep you busy."

"There was a flu epidemic last year. The most amazing thing about this area is that there are so few babies born here. They told us in school that new babies would keep a GP going, but that's not the case here." He paused. "I believe it's cooler in the other room."

They went back into the smaller room and he closed the door. "What will you do here, Ira, do you have a trade?"

"No. I don't have much education, other than reading a hell of a lot of novels. I only have a year of college. I was in the army, but I didn't learn anything of practical value. Then I messed around with newspaper circulation, and later, for three years, I loaded trucks at a packinghouse. I was a part-time student in college, then."

"But you'll have to find work, eventually, do something about the King Store?"

"Yes. Maybe I'll get a loan to rebuild it—but I don't want to be in the clothing business—there's really not much I can do. I'm a damned good artillery forward observer, but there's really not much call for that outside the army. How about another drink?"

"Sure, let's have another—two's my limit, because I have office hours this afternoon."

"I want to get back to work soon, maybe the packinghouse, a man can't just sit around and think all the time, he'd go nuts." Ira spoke as he watched the doctor pour his fresh drink. "Being here in this house is like being nuts, in a way. Sitting here in this bright carpeted surgeons' lounge drinking Scotch whisky. Looking close I can see, through your new paint, the old grease-splattered wall behind where the cookstove used to be."

"I hoped you wouldn't mind the way I moved in here and changed things all around."

"Oh, no—not at all. It's like a crazy dream, though. A nightmare dream, us sitting here in fine chairs, relaxing in a surgeons' lounge, drinking. I can see the spot through the carpet, under the bookcase, where the half-a-snake smeared blood." A long silence followed. Ira broke the silence with a question. "Did you ever look at one thing and see something else?"

The doctor regarded the drink in his hand. He responded slowly, "Yes, I have."

"What was it?"

The doctor knitted his forehead, as if he were trying to form an image in his mind. "My wife," he replied.

"What did you see?"

"We were high-school lovers, and then she was a secretary in a sawmill while I went through college. I wanted to be a doctor, but, like I said, I didn't know that med school teaches you things you're better off not knowing. Speaking for myself, if I had it to do over, I'd be a naturalist."

"My friend, Delaney, was an amateur ornithologist."

"I studied biology in college. I enjoyed pure science."

"I *really* should have finished college," Ira said. "I try to make up for it by reading novels, and history books, and listening to good music on the late-night radio shows."

"Are you married?"

"No. I met a woman when I was in the army—an Indian. When I left the army and moved to Fort Worth she came down from Oklahoma on the weekends. I wanted to marry her, but she wouldn't."

"It would be good for the girl to have a woman in the house."

"Janet wouldn't have liked the girl, she said she hated kids. I've been thinking I might load up and take Jean back to Fort Worth, return her to her uncle—I'm not the sort of fellow to take good care of a girl."

The doctor looked at his watch, feeling awkward that he and Ira had talked so openly. "Well, Ira, I've got to keep my word. Two drinks. By the time I get back to town it'll be three o'clock. I'll drop you by your place. Thanks for the company."

"Not at all. I'll walk down the river. It's a nice day for a walk. Thanks for the drinks."

"Sure. It's a pity you don't play poker, but do come by again soon. Like I said, I'm here every day from two to three. Don't forget about tomorrow?"

"Good. Good-bye."

When Ira got back to the fishing cabin he found Jean waiting on the front porch. She said, "I made some coffee for you. It's on the stove."

Ira looked at her, almost as if he'd never seen her before.

"Really?" He shook his head, feeling the effects of the doctor's Scotch and the exertion of his walk home. He went inside and poured himself a cup. She'd gone a bit heavy on the coffee, but he liked it strong. He tasted it carefully, then took the strainer full of grounds out of the pot, checked the door to see that she wasn't looking, and added a cup of water to thin her brew. He turned the burner up high to reheat the coffee, poured himself a cup, and took it out to the porch. "Thanks for making coffee, Jean."

"Sure."

"That man who was here is a doctor."

"Oh."

"Have you ever visited a doctor?"

"Yes. When I was sick."

"What made you sick?"

"I had the flu, and one time I broke my arm."

"Well, he thinks you should have a checkup before school starts. So you'll be healthy for school."

"OK. But it'll cost money. It cost twenty dollars when I broke my arm."

"He's a friend, he won't charge much."

The next morning Ira told her to put on a new dress. They drove into Tongs, and Ira walked her to the doctor's office. Mrs. Forsythe was expecting them. She said, "Hello, Mr. King; hi, Jean, how are you both doing?" The doctor's wife was showing pregnancy. She put her arm around Jean and pulled Jean close to her side. "Mr. King, if you'll wait here and read a magazine—the *Time* is new—we won't be long. Come in here, dear. That's a beautiful dress, it goes with your hair."

"Thank you." Jean blushed.

They disappeared through a curtained doorway for half an hour. Then the doctor came out and smiled to Ira. "It's all set, Ira. She's a fine, healthy girl. Martha's giving her a list of drugstore things. You might just give Jean five dollars and let her take the list to Mrs. Weems. Martha's going to call the drugstore and tell Mrs. Weems to expect you."

"Thanks. Thank you very much. Will you give me a bill?"

"I'll send it to you."

Jean came through the curtain. "Good-bye, young lady. Come see us again sometime."

She smiled at the doctor and left his office while Ira held the door open for her. On the way to the drugstore she told Ira, "You know, she's his wife, but she called him Doctor Forsythe all the time?"

"That's because they're professionals."

"What's professionals?" Jean asked, looking up at Ira.

"It's people who do their job well."

"Was Clyde a professional?"

"In a way he was. He did a good job at Swift's."

"But he was mean." She looked at the street, biting her lip.

"Maybe it takes a mixture of kindness and knowing your job—maybe it takes both kindness and knowledge to be professional. Let's think about it. Here's some money. Did you want to buy anything at the drugstore?"

"How'd you know that?"

"The doctor told me to give you some money."

"What for? Did he tell you?" she asked, suspiciously.

"No. He just said I should give you some money."

"He's a professional, that doctor."

"No doubt."

"Did you know his wife's going to have a baby?"

"Well, yes, I noticed that."

"She let me feel it. I put my hand right on her stomach. She told me to."

"Well, here's the drugstore. I'll wait in the car for you."

❊   ❊   ❊

But Ira didn't sell his burned-out store. The Winslow boys talked to him three times, trying to get him to set a price, and they decided he was crazy. Chuck said, when they were leaving the last time, "We'll give you three thousand dollars *cash money!*" But all he got was a silent shake of King's head endorsing his comment that the store was not for sale—to them—at any price. He didn't tell them, but he wouldn't sell to them because they took Delaney into The Falls when he drowned, and because they wanted to put a Piggly Wiggly where King's Store had been, where Ira had lived for nineteen years, where he'd been born.

They thought he was crazy, and they thought Paul Jacobs was almost crazy. Ever alert, they'd priced some vacant lots not four blocks from the King's Store, and found that a man could buy any of several nice ones for a thousand dollars, but when they told Mr. Paul about the other lots he got red in the face, said for them to do what the hell they were told to do, that he wasn't paying them to think.

That afternoon, after the Winslows left Ira's cabin, a hot rain fell. Ira watched it rain, and he missed the discipline of going to work. He missed the clean white coveralls and the crisp white paper cap that he'd worn at Swift's. He thought of going back to see Mr. Reams in Beauville to ask for the job. When the probate court turned the few hundred dollars from his father's bank account over to him and gave him title to the store, he'd asked the bank in Beauville for a loan to rebuild it, but they turned him down.

He thought about that, and he thought about having to put a heating stove in the cabin, and work an hour each day cutting firewood for it. He thought about putting Jean in the Tongs school, where he'd gone to school, and he thought about taking a walk up to visit the doctor—it was two o'clock—when he heard Gappy's knock on the front porch. Gappy was nervous and declined to come inside, so they talked on the front porch.

Gappy told Ira that he'd always had strong feelings for the King family, and there was something that he just couldn't keep from telling Ira, for old times' sake. "Now you know I keep my ear close to the ground, Ira? See no evil, hear no evil, speak no evil, that's my motto. But sometimes you can't help it, there's evil in the world, like it or not. Now I heard something the other day, and when I heard it I thought to myself, 'Wouldn't that just make you sick?' Paul Jacobs put those Winslow boys up to buying your store to get you to leave town. They couldn't get you to sell it, so he found another way to get you to leave town."

"To get me to leave town?" Ira looked deep into Gappy's face. "Why?"

"Think about it a minute and it's pretty simple. He traced you back to Fort Worth and found out about the girl. He must've bought off some city officials there, because he's got them to send an extradition for her. They're going to put her in an orphanage."

"That's silly. Why would they? I begged those people to take her before I left, and they didn't have time to listen to me. Besides, why would Paul care anything about me or the girl?"

"I believe it has to do with Melissa. He's a trustee for the estate that Mike Natale left, he's made it grow, but it belongs to all three daughters and the mother. He's afraid that you could sweeten up Melissa and speak for one-fourth of the estate, maybe more if you got the little girl and the old woman on your side, and Melissa tells them two what to do. He wants you to leave Tongs, for good."

"But I haven't been served with any papers."

"He's told the sheriff to wait. He let the word leak out so it'd get to you and you'd have time to think it over. He's giving you a chance to run and cover your trail."

"Did he send you to tell me?" Ira looked him hard in the face.

"Yeah, Ira. You could tell?"

"Well, Gappy, you were pretty shifty-eyed, telling it. Did you see any papers?"

"No. But he's got 'em. He said he wasn't faking. Don't think I'm telling you this because of any love for Paul Jacobs, Ira. I liked him, at first, everybody liked him. He was the town hero, the way he come into all that money. But I see him in the shop all the time, he's pretty underhanded. Some of that land he owns, the people wasn't exactly falling all over themselves to sell it. You know, people feel funny about their land. Even if they have to sell it, sometimes they hate for one man to get it all."

"And you're sure he has the papers?"

"Far as I can tell, he really does."

"Is there anything else that he *didn't* tell you to say?"

"Now, Ira, all he told me was get over here and tell you it was a rumor that he had papers to serve on the girl. That's *all* he told me. That other stuff, it's my own thinking. I might have done you a bad favor, tellin' what I did about Melissa, and about his property being divided amongst the women. I might of put a bad idea in your head."

"No. No, Gappy. I could have figured that out by myself. Does Melissa have any men friends, now?"

"Shit! You kidding? She's just like a ghost. I only see her once a year. She stays up on Mill Creek. I swear, back in the old days people would have called her a witch. If some cows was to die, in the old days I mean, near her place, people would be out looking for her—she's that spooky."

"Well, thanks for the information."

"Don't mention it. I've got to go. I've got to live in this town, Ira, after you're gone, you know."

"Sure, Gappy, 'bye now."

"See you, Ira."

Ira went in the cabin, where Jean was looking out the window. She'd been listening. Ira brewed a pot of strong coffee, hot coffee, twelve miles from the Mississippi town of that name—a town famous throughout the state. He drank the coffee steaming hot, one cup right after another.

At three o'clock the slanting hot rain stopped. A windy front moved in from the Gulf Coast, kicking an endless chain of high clouds above Tongs toward the northeast at twenty miles per hour. It seemed to Ira that it had cooled dramatically. The trees were still, but the high scud of clouds marched across the sky, making it appear as if the earth were on a treadmill. Ira opened all of the windows and doors for fresh cool air. He pulled on his walking boots, indicating to Jean that she could come along, if she wanted.

He left the cabin open, and she followed him, sure-footed in the mud. Ira cut a sweet gum limb with his folding knife, trimming off the branches while they walked. When they reached Pittman's station Ira was struck by the fact that the empty cola bottles were stacked in the same place where they had been nine years before— when he and Cassfield had stolen cases of them to pull off the glass rings, then strung the rings of glass in a pine tree.

He saw the red Indian motorcycle that killed Stanley. It was propped on cement blocks behind Pittman's station, but he didn't know that it was the same machine—he just saw it as an abandoned wreck of a motorcycle. Tendrils of the succulent kudzu vines twined up to the handlebars, not expecting the pending frost, and Ira slapped the rotten leather seat with his sweet gum walking stick as he passed, remembering, "You'll steal them bottles one day and come here the next day trying to sell them back to me, you bums!" "Let's throw them in the Okatoma, Cassfield, and burn the boxes, so they won't know—we can't take them back, they ain't no good with the rings pulled off." "Hit him on the shinbone, cut his damn head off!" He looked toward the river, "I got an eel, Stanley, big as a goddamn cottonmouth, bigger!" "Ira, tell him 'bye. They won't never let him come home again, tell old Cass 'bye."

Jean and Ira turned onto the blacktopped road at the station and followed it up to the Tongs Bridge. When they topped the bridge they could see the steep hill rising into Tongs and the white Baptist Church on the right. They crossed the bridge and turned left, north, upstream, toward Essie's old place, the new doctor's place, and when they got to the mouth of the clear creek, Mill Creek, they followed it toward the small house. On the trees the green clusters of pecans were star-fingered against the scudding clouds, and the black crows defended the pecan grove with caws and false alarms, setting a tone of desolation for the little clearing and the house which shone like it never did for Essie King, Cassfield, or Ira's uncle. The eaves of the cabin were turning drops of accumulated rainwater—water was beaded on the windowpanes and the freshly painted frames and sills. The doctor's car wasn't there, and Ira whacked the chinaberry tree with his walking stick, disappointed that he'd missed the doctor, the man he could talk with freely, the man who he felt to be so much like himself that he could have been his brother. He went around to the front yard and saw the hollow stump that Cassfield had cussed every time he'd stumbled over it and many other times when he just felt like cussing it.

They walked out the sandy road and turned right at the asphalt road and walked onto the bridge, passing under the arched girders, passing the overpainted scar that the red Indian had made in the bridge railing. Ira was wondering what people had done to get across this place in the winters, before the bridge was built. He decided that they must have had a ferryboat of some sort, but no one could be sure; most people seemed to prefer to forget about their past, or else lie about it. Tongs did appear in the Civil War atlas, under the name of Zion Seminary, but there had been no battle here, nothing was written down about Shiloh Crossing.

Back in the cabin he and Jean sat close together at the folding table. Some connection had been made, some switch in their minds had been tripped, for he felt that she knew everything. He knew she'd overheard Gappy's conversation.

"Well?"

"Well. If that man comes to git me, I guess I'll have to go."

Ira cleared his throat. "I don't think you'd like it—in an orphanage."

"No. I wouldn't. I hell-fire wouldn't."

"I guess he could do that. He's got a lot of money."

"I hate to be trouble to you."

"*You're* not trouble. *He's* trouble. Paul Jacobs is trouble."

"Oh."

"See, he married the sister of my old girl friend?"

"Yeah." She didn't see.

"And besides, we just plain don't like each other. From the first grade, the teacher sat us on opposite sides of the room."

They started to pack their accumulation of personal things. He gave her a stout cardboard box for her new clothes, and he started packing another such box for himself, putting his folded black socks and underwear and trousers and extra shirts into it. He packed Delaney's bird guides and binoculars. He stripped the covers from his cot and put them in another box. Finding Delaney's pistol under the mattress, he put it in the box, too. Then he poured the gasoline from the lantern and the camp stove into the car tank and put the rented camp stove in the trunk so that he could leave it off at the station. He put their boxes in the car and checked the cabin to be sure that they weren't leaving anything. They crawled up the muddy road in first gear, the old car complained, but it didn't spin, for it had a lot of weight and fair tread on the four tires.

The kid working Pittman's station wasn't surprised that they were leaving. He obviously didn't care. He took the camp stove to the door of the station and carelessly dropped it inside, agreeing that the rent was paid up. He said that he'd like to get rid of the stove, asked Ira if he'd buy it for five dollars. Ira paid him that, and put it back in the car.

Ira needed gas, he had half a tank, but he didn't want to buy it from Pittman's station. He turned on the blacktopped road and ran the old car up to forty, hugging the center line. He slowed and turned left when they got to the highway intersection, driving south toward the Gulf. In half an hour they were well out of Chambers County. The pines were green against the brown broomstraw, and some of the underbrush and hardwood trees were beginning to turn fall colors.

Then it was dark. When the car slowed for towns or railroad crossings Jean felt the brakes grab, and then she felt the series of gentle lurches while Ira shifted the transmission up to the faster gears. There was enough moonlight to outline tree forms, and the headlights scanned reflecting billboards, fencerows, and the continuous bar ditch. They didn't talk. She slept.

CHAPTER 15

IT WAS AN EASY, FREEWHEELING FEELING. IRA SAW IN HIS IMAGINATION that the four wheels had so smoothly honed their relationship with the axles that the wheels knew the axles, the wheel bearings were smooth and burnished bright. There was no friction, no jolt, no hill to impede the relentless steady onward flow of the old car that enfolded Ira King and Jean Harlow. It was all hanging together in a harmony of rhythms. There were regular sounds like the slap slap of a bald tire on the asphalt or the thump and thump of a tire boot coming down like a clubfoot on the road. They hummed along. The horny steering wheel was smooth and substantial, big enough for a good grip, and the linking mechanism had so much slack that Ira could move the wheel a quarter of a turn before it nudged the front wheels. Then the whole front of the car with the bumper and the chromium ram followed that nudge to the left or right. The seat covers were the original ones. They had been velvet or plush and the color was faded out and they were threadbare, but the springs were good. They were so taut that it felt nice to run your hand across them and feel the quality that had been there. Ira could imagine the pistons bobbing up and down in strict Prussian order. The camshaft turned, and valves opened and closed above the heavy splash of thick crankcase oil, embraced by the rusty labyrinth that the cooling water followed all through the engine to the radiator and back again. The coolant water flowed through the motor block like his own blood flowed through him, Ira thought. He thought that blood was life, and thinking that, he remembered the old rumor in Tongs that they put the blood from the Beauville Funeral Home in the river. That meant that their blood was in the river water—where he and Jean had bathed, where the country Baptists (not the Tongs city Baptists) immersed their sons. *There is a fountain . . . filled with blood. The blood of the Lamb.* Of kinship. *Flesh and blood —Blood is thicker than water.* Ira had only to press down the accelerator ever so slightly to make everything turn and flow faster—yet it kept the strict, formal order.

The moon was up good, and occasional clouds slipped quickly across her face, throwing dark blotches on the roadway and the bar ditches. Jean was too big to curl up on the seat beside him, so she slept, propped against the right-hand door. He saw that the lock button was not pressed down, the one that pulled off the threaded locking rod when it was pressed down, but before that night drive he hadn't had much reason to lock the old car, not since he bought it in Fort Worth. Ira reached across Jean and pressed down the button, locking the door, knowing that the way it stuck, and the way the button pulled off, he might never get it unlocked again.

He thought of Fort Worth and the money he'd saved to buy the car. The steam and stink of the pig-squealing packinghouse was a crisp memory, frozen in time and space. He remembered the story that the old-timers at the packinghouse liked to tell new men, about the time before they made the rule that workers on the killing floor had to rotate jobs every week. The story concerned a man who stuck pigs. He worked up on the third floor, above the cafeteria where employees could buy a bowl of beef stew full of beef, a big bowl, hot, for twenty-two cents. He wore a big rubber apron and rubber boots—like they still wear. The pigs and shoats and sows rolled into his room squealing, hanging by their back-leg tendons from iron hooks on an overhead conveyor. They passed him slowly, about twenty per hour, and he stuck them in the throat as they passed. They screamed and bled freely. When they left his narrow room flinching, yet not quite dead, they slapped through rubber batwing doors into the scalding room where jets of high-pressure steam cleaned and softened their skin and loosened their hair. A constant din and rattle and squeal and hiss of steam, the mechanical sounds, continued for hours—steady, monotonous. A trained ear could distinguish the indignant terrified squeal and snort of the incoming hog from the shocked and paralyzed scream of a dying hog when he slapped into the steam. They sometimes joked that every part of the hog was marketable except the squeal.

The story was that one hogsticker went mad on the evening shift. He pulled the emergency overload switch that stopped the conveyor and lifted the squealing unstuck hogs down from the iron hooks. He took off his apron and rubber boots. Standing barefoot— he was six-foot-six—he wiped his sticking knife clean with his sweat towel that hung beside his lunch box. The freed hogs milled toward the employees' door, and the foreman tripped over them when he came in to see why the line had stopped. He slipped and lost his dignity, fell on his butt, and sat on the hot steel floor among hogs amuck. The professional knife in the professional hand stuck his throat, and then the mad pigsticker went down to the processing floor and stuck five more hot men in their throats before the security guards finally got him to put down the knife. That's why they rotate pigstickers, according to the oldtimers.

The gas tank wasn't full when Ira left the fishing camp, he remembered, and he noticed that the indicator needle was nudging E. Keeping both hands on the wheel, he speculated on how much cash there might be in his billfold, seven or eight tens and some ones, he thought. The funeral had come out of the bills he brought from Texas. There were the travelers' checks. There was more money in the bank, a little bit; there was that black char in Tongs. The house and store where he was born. Some water pipes that had served the upstairs bathroom were still standing, but the walls and floor that had been around and under them had burned away. The washbasin broke off and fell to the foot of the two pipes that fed it, but the toilet bowl was heavier and probably had heavier pipes, for it had arched gently to the ground. Ira surmised that while the pipes were hot and soft they had slowly dropped down, and then as they cooled and hardened they made a rainbow curve over the burned-out store.

Ira didn't want the lot, or the charred beams and lumps of melted plate glass window. He didn't want the graceful toilet bowl pipes, or the accusing stare of the burned-out lot that looked like it was a face with eyes somewhere within that pile of things, things that regardless of their annealed twist or melted form he could still recognize for what they had been—before the fire. The face had eyes somewhere, but the overpowering image of the face was shaggy tormented eyebrows, ash gray, char brown, soot black.

"And what happened to her wisteria vine that was eighteen years old and ran up special wires that he fixed for her all the way to the window of the back bedroom, what happened to the Indian-head pennies that were scotch-taped inside my history book, the conch that came from Gulfport, or Biloxi?" Ira thought.

Going to the Gulf. The idea took shape in his mind. Ira was going due south, toward the sea. A map was etched into his mind. "Lateral movement to Oklahoma and Texas was perhaps necessary movement, but it was negligible movement. The Mississippi River runs south to the Gulf. Sherman marched southeast to the sea. Just as surely as north on a map is up, all that goes up must come down. The pond overflows into a branch that meets a creek that flows into a river that joins another river that flows into the sea. The water that washed Delaney is now in the sea. The water in the radiator is doing its job, but the gas needle is on E."

The old engine was a cat. Ira could imagine that he heard the pistons slapping, filling their chambers. It ran so quiet because the tolerances were all worn smooth and comfortable. Maybe the compression rings were worn; nevertheless, they were oiled and smooth. But the needle was on E. He knew that any gasoline station that they might pass would be closed, but Ira started consciously hoping for one, even if it was dark and empty. In the darkness ahead of and above the cloud of light that the old car generated and cast out, Ira King saw a mirage of a new Magnolia station. It sailed before them like a warship in the night, like a destroyer, everything was bright and new and freshly painted. It had a compressed-air lift which rose in the lube room on a burnished steel pillar as big as an elephant's leg. There were giant unseen underground storage tanks for the different grades of gasoline and Diesel. There was a new, black, coiled air hose for filling tires and a long-spouted water can, galvanized, for overheated radiators. The gas pumps stood like marines at parade rest, while four ladies in big pretty floppy hats and white gloves and magnolia blossom corsages were pouring punch and serving squares of frosted white cake—for it was the grand opening. An attendant in uniform was serving cookies to small boys and giving them free rides on the auto lift, pushing first the up button and then the down. There was a shrill sound of escaping compressed air when the lift came down, and the boys' giggles in anticipation of whose toes would first touch the cement floor, which was complete to the smallest detail, gently slanted so that the water could drain, when they washed cars. The manager stood inside the station behind a new plate glass window, and he straightened his cap and smiled, even while he kept his eye on the cash register. One of the serving ladies was the nurse. "What was her name?" Ira tried to remember. "Sarah. The Spanish lady. The one who I knew was going to follow me down the hallway." Ira knew that she would talk and smoke and talk and smoke and then follow him down the hallway. She'd asked—was Ira old enough to buy wine? Did he know the way to the liquor store? She smiled with the same mouth that had kissed Ira, and she gave a man in overalls some punch, some strawberry punch. Sarah. He tried to focus and see her more clearly, but the picture faded and dissolved. The gasoline needle had stopped its pulsations and lay dead against the bold-faced E.

Then Ira saw a real station, a dark station, and eased off the accelerator. The smooth car grew quiet, and when he nudged the wheel she simpled from asphalt to gravel to the concrete driveway behind the shadowy pumps. It was impoverished and dirty-smelling of motor oil and boredom and sweat. Signs in the dirty window appealed for him to smoke Camels and drink Coke and put Bardahl in his motor oil. The motor was idling, and he put the car in gear and rolled off the driveway to park on the gravel beside a fifty-five-gallon drum that overflowed with empty oil cans. Ira switched off the motor and got out to stretch his legs, closing the door softly, so as not to wake Jean.

Remembering the time when he and Cassfield stole the bottles, Ira didn't go too near the station, for fear that somebody might see him and think he was a bottle thief. He guessed it to be about one-thirty, and figured that the station wouldn't open until seven or eight. He couldn't yet smell or feel salt air on the breeze, but he thought of the Gulf when he noticed that what he'd assumed to be white gravel underfoot was crushed oyster shells.

Somehow, the night reminded him of the one that he and Delaney had talked through. "Whiskey is good with someone like Delaney," he thought. "How many stockpiled bottles melted in the fire? What does a bottle of ninety-proof do when it gets that hot? Wouldn't it get hotter and hotter until it burst, and then spread out and burn with a blue flame?" Ira needed a drink to put him to sleep, to stop the endless and anxious floodgate of faces and places from running through his head, but there was no drink in the car. He knew there was whiskey to be bought, illegal whiskey, somewhere within a mile of where he stood, but Ira was a stranger here—it couldn't be bought by him. He quietly opened the rear door, put the things from the back seat down in the floorboards, and lay on the seat to try to sleep.

Jean was snoring, softly like a woman might snore, but then it occurred to Ira that he'd never heard a woman snore. No wonder nobody would marry her. Willard Ford wouldn't. Willard Ford would take a trade. It was like a story Ira read in *Playboy*, that business. "How much money in the bank? Hell, I've saved five thousand dollars, most of it waiting for Janet to decide to marry me."

Then he remembered his dream of Willard Ford making a trade to do the carpet, the woman wanted carpet so much—Willard knew that only women want a carpet, men would never spend the money for carpet, if it was left up to them—Willard was trading, she knew her husband wouldn't let her pay a hundred fifty, so Willard made the deal for a hundred and took the fifty in trade. The husband came home, and Willard Ford's panel truck was out front, and Willard rolled up and hid in some new carpet, and the husband didn't know. He sat down on the roll of carpet and Willard couldn't breathe and the wife was scared to death and the husband said where is the carpet man and she says he's gone off somewhere and the husband says his truck is out there and she says do you want a cup of coffee and the husband says no I want a quickie and they went in the back of the house and Willard went out the front of the house.

"Why is it that no matter how hard or how long you stare at a woman," Ira wondered, "you can't see through her clothes, not even if you blink your eyes as fast as the frames flash in movie film and think about the nude statues in the capitol building. Even with the nude pictures in the men's magazines, there's no real idea of what a real woman looks like, there's no real idea of what Janet looked like, what she felt like. Nurse Sarah followed me down the hallway. She was crazy. She was a nympho. She was a wino. I told Willard Ford about her coming into my room that night. The next morning I was beat, I'd gotten no sleep—he could tell. He said you had quite a night, I told him how she came down the dark hallway, avoiding the creaky board, how she softly opened my unlocked door. Willard wanted specifics, he knew which questions to ask. Stanley asked about Melissa, what was it like, he didn't know which questions to ask, Willard did. I got the feeling Willard liked it more than I did, just hearing about it. When Delaney followed me in Madam Pow Wow's trailer house I know he expected to see more than he did, for he said to her, mad, 'Is that all he gets for five dollars?'—he was my second-cousin. What about Melissa? Delaney brought a parrot through Tongs one time that could talk. It said 'hooker, hooker, and kiss it, baby.' Delaney said parrots live fifty years because they have good stomachs and short guts—he said she was a hen and called her Dora Belle and said she'd never ever laid an egg." Other thoughts came to Ira, or dreams, for he was asleep.

He slept until daylight, and as he waked he felt somebody looking at him through the window. Jean was sitting up, looking out at a man whom Ira took to be the station attendant. He was slim and had small red eyes set deep in his head. His hair was thin and black, and he seemed unsure of who he was or what he was doing. Ira crawled out of the car and spoke to him, feeling the oyster shells crunch under his feet. Ira told him that he was out of gas and had stopped to wait for him to open up. He looked like he didn't believe Ira, or didn't believe Ira had any money. Then Ira told him he was completely out of gas and would have to push the car back to the pump. Ira didn't know why he wanted to lie—it seemed that he had to do it, to make himself more real and believable. He'd been lying right along, he thought. He'd lied to the welfare woman, and he'd lied to Mr. Reams. He lied and ran away from Paul Jacobs's threat, because it was a windy day, or because the clouds were blowing.

"OK," the man said, "but hit's in gear," as he leaned on his thin hands against the hood and pressed the old car backward toward the driveway. Ira slipped under the wheel and, pressing in the clutch, knocked it out of gear. Then he walked around beside him at the hood, ready to push. The man looked at Jean, who'd climbed out of the front seat and was standing off to one side watching. He said, "Grab a holt, girl," and jerked his head for her to come help push the car. Maybe she heard, maybe she didn't, but she came over beside the man and pressed against the car like they were doing. Then they all pushed, and the Dodge crunched back up over the little bump onto the cement drive, toward the gas pumps. All Ira could hear was "Grab a holt, girl grab a holt, girl," echoing over and over, ringing in his head.

The attendant put in eleven and seven-tenths gallons of regular while Ira checked the oil. He added a quart. It was the last of the case he'd bought in Texas, at the railway salvage store. By the time he got it poured in, the attendant came around to the front and asked if he needed any more. They like to sell oil, they make double profit on oil. Ira said, "Yes, I need three quarts of two-bit oil." Then he went inside to pay for that and the gas. Ira handed the attendant a ten from his roll and asked how far it was to the Coast. He pointed to a highway map that was tacked to the inside of the door which opened onto the lube bay, saying that there was a red X on Highway 49 where they were, and that Ira could use the string to see how far it was to any place that he might want to go, as long as it was in southern Mississippi, Louisiana, or part of Alabama, since that was as far as the map went. Ira found the red X and the string. The string was about a yard long, black, braided nylon fishing line. One end was tied to a nail in the map, which was just west of Myrtle, in Union County, and the dangling end had a small lead weight that caused the string to hang straight down, bisecting the map from north to south. When it hung still the lead weight was south, about half an inch in the Gulf, but there was a faint, gray line where it had rubbed a pendulum's arc across the map from every jolt and slosh of opening and closing the door. The gray line cut inland making land at Pass Christian on the west and Pascagoula on the east. Further inland, it passed through Mobile Bay on the east, and it went north of Lake Pontchartrain on the west.

There was a linear scale in miles at the bottom of the map, and Ira measured his distance to the Gulf by marking the map distance on the string, pinching off the distance with his fingertips, and then holding that section of string up to the linear scale. It looked like it was about twenty-five miles. Ira asked the attendant how far it was to the next cafe, but he wouldn't tell him in miles, he stepped over to the map and put his finger on a spot south of the red X. Ira put the string to it and guessed that it was about ten miles. When he dropped the string against the map it bounced two or three times and settled into a short, ever-decreasing swing, following its own gray line. Ira looked at the lead. Having previously paid more attention to the string, and seeing that it was a fishing line, he'd supposed that the weight was a lead fishing sinker, but it wasn't. It was a spent bullet. A .30 caliber bullet. Ira took it in his hand, feeling that it was flattened on the nose and bent to one side, as if it had hit a bone, or a hard surface. The string was tied to the bullet through a small hole. There was an indention or opening to the hole on one side (a nail had been driven through the bullet to make the hole) and a flattened burr on the other side (where the nail had come out). The nail had displaced the lead when it was forced through the bullet—if the person who made the hole had used a small drill, it would have removed the lead within the hole, and that would have been a neater job—there would have been no flattened burr. Also, by driving a nail through it, the person had distorted the whole bullet, for the soft lead had been forced to expand to accept the nail. This bullet couldn't now be fired through the bore of a .30, for it was too big.

Ira dropped the bullet back to the end of its tether, wondering why it had been chosen as a talisman. Jean, sensing that he was ready to go, had gotten into the car. As they left, Ira didn't thank the attendant for his service, and evidently he didn't think enough of their patronage to thank them, or ask them to stop again.

Ira couldn't remember when he'd eaten last. "Surely Jean's hungry," he thought. She looked straight down the road, south, and Ira thought about eggs and ketchup and grits and a breakfast steak. He thought of coffee. Somehow the presence of Jean reminded him of the smell of coffee, or the freshness of coffee. He told himself that he would get her some Breck Shampoo for her blonde hair. Then he thought again of the lead slug that seemed to fall from north to south through Mississippi and into the Gulf. There was a man he'd known in the army, Stephens, who would ask, "What is gray-green and lives under the ground about two feet and eats rocks?" The answer was a gray-green rockeater. Stephens would wait a few minutes and then ask, "If you could, realizing of course that it's impossible since the center of the earth is molten nickel, but if you could, this is a hypothetical question, if you could drill a six-inch hole right through the center of the earth from Georgia to China, and if you were to drop a rock into that hole, would it, number one, fall to the center of the earth and stop? would it, number two, fall past the center of the earth and stop, fall back *up* past the center of the earth and then stop, and then fall back down, et cetera, in decreasing distances until it finally remained static at the center of the earth? or, number three, would it simply continue to accelerate as it fell through the earth and just shoot out the hole in China and break away from the earth's atmosphere and launch itself as a satellite?"

Thinking that one of these answers was correct, a person might pick number one, two, or three—most people picked number two, but they were wrong, because Stephens would say, "No, you dumb shit, the gray-green rockeater would grab it when it fell just about two feet down the hole." Ira thought that if the bullet were the rock, and if it were falling down the map of Mississippi, he might be the rockeater—or he could be the rock and be falling down the map of Mississippi. "If Jean was the rockeater, would that make me the rock?" he wondered. Stephens's trick question seemed important to Ira, because it showed that things usually aren't so simple as they seem: the obvious answer may not be the right answer. Last night he'd dreamed of leaving home and the things connected with home before he left, before the fire, before all that. He dreamed of the secret places in the store, loose boards in the attic, the movie house with its midnight shows and its white bed-sheet screen, and Melissa. She had a feminine shape, and her arms and shoulders were soft. She smelled of Rose Hair Tonic, or perfume—not little-girl sweat as she did when she was two grades behind him, yet even then she was his size, when he was in the sixth grade and called her Palmolive. Her eyes were big and black, dark in the sockets, and her cheeks were smooth like an Eskimo. Ira dreamed that he'd lied to his father about her, that she really was pregnant, and Jean was her daughter, and she gave Paul Jacobs the farm so he'd let her send Jean by Clyde Ponder, to him.

Ira felt Jean's eyes flicking to the left—up ahead—to the left, to a cafe. He stopped dreaming and followed her eyes to the cafe. Then he slowed the car and prepared to turn in at the cafe, thinking, "Delaney should be with us now. Nobody could enjoy a big cafe breakfast more than Delaney. He liked Jean. He took her fishing. Delaney was a good man with kids. He always took the scouts on bird walks, and wouldn't he take a fellow to the County Line, when a fellow got old enough?"

Jean and Ira were both hungry. Her eyes followed the regular, jiggling advance of the cafe. They both smelled the hot grease and fresh-chopped onions, the slices of ham searing on the flat grill, as one man's eggs spat sunny-side-up beside another man's hamburger. Sliced red tomatoes and hot grease and bacon and mayonnaise, all the smells mixed together in the warm cafe, the smell of coffee over all. Ira stopped the car, thinking, "I'll bet they have a fat cook who's starting some greens and beans and beets and meats and gravy for the blueplate lunch—or the merchants' lunch, whichever they happen to call it. There was no whiskey last night, but I'm hungry. We stop in the old car between a pickup and a new Chrysler, and I turn off the key, cutting the engine to a slappety-slap stop. Then she pulls back on her door handle and I remember locking it last night, thinking that it would stick locked forever, but it works just fine, and she opens it from the inside."

Jean got to the cafe door first, but she waited for him, and following him in, grabbed the screen door to gentle its slam. She trailed him to a table beside a dark television set. There were menus on the table, caught between the chrome napkin holder and a tall chrome-capped glass sugar jar. They both took a menu, and Ira asked her what she wanted to eat. She looked at the menu, and she looked at him. A man at the counter, smoking a cigar, told the straw-colored waitress that the Chrysler outside belonged to him, that it would run a hundred and ten, maybe more. She seemed to be impressed, topping off his coffee, letting Ira and Jean wait. She gave him a view of the thrust of the profile of her trim breasts, and it looked to Ira like the man had something cooking.

Ira watched the steam rise from the man's coffee cup, and thought how much he needed coffee. He wondered if the waitress would give him coffee, if she knew how much he needed it. Jean read her menu, not knowing what to order. Then the waitress came to their table, reluctantly, to take their order.

"What do you want, Jean?" Ira asked.

She pursed her lips, pulling back a strand of blonde hair that had fallen over her right eye. The hair was clean. She looked hard at the plastic-backed menu. "Could I have," she paused, the waitress waited, impatiently, "hot cakes?"

"Yes."

"—and bacon?"

Ira watched the waitress's pencil move. Then he said, "Two eggs up, sausage, grits, and we both want coffee."

The waitress scratched out their order, scooping up the menus with her left hand just as her pencil made the last stroke. Ira looked straight at her. Because he was seated, and she was standing, he saw the curve of her breasts and the tight-dressed curve of her waist.

When she left their table, he looked at Jean. She was a pretty girl, but he'd like for her hair to grow out longer. She had slept well, for her eyes were bright, and she looked to him like she was relaxed, happy. She was still a bit sleepy, for she hadn't waked up fully, and she ate all of her hot cakes and bacon.

*   *   *

It was midafternoon when they saw the Gulf. Through the morning's drive, Ira kept seeing the profile of that waitress, and then he saw her profile in the Gulf surf. It was in the sharp-angled tip of each knee-high wave, and it was in the rounded curl at the crest of each wave that broke and floundered on the jetty, and it was in the solid and round curve of the Gulf as it went out to the horizon to where it, sloping down like a meadow, fell with part of the sky out of sight. Then Ira saw the waitress squirming, naked, in the breakers. Jean didn't see any of that, and Ira wondered what visions she was seeing. He saw Melissa with great olive-green thighs in the rocks, where some seaweed in the water twisted and moved like long dark hair. "The water is warm and the Gulf is a woman," he thought, "and all the underwater receiving flounder and redfish and weakfish are shes, but the horny, sideways-bubbling dry-backed fiddler crabs and the dead fish and dead shells torn on the sand are hes."

Ira hadn't known, when he'd visited the Gulf once before in his life, that there was sexuality in sea things. He was Jean's age then, or perhaps a year younger than Jean, and his cousins lived in Biloxi, and it all smelled sour and salty, he remembered. He was barefoot —closer to the ground, then—and he remembered the sharp oyster shells underfoot, and the smell of pee in his cousins' yard, and the great wooden bowl of rice on their eating table, and the smell of pee in the corner, and looking up at Joe, saying with his eyes, "Aren't they terribly poor, my cousins?" All they had to eat was rice, a big bowl of rice amid kerosene lamps, smoking black. His mother's kitchen had chairs, and a tablecloth, and nine or ten bowls of different kinds of food. Ira remembered that Joe didn't eat much rice, but he drank from a bottle with his brother, Ira's uncle, the cousins' father, and after supper Ira's big cousin, Clark, talked about things that Ira didn't know about, and demonstrated them in the dark of the porch, with another cousin strangely named T. Bo—and then Ira remembered the time the cousins all went out on the railroad trestle at Back Bay and fished with handlines for sheepshead and got scared by a train. They all hunched out on the tips of crossties and closed their eyes and held their breath, while it thundered on the rails just an arm's length above them. The long train was going sixty-five miles an hour, Ira's cousin said.

But Ira couldn't tell Jean about that, so he walked with her down the cement steps and through the soft dry sand to the hard-packed damp sand right at the water. Ira watched her, wanting to tell her something, for she reminded him of himself. He liked her, she'd been smiling since breakfast. That was the first time he saw her play, or do anything childish, or act like a kid.

Wearing his trousers and shoes, Ira waded out into the surf. She followed, trying to step over the small waves that were breaking about her knees. She laughed. Then the gulls found them and wheeled down, crying and hanging from their mock-bird wings on the softest possible puffs of a sea breeze. If they'd had some bread scraps or chopped mullet, the birds would have come to their heads, but the gulls quickly judged that the man and girl were paupers and rode the breeze higher, off to the west.

Jean and Ira splashed for an hour, then they left the water and walked along the hard-packed sand, noticing and searching every bit of fluff or plastic or bone. It was a public beach which had a wide assortment of the refuse of people's public things, most of which were vaguely connected with pleasure—beer cans, Popsicle sticks, suntan lotion tubes, cigarette butts, flashlight batteries, two copper pennies—and a radiator cap.

Ira knew that he'd been thinking about Jean for several days, but while they walked in the surf an unconscious awareness that came from a growing affection and responsibility began to color his reactions to her. Why else had he so quickly run from Paul Jacobs's threat, he wondered. It could have been, he reasoned, that muddy picture of dumb idiots and epileptics chained to wooden benches in the state asylum where they'd taken Cassfield. They'd tried to leave him there, Essie and his father, but on visiting Sundays they saw him among the other patients, and Essie brooded over the chains and cane-bottomed chairs (used like the lion tamers') until, in a nightmare lather, she ran to get him out and bring him back home, but that was before he and Ira stole the bottles and pulled the rings, when Cass hit the man, because after that they never let him out again.

It's surprising how quickly the water and sand tires a man's legs. It's tiring, like a man walking across a hot plowed field in low-cut Sunday shoes, when he tries to put his feet down and then lift them neatly, so that none of the hot loose dirt spills into his shoes. Ira's legs got tired from high-stepping, but willow Jean was fresh.

Their clothes were wet when they got to the car, but the old seats didn't complain. It surprised Ira to realize, after he'd started the car and turned around, that he was unconsciously driving slowly, watching for a phone booth so that he could find James Goff's telephone number and call him up. He was surprised at how smoothly it worked, for he'd known all along that James lived here, somewhere between Gulfport and Biloxi, yet he hadn't consciously planned, when he fled Tongs and drove south, to call or visit James Goff. Perhaps, he told himself, it was because James was the only one left alive who he knew from before, in Tongs, when he was number one at graduation, when their store was the biggest building in town, when everyone thought he'd be the one, he or James, to go to college.

CHAPTER 16

WHEN JAMES ANSWERED, IRA TOLD HIM WHO HE WAS, AND WHERE he was. James sounded pleased and surprised, repeating Ira's name as if he were making sure that Ira knew, himself, who he was. "Ira, Ira, Ira." He pronounced the name different than he had before, when they were boys in Tongs.

He told Ira to follow the beach highway for two miles and then turn right at the Owl Cleaners, the place with an owl on the sign which rolled its eyes and hooted "Twenty-four-hour service." Ira said, "Sure, we'll be right over."

James asked, "Who's *we?*"

Ira told him that it was a long story, too long to start over the phone.

Ira easily found the owl sign and turned right. He followed a winding, potholed shell road for two thousand yards until he found a mailbox with James's name on it. It read Number Seven Cove Drive. All of the area behind the mailbox, clear back to the telephone-pole stilts of the house, was paved like a large parking lot, the kind the Gulf Coast cafes have of oyster shells supplemented with asphalt roofing tabs. Off to their left, a drooping bedraggled palm fluttered in the sea breeze, looking like it had been nipped by too many winter frosts. It showed a swollen lump in its fibrous trunk and a crosshatched pattern that had been caused by the annual cutting of fronds as it grew taller. It seemed to cry out that it

—being too far north—felt out of place, unproductive, exotic.

The parking area was solid and well packed, and there was even room for a large boat or a car to be parked underneath the stilt house. Ira parked near the foot of the steps that led up to a little square entrance porch with an aluminum awning. Jean was inclined to stay in the car, where in fact she sat while Ira got out, but as he climbed the stairs, he saw that she was quietly closing the car door, coming over for a closer look at the underside of this strange house built on stilts.

From the porch Ira saw pines, acres of blowing sea grass, and the reflecting fluttering whitecaps of the bay. James had an engraved brass door lock, with a knocker built into the handle of it. The handle was a dragon's head, and the knocker was its forked tongue. Ira rattled it lightly, but James had heard their car, for he opened the door just as Ira knocked. Ira was shocked to see that James's hairline had receded. He wore an expensive-looking shiny shirt with a plaid jacket, over black Bermuda shorts.

"Water under the bridge" was the phrase that came into Ira's mind. James didn't talk like he had six years before; he talked faster, longer, and with different emphasis. He smoked extralong cigarettes, and he said that it was just about time for his afternoon cocktail, that he always had a cocktail about that time.

"Well, sit down, Ira, here," he said. "I don't mix them too strong, and I use lots of ice, just an afternoon refresher, that's all."

"It's a nice place you have here, James."

"Pleasant, yes. Good air circulation up high like this, I get the breeze. I saw you admiring my view out on the porch. See? I have a tiny periscope there in the door, so I can see who's knocking before I open the door."

"Yes, I was looking at your house."

"You'd be amazed at how economical it was to build. There was an old gas station here, and my contractor used its cement foundation for footing my poles. That's why the wonderful old palm tree is here. It must be fifty years old, if it's a day. It was undoubtedly planted by whoever built the station. I got free house plans from the government, Department of the Interior, or some such. But let me open the drapes. It's actually prettier from inside here, across the cocktail table and across the window ledge and past the palm tree to the bay.

"Oh. See that piece of iron set in cement this side of the palm tree? It looks somewhat like a tree stump. That's where the gasoline pump was. It was one of those old jobs with a glass cylinder on top that was marked in gallons, and you could watch the gasoline fall from one mark to the next while your tank filled. There was only one pump, because there was only one grade of gasoline then, not three or four like we have now.

"I'm sorry about your folks, Ira. I read about the fire, of course— but I didn't know about you and the girl. You want to watch yourself, boy. Gee, but you look nice. You needed a few years to mature. I *should* have gone up for Delaney's funeral. It was *too* sad. I don't know why I persist in taking that Beauville newspaper, only to read about nice people dying, it seems. He was a tremendous friend to me, you know. Here, let me show you the inscription in the copy of Peterson's *Field Guide to the Birds* that he gave me: 'For James Goff, so that he may learn the birds, and knowing them, love them as much as I, Delaney.' And I did learn them, I keep this field guide here by the window, and I check everything that I'm not sure of with it. There's a whole ecology of the salt marshes, Ira, species that I'd never seen in Tongs—clapper, sora, Virginia rails; piping, snowy, ringed plovers; ruddy turnstones; black skimmers. Here, under Delaney's inscription I wrote some lines that I call "Delaney."

> *I have touched the valve that stems the flow,*
> *I've made a rock-high statue grow,*
> *But I fear to think, and I doubt the gods,*
> *I'll try to sell my fishing rods.*

"Do you like it? It seems so much like a way that Delaney had about himself."

"I understand you're a schoolteacher, James?"

"Well, I'm not teaching just now. I'm keeping private and working on a book of poems called *Masters of Flurry and Stagmen of Hope*. Last summer I took a bartending job in Florida. What *will* a schoolteacher do to keep alive, huh? That's something you should

154

try if you ever get truly bored, to get bored in a quiet bar, working there, I mean, is to be really *ennui* bored.

"There was a bored girl there, a cocktail waitress, who suggested the title to me. She held that the bar where we worked was the universe, and that all women were the same, exactly, but that there were two distinct types of men. That's what kept the universe going. She said that the one type were the Masters of Flurry, sort of in-charge types, like ships' captains—who have the power over the flurry or whirling dervish of reality and kaleidoscopic sensations—who have power over Flurry, furry, pussycats, and women. According to her, the other type of men were the Stagmen of Hope. The Stagmen of Hope always have hope, but they never get anything. They sit in dark corners and drink Tom Collinses. They pretend. The stag means they're alone, and it means horn—maybe the irony of it is that they're wearing horns, in Shakespeare's sense, while they ogle her cleavage in the dark bar, maybe while they ogle the cocktail waitress, their stay-at-home wives are giving them horns, I don't know. But she knew the two types well, and she kept a big, ramshackled family of cousins, brothers, and sisters with various children fed by picking out the Stagmen of Hope. They tipped her heavily, pretending and hoping and thinking that they were Masters of Flurry. Which type are you, Ira?"

"She was wrong. I don't believe that system," Ira replied.

"Ah, Ira King, let me fresh this up for you, you're a regular straight arrow, and I'm proud of you. Oh! There she is, a windy-haired waif by the coconut palm, flapping her arms to cast shadows on the ground, like the wings of a great bird, look, the treetop shadow is the bird's crested head and the trunk is its neck and she's making wings. How clever is youth. What's her name, Ira?"

"Jean Harlow Davis."

"My God! I'll bet her mother *loved Red Dust.*"

"I don't know about that."

"You *must* bring her up, Ira. Right now, while I rummage up a glass of orange juice or milk and a cookie. How wonderful is youth."

Ira went to the door and called her. She came slowly to the stairs, as if she knew that she wouldn't like the house, or James Goff. She waited at the foot of the stairs. He asked James, "How do you manage, how do you get by, such a nice house, without teaching? Bartending?"

"Oh that, and my savings. I've another job next term. It was a mistake for me to choose schoolteaching, Ira."

"I think you're probably a good teacher, James."

"Yes. A good teacher. But I fell in love with a student. I couldn't resist him, and he knew it. I had a garage apartment in Biloxi. Some boys broke in on me one night and smashed out the windows, ripped the drapes, threw all my books on the floor—I couldn't teach there any longer, you see?" Jean came in the door. "Hello, you're the famous Jean Harlow? Come here, here's a cookie. Which do you prefer, milk or orange juice? Right, Ira! Look at this beautiful, soft, blonde hair, and those beautiful, *serious* eyes! Come here and sit on Uncle Jamie's knee."

She hung back. James lit a cigarette.

"Such a serious face. Such a beautifully thin little body. I'll bet you didn't let Delaney hold you on his knee, either, Jean Harlow. Poor Delaney. And poor everybody, it seems, who stays in the Piney Woods too long." James tried to brush her hair, but she pulled away. He gave her candy and stroked the palm of his left hand with his silver-backed hairbrush.

Ira fixed stronger drinks and watched James smoke cigarettes, blowing smoke clouds toward the bay until they flopped against the big window and curled back into the room, and Ira did a lot of thinking—about Joe and wisteria vines and Gappy's barbershop and globs of melted plate glass window and Delaney and Paul Jacobs. Jean sat on the floor, on a square red and white Persian carpet, and Ira wondered if she was taking imaginary rides as he was. Then James fixed a third drink, and the automatic thing started working in Ira's head, telling him that they'd made it to the Gulf, and the gray-green rockeater hadn't gotten them—they'd waded in the surf with the stingray, and they were safe, but at the end of their rope, and they would have to do like the ugly man at the station with a bullet on a string had said, they'd have to grab a holt, girl, and climb their way back up the rope, hand over hand, like basic training, if they wanted to stay alive.

James moved toward Jean with his brush, but she deftly side-stepped him and ran out to the porch and down the steps.

"The last drink I had, James, except for an afternoon drink with Dr. Forsythe, was two weeks ago, late at night, with Delaney. We were sitting on the porch of a fishing cabin, at Shiloh Crossing, down behind Pittman's station, on the Okatoma."

"I see." James rattled the ice in his glass.

"I came back from Texas to see my father. Delaney wrote me a letter from Beauville that the store had burned and that Paul Jacobs had taken Essie's place away from Melissa. Delaney wanted me to come back and get that place, but when I got to Beauville, Joe was dead. He didn't even know that I was coming, because the clerk at the hotel lost the message I left when I phoned. And when I got there Delaney was drunk."

"You'd been in Texas all that time?"

"Except for the time I was in the army. A fellow who killed rats at the slaughterhouse where I was working dumped Jean on me. That was in Fort Worth. I couldn't get rid of her, so when I got Delaney's letter I brought her with me. I *tried* to get rid of her then, and now I'm afraid they'll get her and put her in an orphanage."

"They who? They shouldn't care, if you're taking good care of her. Who would want to put her in an orphanage?"

"Paul Jacobs. He threatened me. He sent the Winslow boys to buy my burned store so I'd leave Tongs, but I wouldn't sell it to them. Then he waited a day and sent Gappy to tell me that he had papers to send her back to Texas. Said he'd have them served, if I didn't leave town—for good."

"Paul Jacobs, no! That little piece of excrement."

"It's because he's afraid I'll marry Melissa and sue him for the farm—he sold it to a doctor. Anyway, I was scared. I left. I couldn't look at that burned-out store any longer. Tongs is so dead and bloody. When I left I thought about the Tongs Bridge and remembered all the people who had died and been put in the Okatoma for the alligator gar; even if they took them to the Beauville Funeral Home the blood would still get back in the Okatoma and run downstream to Tongs."

"That's not true, Ira, not now. I know they say it, but it's not true, they don't put the blood in the river, that's a superstitious lie."

"Well, they say it's true. I think it's true, because there are different kinds of truth—I'm sure of that. I think the water purifies the spirits of the dead, and they keep on living in their old trees and houses and barns and such. Some have to live in ditches, and some have to walk the roads by night, but they all go into the river and come out again. Somehow it reminds me of the story about the King boy who washed his guts in the Okatoma, he seems like the only one who put his blood in the river and lived, but then he died too—eventually.

"I have a sharp memory of a stump where a tree had been cut on the bank of the river, back in the Depression, Aunt Essie said, and the old river changed course and washed all the earth from the bank and left it bleached and solid, standing in the river like an island or a single tooth. I was twelve when I swam out to it. It was June. I crawled up on it and pulled the string, towing my fishing line and can of worms—Prince Albert can. It's impossible to describe to you how hard he bit, the big eel, as long as my arm and that big around. The broad hook went deep into his jaw, but he couldn't straighten it, nor could he break the sixty-pound line. He wrapped himself around an underwater root and I took a turn on a knob of the stump. We waited. I pulled, he pulled, and we waited some more. By that afternoon I was winning. Although he was stronger than me, I had more brains than him. Then I got his head out of the water and snubbed the line to the knob, oh, pearly polished knob, a good belaying pin. Of course it scared me to look down at him. His eyes were two inches apart, evil black dots, and his mouth gaped open and then snapped shut, clipping chunks off the hardwood stump. A thread of his blood drooped into the river, and although he couldn't breathe the air—he wouldn't die, and I waited, staring into his open mouth, afraid to swim him back until he hung perfectly still, and his eyes glazed over. Later Stanley and I skinned and gutted him. He had wonderful long guts, and we sold him to The People for a dollar. Stanley sold all his game to The People, but he'd never gotten a dollar for an eel before."

James smiled kindly. "Stanley. Always parading around in a red plaid cap, twisting rabbits out of the hollow gum trees, setting traps for bandit coons, or following some snuffling midnight hound up the cottonmouth bottoms. And he sold what he killed for meat."

"The People bought from him because he cleaned stuff nice and wrapped it in wax paper, and if he sold them a rabbit he'd leave one foot on, so they'd know it wasn't a cat."

"I'll tell you something you probably didn't know about Paul Jacobs, Ira. He and Monk Farley caught a possum in his mother's chicken house, and they sulled it up and took it out to the hollow on Monk's Service-Cycle. Paul asked that big nigger, Henceforth, if he'd give a dollar for a possum, and Henceforth was mean, I mean real mean. Henceforth said, 'You get yore white ass out of here 'fore I beat you over the head with yore goddamn possum!' Monk told me about it. He thought it was funny."

James lit a fresh cigarette. "The People, Stanley, Delaney, perhaps they all walk the roads at night, dead and alive. The girls and boys holding hands, the Winslow boys—you know they married twin sisters, the Muncey girls, a matched pair of beautiful girls, and any children that they have will be double first cousins, I read that in the *Beauville Clarion.* Delaney told me once, Ira, before I left Tongs, that his life had been ruined because he loved his first cousin, Essie, and their parents wouldn't let them marry, because of the old blood taboo.

"And old man Natale dying and leaving Paul Jacobs thousands and thousands in cash—it's absurd. Like the way you say you got this girl, not even wanting her—absurd. I'd give my life for such a pretty girl."

"Sometimes, James, I get the idea that she's Melissa's daughter, except she's so blonde, and then I realize that she couldn't be her daughter. Other times I imagine she's Janet's girl, but she was dark too, part Indian. I knew her when I was in the army, I guess I was in love with her, and sometimes I imagine that she got pregnant and kept it a secret, and when Jean was born she paid the rat shooter to bring her to me. But of course not enough time has passed, not a third enough time. It's crazy, but it's also crazy to think that dead people keep on living in their old houses, old man Natale living out there with his widow and Melissa, Delaney sitting in Gappy's barbershop, Cassfield walking around in Aunt Essie's little house. My folks' store burned down, and they either live in the ashes or else they have to walk the roads at night, they all go into the river and come out again. It even seems that Stanley and Delaney were impatient to die, they went straight to the river."

"So you just left Tongs and drove down here?"

"Yes. I was driving at night and I saw a dream vision of a new service station, a Magnolia Oil Company station having a grand opening, and there were people that I knew, but when I pulled off the road and stopped it was an old, dirty, run-down station with a bullet on a string."

"A string?"

"And then I got in the back seat and tried to sleep, dreamed about a long mule and plow. It was about a mile long. The mule had big soft ears and glassy eyes. From his blinders I traced the leather down to the bit and then the reins all the way back to where they were looped over the handle of the plow. I traced the trace chains from the collar to the back band, then drooping down to the single-tree. I traced the wooden beam of the plow, it was a Georgia stock, back to the plowpoint. Then I saw the plowpoint off the plow, it was a broken, rusty piece of iron then, laying in the weeds behind a shit house, and I saw Melissa come with a pink baby wrapped in a pink shawl. She got the broken plowpoint and wrapped it in the shawl with the baby. She tied the four corners of the shawl across the top like a laundry bundle and took it and threw it in The Falls."

"What does it mean?" James had listened intently.

"You tell me. Maybe that's why I came down here to see you, to find out. You deal in poetry, riddles, symbols."

"Well, Ira, it means what it means. I could guess that it means you have a subconscious desire to legitimatize your relationship with the girl—maybe that's what it means. At any rate, Melissa probably never had a baby."

"Of course not, not unless—"

"No. But what was so important about a bullet on a string? You mentioned that?"

"It was in the old service station and it fascinated me. It was like a cow on a rope, or a boat tied to a dock, and it was hanging down through Mississippi, like I was going down the map of Mississippi. Now I know why it was important—because it was tied to Mississippi, like I am tied to Tongs, and to that place of Essie's, where spirits walk. I knew when I hit the Gulf and was wading in the salt water with laughing Jean that I'd have to bounce back up there, up to the Piney Woods, like the rock that falls through the earth, if the gray-green rockeater doesn't get it."

"I see. That's poetry."

"Maybe so. What it means is that water responds to gravity, runs downhill because of gravity. Gravity is why water moves, why men walk, it's the strongest force we know. If the string didn't hold it, the bullet would fall. Gravity tries to pull the rifle ball to the ground, and if you're far enough away from the man who shot it at you, the bullet will fall short and hit the ground."

"I see. You'll go back up to Tongs?"

"Yes. I haven't thought it out yet, but I have an idea that I'll trade cars and find a place to live that isn't too far from Tongs, for I'll be in hiding. I believe if Paul Jacobs finds us out, he'll surely have Jean sent away."

"Of course it would be simpler to stay away from Tongs. Nobody cares if you keep Jean, apparently, nobody except Paul Jacobs."

"That's just it, James, I never cared *where* I was before. I didn't give a damn about Tongs when I left it to go out west, but now it's gotten hold of me. All the Kings are dead, all but me. There's names of Kings cut on a beech tree on Essie's place with dates back in the 1880s, it was a King who got his guts cut out in a fight and rode twelve miles back to Shiloh Church and washed himself in the clean water and lived—I'm tied to that place."

James said, "OK," and asked Ira if it wasn't suppertime. He steamed some rice and warmed a can of chili to pour over it. He put a small can of whole-kernel corn in the chili and sprinkled in a bit of red pepper. Ira went out on the balcony porch and waved to Jean. She was sitting in the car. James put three plates of the rice and chili on the coffee table. He gave Jean a Coke and fixed some instant coffee for himself and Ira, and while they drank the coffee, a cool twilight started to gloom the bay. James said, "Paul Jacobs is a stupid ass, don't worry too much about him. If you ever do get in a *real* tight, however, just put Jean on a bus and send her down here, nobody would look for her here. I'll hide her for you." He wrote his phone number on a note pad for Ira.

Jean caught his eye. She said with her eyes that she was afraid of James and his house. Ira said, "Thanks, we'd better start back. We can get across the bay before dark."

"Don't leave now, Ira. You can stay here and get a good early start in the morning. You've had several drinks."

"No, really, I like to drive at night. There's less traffic, and we can make good time."

"Well—at least take another cup of coffee. You've had three or four drinks."

"I'm fine," Ira said firmly, feeling, for some reason that he didn't understand, uncomfortable. "Thanks for the visit and the supper. Come on, Jean, we've got to get on back up to the Piney Woods."

While James walked them down the steps he touched a secret switch, turning on floodlights which lit the whole place, the house, the car, and the palm tree, like a supermarket parking lot. It really wasn't so dark that they needed the floodlights, and the lights combined with the natural twilight to make a strange glow. Ira wondered if James had the floodlights to keep boys from rocking his house. He wondered if the old car would start, and he tried to guess how many times he'd turned on the ignition key and pressed the silver starter button. James watched them with a pensive smile, and the wind lifted a layer of his hair and held it straight up, away from his head, showing a patch of pale scalp in the artificial light, and it seemed to Ira that neither he nor James had achieved his high-school potential, when they tied for "most likely to succeed."

The old motor kicked over, sputtered once, and warmed to a steady idle. Ira turned in a lazy circle on James's oversized parking lot, packing the oyster shells a bit tighter in the process. James kept one hand in his jacket pocket and waved good-bye with the other. Over James's shoulder Ira saw the palm tree, and beyond that sad tree, the house on stilts.

CHAPTER 17

IRA MADE FOR THE BRIDGE OVER BILOXI BAY, WANTING TO CROSS IT before full dark and intending to find a fishing camp that rented cabins and boats. Maybe this had been a long trip for such a short stay, he thought, but at least he could make it worthwhile by fishing in the morning, and he started planning his strategy as he followed road signs to the bridge. He noticed a mileage sign to the town called Wool Market and showed it to Jean. She thought it was a funny name.

When they got on the bridge, most of the cars that they met, even though it wasn't dark, had their lights on. There was little traffic. The water was choppy, but there were no whitecaps. There was wide water on both sides and in front of them. Ira imagined that the old car was a submarine running at dusk to recharge her batteries. Jean, having figured a way to sit on her tucked-up feet so that she was high enough to see everything comfortably, looked out her side window. She said, looking out the window, "Ira, I guess your friend James is pretty smart, huh?"

"Yes, he is. He's a schoolteacher."

"That was the prettiest house I've ever been in."

"It's a nice house. It's well decorated inside."

"But from the outside, it's creepy. It looks like a daddy longlegs. Wonder why it's so high? In case of floods?"

"Dunno."

"James is nice. But I didn't feel good being in his house."

Ira wanted a lot of things for the morning, and he figured he'd try to make a package deal to include the cabin with twin beds, breakfast, a boat and motor, two rods, and bait, thinking, if it's a clean room—I'll give twelve dollars for both of us, package deal.

The man woke them at five the next morning. Ira put all their things in the car and locked them up. Then he and Jean drank coffee in the cafe while the man's wife fried eggs. Ira cut Jean's coffee with sweet milk, and outside, at the wharf, he heard the man priming the motor. His wife was pleasant, she even asked if they wanted more sausage. Ira said, "No, thank you," and ate a piece that Jean left—it was good, hot sausage. The woman said it was homemade. Then they hurried out to the wharf. He had the motor running, and he gave Ira a cigar box filled with extra hooks, swivels, and sinkers, as Ira stepped into the boat.

"You a fisherman, honey?" the man asked Jean, smiling.

"Yes."

"Then you can take these bait"—he handed her a bucket of live shrimp—"and dump them in the bait well." He spoke with an even tone of voice that flattered her ability to handle the heavy, fishy bucket. She toted it to the edge of the wharf, where she handed it down to Ira. He stood, wide-legged, balancing, in the boat, and Jean remembered her first fishing trip, when Delaney hunkered flat, hugging his knees up under his chin, like a kid, in the bottom of that round-heeled steel boat at The Falls.

Ira poured the shrimp into the bait well under the middle thwart and gestured for Jean to get up in the bow. The man handed her two rods, then he shoved the boat off with his foot, saying loud over the motor that there was no use staying after nine-thirty, because if they hadn't caught a mess of fish by then, it would be too late. "Go for the open water, straight out that way, and get your hooks wet as soon as you can," he said.

When they got out of sight of the wharf it was chilly, and the little aluminum boat kicked along obedient to the twelve-horse Johnson. It was first light, and Ira could see five or six other boats out ahead of them. Jean followed his eyes. There were some gulls. It looked like it would be a nice day. When they'd cleared the salt-marsh grass by three hundred yards they were still a long way from the boats that were fishing, but they were close enough to see men in different boats pulling in fish. Ira turned the throttle harder to the right, but the old Johnson wouldn't change speed. It was so loud that he couldn't talk over it. Jean divided her attention between the boats that were catching fish, the fishing tackle she was holding, and the haze of blue smoke which the motor was spreading across their wake. Figuring it wouldn't hurt to try, Ira pointed at the bait well and crooked his index finger in the shape of a fishhook, or a shrimp's tail. She cocked her head to one side, like a robin hunting earthworms, then she nodded and scooted up to the bait well. She placed the tackle between her feet and used the small dip net that was tied to the cover of the bait well to catch a live shrimp. She hooked it straight through the back, which was OK. Her baiting the two rods with live shrimp took several minutes—when she looked back at the other boats they seemed to have doubled in size.

Ira didn't want to get too close to them. The marsh grass behind him seemed to be half a mile away. He cut the motor. Both rods were rigged with red and white slip corks. Ira moved up to the middle thwart. Taking one of the rods from Jean, he cast it out about thirty feet from the boat, set the click drag, and gave it back to her. Ira then cast his rod on the opposite side of the boat and turned his back to Jean, but before he got settled, he heard her winding in the clicking reel against the pull of a good fish, for as she tried to reel it straight in, it ran with the line, pulling the cork underwater, bowing the rod, and stopping the reel until its lunge ended and the line bellied slack again. She got it alongside, and Ira grabbed the tight line. It was a speckled trout. The man hadn't given them a landing net, so Ira used the line to pull it halfway out of the water and grabbed its open mouth with his free hand. They are pretty fish, healthy and scrappy, but with mouths so soft the hook pulls out easily. Some fishermen call them weakfish. Ira held the fish still in the bottom of the boat and rebaited the hook. Then he put it in the bait well and cast his line back out. Another fish hit while he was handling the rod, which he quickly gave to Jean. He turned his back and watched his own cork, letting her do it all

herself. The fish hit good, for the next half hour. Jean landed two
more fish and Ira got three, for when they stopped biting there were
six speckled trout huddled in the bait well, all spooky and alive and
the same size. Ira threw the eight or ten shrimp that were left over-
board, thinking the man wouldn't want them.

Jean was proud of her fish. She said, "Delaney told me I'd have
to learn to fish if I stayed with you."

"Yeah, you did good," Ira said. The other boats were starting their
motors. He latched the cover on the bait well and fastened the
hooks to guides and reeled them tight against the clickers. The
motor started on the first pull and purred them steadily back to the
fishing camp.

After Ira cleaned the fish at the dock and wrapped them in paper,
he took them to the cafe and asked the woman to cook two of them.
She put the other four in a gallon mayonnaise jar and packed ice
around them. Then she gave Ira coffee and Jean an orange drink.
She cooked the fish whole in the deep fryer and fixed a regular plate
lunch, with boiled potatoes and sliced bread. Ira ate fast. They were
both hungry, and he watched Jean to see if she knew about fish
bones.

Ira was glad that the car was all packed and ready to go.

She charged one dollar, a fair enough price, for cooking the fish.
She ate a piece of what Jean left and declared it was very good. Ira
didn't see the man again. He put the fish in the trunk and wrapped
an old quilt around the jar to insulate it, thinking, "Of course Jean
knows about fish bones, she ate the catfish she and Delaney caught."

The day was cool enough for them to drive with the windows
rolled up, and as they hummed along the black highway Ira caught
himself watching for the cafe where they'd had breakfast on the
way down. When it finally popped up on the right, he speeded up a
little, uncomfortable at the thought of stopping and seeing the
straw-colored waitress who flirted with the man who drove a Chrysler, but then he felt foolish as they passed, for there was no parked
Chrysler, and he thought, "She's probably off duty on top of that,
like Nurse Sarah was often off duty, and besides, it's a long way to
the next cafe." It wasn't important. The gas tank was three-quarters
full, indicating that they wouldn't have to stop at the dirty gas

station with the bullet on the string. Ira thought, "I could get a quart of gas for the camp stove at the next station. Then we could stop at the roadside rest area and fry the fish." Was there cornmeal and grease and salt in the jumbled cook box, he wondered, deciding that there was no salt, remembering that he'd been out of salt when they left Tongs. "I'll need to stop at a store, or better yet, detour through the next town and find a supermarket," he thought.

Then they saw the dirty station on the left, squat and dry in the brightening sunshine. After they passed it, Ira noticed there were several hills that hadn't seemed so pronounced on the trip down, at night. Either that, he thought, or the motor was going out, or he had some bad gasoline, for it became hard to keep up a good sixty. Could it be that on the trip down the hills weren't as steep as they were on the trip back north? He didn't think so, but then it occurred to him that there was a gradual loss of altitude from Tongs to the Gulf, else why should the creeks and rivers run south? It became more than idle speculation, however, because Ira heard a big tractor-trailer booming up on his tail with a full head of steam. He wanted to pass, but couldn't. There was no climbing lane or shoulder for Ira to move onto, and near the tops of the hills he couldn't do more than fifty-five, while the trucker wanted to go seventy. If he hadn't been so close, Ira would have slowed down and eased onto the sharp-angled roadside, but he knew that he couldn't jump off there at fifty-five, or even forty. Ira saw the truckers' big face in the rearview mirror. His big elbow was cocked out the window, and he had a pleasant face, smooth and expansive, but he was in too much of a hurry. It occurred to Ira that he could have been Nurse Sarah's man—her truck driver Big Pill who bought cows in Stillwater with a hot check drawn on a Kansas bank, ran the cows to KC, sold them, deposited the money in time to cover the check, and thought that that flurry of activity made him a business-man, a wheeler-dealer, and thought that she was reading *True Romance* all the while and waiting for him when she was, in fact, walking with the college boy in a downtown park, sitting beside the goldfish pool, eating their picnic lunch, very nice, chewing slowly, thinking—anchovies are so salty and wasn't it clever of him to pour the cold 7UP into the sink and refill the chilled 7UP bottles with

Sauterne and snap the bottle caps back in place, put the bottles in the corner of the basket, for if you give them half a chance they'll spill, keep the sandwiches dry, keep your powder dry, powder your nose, lipstick—and after the sandwiches they drank straight from the 7UP bottles, kissing, in a way, the little glass rings on the tops of their bottles, rings like those Ira taught Cassfield to pull off, and they giggled at the two boys who were talking so earnestly, wanting to hold hands, while they both smoked his cigarillos.

Ira wondered if he'd really known about Delaney before he left Tongs. "I must have known," he thought, "for sometimes I know things without realizing it, and only later do I realize that I knew them." Then he wondered just when it was that he decided to keep Jean and take care of her. "Was it in Texas, our last night there, when I was going for hamburgers, or was it when I walked her back from The Falls on the day Delaney died, or was it in the Gulf surf, or was it in James's stilt house, or was it when she reeled in the speckled trout, or was it just now?"

Then Ira topped the hill, and there was clear highway for a mile. The truck driver put his foot on his carburetor and spewed black plumes of Diesel smoke, and Ira foolishly floor-boarded the old Dodge, but the trucker was confidently out in the other lane passing them easily, and Ira's fanciful memory proved to be true, in part, because it was a cattle truck. It was a double-decker loaded with wild-eyed scrub calves from the coastal plain, headed north with too much speed, and the trailer seemed to be striding in giant slow steps as it rocked from side to side. Ira took his foot off the gas when the sudden acceleration of the truck showered calf shit out the tailgate and down onto the pavement and even partway into the bar ditch.

Then the pressure of the tailgating truck was off, and Ira didn't push the old car so hard. In the next town he stopped in a super-market to replenish the food box. At a hardware store across the street from the supermarket he got a gallon can of Coleman stove fuel and a box of .38 bullets for Delaney's pistol. He didn't know why he bought the bullets, it just seemed awkward to have a pistol with no ammunition. Then they drove through the town looking for a cheap motel, and on to the outskirts of town where he parked under roadside pines and set up the camp stove. He was afraid the fish wouldn't keep until the next day, so he cooked all four of them. They ate them with bread and ketchup. Then Ira wiped out the skillet and plates, packed the food in the box, put the camp stove in the trunk, carefully, so that it wouldn't leak fuel, and drove back to check the motel he'd spotted in town. He signed the register card, telling the man behind the counter that his daughter would need a separate bed.

The town was Cumby, twenty-eight miles south of Tongs. Ira went to the Planters' Bank of Cumby the next morning and asked to see the president. Ira told him that he was working on a land speculation deal and wanted to build up an account so he'd have money handy when the deal was ready to close. He deposited the travelers' checks and the money his father left, except for three hundred dollars, in the new account, saying that he didn't know how long it would take to complete the deal. The banker was pleased, since the account came to something over five thousand dollars, and it wasn't a savings account. Ira asked him if the bank, with a power of attorney, could sell a piece of property and add the money to his account. He said "Sure, Mr. King," and Ira gave him the legal description of the lot in Tongs, while his secretary typed up the power of attorney. Ira said, "Sell it for the highest amount you can get— say, in two months." They signed papers, and Ira told him to write to him at General Delivery, Beauville. Then they shook hands, and Ira put the slim bankbook in the zipper pocket of his billfold and went back to the motel to get Jean.

He liked the look of Cumby, there was a college there, and Ira envied the college people. He loaded the car and drove twenty-six miles to Laurel, where they got lunch at a drive-in cafe. A pretty young girl took their order. She wore a green high-school band sweater, and it reminded Ira of other high-school girls and other sweaters. She brought the sandwiches on a metal tray that had to be brought into the car, for there were no hooks to hold it on the window. Ira thought it was a backward way to serve cars, and asked her why she didn't have the outside-the-car type. She saw his quarter tip on the tray, among the rings of water from the glasses, and she thought he was trying to flirt and make conversation. She hung her head and moistened her lips and said that she didn't know, maybe this kind of tray was just more homey.

Ira saw the flush on her cheeks—thought about her answer, and had no apt reply for it. He couldn't avoid looking at her breasts and hips as she stood there, swinging her weight to one foot, but looking at her that way with Jean in the car embarrassed him. In an awkward silence she waited for his reply until, realizing that he had none, she turned angrily and took the tray to the carhops' window.

Ira drove around the streets of Laurel searching the used car lots for an old pickup truck. He stopped at several places and went in to talk, but they weren't interested in his car in trade. Finally, he found a man who said he wanted the car and would give a hundred for it, on a trade. He showed Ira a faded blue pickup, Ford half-ton, that had a dim, crescent-shaped sign hand lettered on each door—Whitton's Egg Farm. Ira indifferently kicked a tire while he looked carefully at the interior of the cab.

"How much will you give to boot?" the man asked.

"How much will *you* give *me*?" Ira replied.

"The truck's two and a quarter." He got in and started the truck motor, revved it up.

Ira went to his car, leaving the man sitting in his pickup. Ira drove to the pickup and told Jean to put their things in the back of the truck. Then he walked around to where the man sat, foot-patting the gas pedal. "My car and a hundred—cash, you take care of the tax and title."

"Fair enough." The man smiled as he stepped down from the running board. Ira gave him the title papers of the old Dodge, and he went in his little office to write up the transfer. Ira opened the trunk for Jean and lifted out the heavy camp stove, easing it into the bed of the truck.

The man returned with the papers. "She's an old truck, full of gas and oil, uses a little oil, here's my pen, but she's solid. Belonged to an old-maid schoolteacher!" he beamed. Jean and Ira got in the truck, thanked the man, he thanked them, and they bounced out his gravel driveway with Jean watching, through the back window, the man sink his hands deep into his trousers pockets, and walk a slow circle around the old Dodge, staring at it as if it were a strange rhinoceros. At the front grill he put his hand on the chrome ram's head, just as Delaney had done that night he led them, through the dark, to the fishing cabin.

Ira stopped at a drugstore on the main street and bought two newspapers, both weeklies, several days old. Then he drove their new old Whitton's Egg Farm truck west to Leaf River. In a service-station-store by the river bridge he bought candy, pop, fishing stuff, and worms. They turned onto a sandy road that curled around down below the bridge to a sandy turn-around under a grove of nice water oaks. The river was waist deep and clear. Where it bel-lied in a curve, the force of the current had knocked out a blue hole that was perhaps ten feet deep. Ira fixed the lines for perch and cut two green canes for poles, baited one, and stuck the butt of the cane into the sandy bank. Jean fixed her own line, and Ira left her to watch the poles while he unloaded the stove. Putting it behind the truck, he set up the wooden cook box and skillet.

Then he walked back to the creek and sat beside Jean, dangling his feet over the water, wanting to fish for half an hour, relax, think about the money safe in the bank, think about their new truck, and then read through the papers, looking for a small farm near Tongs. The perch were slow to bite, and those they caught were too small to keep. Ira let Jean take them off the hooks and drop them gently into the blue hole.

They had Star Brand Vienna sausage for supper, and Ira read the newspapers by the light of the Coleman lamp, looking for an advertised farm. There were many big farms, but there was only one of manageable size—in Chambers County. The ad read, *Twenty acres house well pond, seeded pasture ½ timber, $200 acre 9 mi. ne Tongs.* "That's just four thousand dollars," Ira thought, "and it has a house. Must be on the WPA road, if it's nine miles northeast of Tongs. I'll go look at it in the morning." He put away the news-papers and used the blankets to make a bed in the back of the truck, knowing that it would be hard sleeping.

It wasn't cold enough to frost, but it was so cold that Ira didn't sleep well. In her sleep, Jean curled up beside him, putting her cold feet on his leg. He lay still and catnapped through the night.

Ira was up with the first light of dawn, hovering over the camp stove, waiting for the sun to come up and the coffee to boil. There were heavy drops of dew on the cab of the truck and the blankets were damp, so he hung them up around the stove to dry, making it look like a permanent camp. Then he got in the truck and looked down at shivering Jean. "Are you warming up?" he asked.

"Yeah. I'm OK. It's gettin' warm already." She spoke pleasantly.

"Stay here and try to catch some fish for dinner. I'm going to look for a place for us to live. I'll be back about noon." Ira watched her pretty face in the rearview mirror while the motor warmed up, and he noticed that she'd grown since he bought the clothes for her in Beauville, for she had on one of the new dresses, and it was too tight. She seemed calm. As he circled under the bridge to get up on the road, Ira saw her carefully rearrange the food box, then she turned down the burner under the tall, thin-spouted enamel coffee-pot. He could tell she knew he was coming back.

Away for the first time, it seemed, since he'd tried to get the job in Beauville, from the shoulder-high bob of blonde hair and sharp chin and sober green eyes and silver thread of saliva when she parts her lips to speak, Ira felt alone as a stone and listened to the motor of the truck, but he couldn't hear the pistons plappety-slap or visualize the oil splashing inside the motor, because it wasn't as smooth as the old car had been. He stared at the gravel road, the unpainted farm houses, unplowed fields bristling cedar weeds, finger-thick sassafras bushes, and broomstraw. His generation from Tongs had moved to the bigger southern towns, or west to California, or the aircraft plants of Texas. On some few farms there were new shining brooder houses built from Department of Agriculture plans. The brooder houses were rectangular, with a specific number of windows in ratio to their floor area, made of pine two-by-fours covered with sheets of tin. They sparkled like fresh pork-and-beans cans in the grass, after the camp-out, before the rain. Ira remembered when there was no chicken business, when people got chicks from the mail-order houses. They came in squat pasteboard boxes with air holes in the sides—usually one or two were dead, and it was always a surprise to see the identical puff-balls of yellow fuzz grow exactly into proper hens or roosters, whichever had been ordered.

Without Jean with him, breathing the same air, listening, quietly watching his every move, Ira smiled madly, drove fast, and ran a quick inventory of women through his mind. It started with the waitress in breasty profile and shifted to the carhop's band sweater and then flashed to Sarah drinking wine from the 7UP bottle and then it changed to Melissa, but he couldn't keep Melissa's face in focus—she seemed pretty, but Ira couldn't make his mind recall her face or her figure, so the image slipped to the welfare woman. Her image was clear. Ira could see and feel everything about her, just as if it had been yesterday, or now—clearer, in fact, for he saw things about her that he hadn't noticed before. Like the fact that she smoked too much and her teeth were stained, but they were handsome teeth. She was well formed; she always ate a big breakfast. She wore a girdle with sterling silver garter belt clips, and there was a little pink nonfunctional bow between the cups of her brassiere. She was a five foot eight Breck Blonde and weighed a hundred and thirty pounds, was thirty-four years old, and she'd never been married. She dusted around her waist with a big powder puff, and she wore too-small shoes. She looked straight into her supervisor's eyes and, breathing deep, she turned sideways when they met in the narrow file-room corridor, so that he wouldn't have to brush against her, but if he had brushed against her it would have been all right, because she'd danced close with him at the last Christmas party when his wife had too much to drink. She was thinking about that when she looked at Ira and saw that he was getting angry. She got up brusquely, took off her coat, folded it, and sat down again with it folded in her lap. She wondered if he would slap her if he got mad enough. She decided that he wouldn't, and that depressed her. She crossed her legs and tried to insult him, but it didn't work. She lit a cigarette, wondering if Ira ever had women in the little shack, then she saw the runnered nylon stocking that Janet had left beside the bed. She thought that Ira was dull and poor and afraid and that it wouldn't work, so she left, and Ira realized that Willard Ford had been right when he said that the ones who asked him to take a break from ripping up dirty carpets to drink a cup of coffee and started talking, in a cautious way, about sex were the ones who wasted his time—time is money—but the nervous ones that fussed and strode around and slapped their thighs with a folded *Redbook* or nail file and kept their mouths shut and crossed their legs when they sat down, they were the live ones. Ira's picture of the welfare woman was nice, and it reminded him of the few times Janet came to visit at his cabin in Fort Worth. They always had Chinese food and beer downtown, Fourth and Main, and when they went back to the cabin, Ira would light candles and put sheets over the windows. Janet liked to undress by candlelight. She liked her body. She'd unzip her dress and take it off slowly, put it on a hanger, and hang that on the wall nail. She'd pull her black slip over her head and shake her hair free. She was slow to undress, she liked for him to watch her. After she took her slip off, she'd get two cans of beer from the refrigerator and smoke a cigarette while they drank the beers. Then she'd prop her foot on a kitchen chair and roll down her stocking. She'd pitch the rolled stockings to the floor near the bed and then cross the room barefooted, slender and flat of stomach, to blow out the candles. Ira tried again to form a picture of Melissa, to see and feel her, to remember her, but she wouldn't come to mind.

CHAPTER 18

THE UNPAINTED WOODEN HOUSE THAT IRA RENTED IS ON THE TOP OF A sandy red-clay hill. It is the nucleus of a worn-out twenty-acre farm. Ira suspected someone had owned it as an investment, as a tenant farm, until the fields were so leeched of fertility and the cotton economy had so changed that they could no longer keep it rented. It is possible to reclaim such farms, to plant legumes on the raw hills and kudzu in the red-clay gulleys and heal them over, but that's a slow process—there's no cash in it.

For its considerable misuse, it is a beautiful little place. The house stares vacantly down from its knee-high blocks across a grassless yard at a decrowned chinaberry tree. Underneath the house, among the shadows, a flock of Dominique chickens blink and yawn. The house is dumb. Her porch is a face—symmetrical, unimaginative, boxy—matching four-paned windows are her eyes, the steps are her tongue sprawling down to the pack-dirt, grassless yard. She has a double-hipped pointed head of a roof that looks like a dunce's cap, and it is covered with cradle cap scales of Masonite shingles.

Vacationers or tourists who, by chance, might drive by and see it would think that there'd be nobody left in the world poor enough to live in such a house. A scaly-backed fence lizard, the kind that likes to bake in the sun, lives on the broken chinaberry tree. He seems to know that the Dominiques would eat him; their forebears might have eaten a previous scaly-back, or something like a Dominique, perhaps a small two-legged dinosaur, might have eaten some of his ancestors, for he has good instincts that cause him, every time one of the hens walks near, to fling himself with a dry rustle to the opposite side of the tree. He hides from Jean and Ira, too.

A recent storm tore the crown from the chinaberry tree and threw it south of the trunk, toward the gravel road. There is no REA line to the house. A covered well is tacked onto the west side of the house, and its Long Johnny Snout bucket hangs dumb on the windlass rope.

Just as easily as he'd ripped up filthy carpets for Willard Ford or gone carelessly to his job at Swift's, when they moved into the house Ira did nothing except cut firewood and sow clover seed in the meadow. The Fort Worth cabin by the reservoir was tight and neat, quite unlike this house. Ira remembered the service station man saying *grab a holt, girl,* and Ira remembered aphorisms that he learned in childhood: *you can lead a horse to water, but you can't make him drink; you can't get blood out of a turnip, the salt of the earth, tar up yore ass wid a tater vine.*

Although he'd planned to buy the farm—there was enough money to buy it outright—for some reason Ira chose to lease it and live off his capital. He had an option to buy later, if he wanted to. He just thought that it would be pleasant to stop jostling across the map or running up and down the map, tied like that bullet on a string, like a grinder's monkey to the organ with the grinder calling the tunes. He was content to have escaped the gray-green rockeater, pleased to have no job of work, just then. The place was beautiful, and Ira realized how much, in Texas, he'd missed the pines and sweet gums and the abundant fresh water and the automatic grits with every cafe breakfast.

Ira bought Jean a plywood chest of drawers to keep her clothes in, with the stipulation that he could use half of the top of it for his toothbrush, mirror, and razor. He bought some used chairs, a table, and a wood-burning heater for the living room. They had a kerosene lamp for light, and well water was free for the drawing. The windows had neither curtains nor shades. Their new crop of twenty chickens grew daily, nearing eating size. Pert and healthy, the chickens ranged from their coop out back, to under the house for dust baths, to clear down to the pond for water. Remembering the old country saying, *possum meat is just like pork,* Ira bought a young bred sow that was due to pig in the spring. Jean enjoyed feeding the fat-faced sow and the chickens.

Jean picked up the habit of looking at birds with Delaney's binoculars, and that prompted Ira to untie the bundle of bird guides and notebooks that he'd found in Delaney's suitcase. It was quite easy for Jean and Ira to identify the birds that they saw. They kept a list of the birds, but they weren't as scientific as Delaney had been. In one of his notebooks Delaney had cataloged every bird in Chambers County, complete with date, weather conditions, time of day, and the bird's exact location and activity.

The stock pond in the low pasture east of the house is big enough to have good fish. Ira can see it from the living room window. His chair is beside that window, near the heater. There's a sweet gum, poplar, white oak, dogwood hollow behind the house for rabbits, squirrels, and grinning possums.

Ira enrolled Jean in the Beauville Consolidated School, where she was placed in the fourth grade. Ira gave her name as Jean Harlow King, telling the principal that her birth certificate was lost. She brought notes home from her teacher, Miss Bradley, reminding Ira that they had to have it, asking him to please apply for a duplicate copy. Aside from those notes, they had no problems from outsiders. Jean liked school. Ira got the idea that he might be able to bribe her principal. Ira knew a man in the army who could forge documents. Discharge papers cost two hundred dollars, drivers' licenses, ID cards, and passes were cheap—it wouldn't take him ten minutes to make a fake birth certificate—but, Ira thought, he's lost, somewhere in the army.

Ira began to cut up the chinaberry tree for firewood, and while he rested, blowing out the frosty clouds of breath and rubbing his numb hands, he thought that he'd get some new novels to read during the winter, and maybe a battery-powered radio for the news and late-night music programs.

Jean asked for the .22, so Ira bought an old double-barreled twelve-gauge shotgun for himself. They practiced behind the house. She handled the rifle quite well. Twice a week Ira took her to the movie in Beauville, as part of her education, and Ira thought that she understood the movies pretty well. She liked them. He tried to pick good movies for her, like *Moby Dick* and *Giant*. She completely outgrew the clothes he'd bought for her after Delaney's funeral.

Ira made two beds in the back room adjoining the kitchen. They were simply large wooden shelves that extended from the north and east walls. They were about waist high, respectively, to each of them, and Ira hung a big Indian blanket between the beds as a partition. He divided his army blankets between the two beds, and they slept warm, even though there was no heat in the back room. From the army Ira had learned the expression, "hit the sack." Jean and he had a joke that they used at bedtime. They'd say, "Well, time to hit the shelf," and in the mornings, to wake each other, they'd say, "OK, sunup, crawl off that shelf!"

When it really got cold, when it snowed, Ira put one of his blankets on her bed, banked the heater, and propped the bedroom door open so that they would get the warmth. The next night it was even colder, so cold that Ira brought the camp stove from the kitchen to heat their bedroom. That's the night Jean crept into bed with Ira and mumbled in her sleep while he lay awake, feeling guilty about the touch of her body, thinking about the cold. At first he thought she was snoring, but when Ira strained hard in the darkness to hear above the moan of the north wind that was splitting the shingles, he could make out her words—it made him certain that she was happy with him.

Ira got a letter the next day from the Cumby banker telling him that he'd waited the two months, as instructed, and then sold the store in Tongs for the best offer that he got, seventeen hundred dollars from Mr. Paul Jacobs of Tongs. He wrote that he'd deposited the proceeds in Ira's account. That helped Ira decide to buy the farm. He drove down to Cumby, while Jean was in school, and fixed it for his bank to transfer the money to the real estate man in Beauville who owned the farm.

* * *

From his living room chair by the heater Ira could see the downhill east orchard, twelve clingstone peach trees, and the pond. He'd seeded the meadow below the pond with vetch and white Dutch clover, but it was covered with snow, and the hard seeds were frozen cold and dormant. There was a light sheet of ice on the pond.

Normally Ira watched the sunrise from that chair, while Jean slept in the back room, and he thought that whoever built this house must have known about the mystery of sunrises, to have put the fireplace room on the east side. The kitchen was on the cold north-west, and if a family were living there, the mother would be in the kitchen just then, baking their morning biscuits.

The tall coffeepot on the heater had not begun to boil, the sun had yet to rise over the pond. Ira knew that it would rise over the pond, for he'd watched it every morning and made knife marks on the floor so that he could keep the chair in exactly the same place. The sun had moved south every morning until it got to the pond, and it kept moving south until it was midway down the pond, actually coming up through the bare limbs of a tall hickory tree on the horizon. The sun wouldn't go south anymore, Ira supposed, because of the date. It was December nineteenth, two days before solstice, and it would hang in the unknown neighbor's hickory tree for about a week and then appear to move north again. Ira knew about appearances, for he'd checked in the Beauville library about the seasons, about the obliquity of the ecliptic, about the Earth sweeping its path around the sun. It was unseasonably early, he thought, for a blanket of snow.

The coffee began to boil, and Ira pulled it toward the edge of the heater. In the false dawn he saw frost on the windowpanes. He got up from his chair carefully, so as not to move it from the marks, and reached for a cup on the mantel. There was a genuine fireplace with a mantel, pothooks, Hessians, and hearthstones, but Ira preferred to use the metal heater, for it seemed more efficient to have it radiating heat into the room rather than heating up the cold chimney bricks. Another good feature of the heater was that it had a flat top where he could boil coffee. Ira used a potholder with a printed advertisement for the Farley Butane Company to pour the coffee and sat back in the chair, checking the marks on the floor. Perhaps the potholder came from someone related to Midge Farley, he thought, the waitress in Tongs who had been Stanley's girl friend. That made him remember Stanley and James and Cass-field and—Delaney—and everybody who had died since the fall morning he left Tongs. He could see the outline of the hickory tree clearly, for a flickering tongue-tip of the rising sun was flashing through it. Then the glowing pie plate of a sun started swimming up through its branches. Its color grew warmer every minute until it was blazing red. It seemed to be snared in the network and mesh of the tree's bare limbs. Ira looked straight at it, protected by the thickness of Earth's atmosphere at the sunrise angle, so the Beau-ville library said, and he watched the thin low wisps of clouds that it was dissolving and the long silvery line of faceted reflections it cast across the ice of the frozen pond. The higher the sun got, the warmer the dawn grew and the more light it cast, but paradox-ically, the colder grew the color of the sun's face, until it would become so cold in color that Ira couldn't look straight at it, yet it cast intense heat. Likewise, at sunset as it left the sky the day would chill while the color of the sun would grow warmer, cherry hot-poker red.

Then suddenly—low and from his right—a flock of ducks flew into the sun. They flew toward the brushy top end of the pond and dis-appeared behind the pines. Surprised, Ira sipped the coffee, savor-ing the image of them flying across the sun. It seemed that there were as many as twenty birds in the flock, and he remarked that it was two days before the winter solstice—the sun was rising through the hickory. If he could make a note of that, Ira thought, perhaps it might forecast their coming next year. He didn't know ducks very well, but he thought the large ones might have been pintails or mallards. Ira got out Delaney's bird guides and his Chambers County notebook to check them.

Then the coffee in his cup was too cold to drink, and Ira went into the back room to wake Jean. When he opened the door it was much colder than the parlor, even though the camp stove was still burn-ing. He looked down at her. She slept on her side, with her mouth open. He shook her shoulder, waking her. She tried to crawl deeper under the blankets, but he stripped them back and piled them at the foot. "Crawl off the shelf, Jean." She rolled partway off the edge, reaching timidly with her bare feet for the cold floor. When her toes found the floor she ran into the fireplace room, dragging from the foot of her bed one of the green army blankets. She wrapped up in the blanket and huddled in his chair while Ira cautiously took the hot camp stove back to the kitchen and refilled its tank. He cooked four eggs, some strips of bacon, and heated slices of bread in the skillet, after pouring off the grease. He fixed two plates. The cold plates spoiled the eggs, but it couldn't be helped, he thought.

While they ate by the heater, Ira said, "There are some ducks down on the pond."

"Really?" Jean was half awake.

"Yeah. Big flock of migrant ducks. I was looking out the window and saw them fly up toward the top end of the pond. They're probably at the mouth of the creek that feeds the pond."

"Can we go see?" She looked out the frosted window. "Ira! It snowed last night! Let's go see the ducks!"

"School, girl. School. After you catch the bus, I might go try to shoot us one or two."

"Aw—it wouldn't take long—I could go with you?"

"You've got twenty minutes till the bus comes," he said, wondering if the unexpected snow would slow the school bus.

"You could drive me, later. I could be an hour late to school. One day I could be late. Hell-fire."

"All right, but if you're going to be late anyway, you might as well help me hunt them. They'll only flush once."

"What's flush?"

"Jump up and fly."

"Good. I'll help you hunt them!"

When they finished eating, Ira brought the shotgun and the rifle from the closet and stood them in the chimney corner. He took the ammunition box down from the shelf and handed her a box of .22 shells. They were small—the box of fifty only slightly larger than a penny box of matches. She held them tight in the palm of her left hand and looked at the guns while she finished eating breakfast. Then she ran the plates to the kitchen and brought her clothes from the back room to dress by the heater.

Ira turned his back while she was dressing and got a pencil and paper from the closet to draw a map of the pond, the orchard, and the house. At first he'd planned to go out to the front of the house, circle around the hill to come up through the orchard from the lowest part of the meadow, from the south, crawling to the dam, keeping it between them and the ducks so that they could shoot over it, but then he remembered that the pond was frozen. They would have to go out the back of the house, north, and cut through the hollow to the head of the pond, where a stream fed into it, for that would be the only place with open water—where the running stream fed in. Not that it was a hard freeze. It would probably melt by noon, but the ducks might be rested and gone by then.

Ira drew a dotted line on the paper from the back door to the thicket, then continuing down to the head of the pond. He showed it to Jean and explained his strategy, making sure she understood.

"We slip out the back door. Don't let it slam. The ducks are probably up here, in the open water. We can walk to here. Here we have to crawl. From here we can shoot. You shoot when I touch your shoulder. Shoot the biggest duck that you see, and don't shoot for his head. Shoot a duck that's *sideways* to you. Don't shoot *into a bunch*—pick out *one* duck and shoot him. After you shoot they'll probably fly, but shoot again if you have time to reload. I'll shoot targets of opportunity." It sounded embarrassingly silly, as soon as he said it, the "targets of opportunity" sounded like he was still in the artillery, but Jean didn't know about that.

He filled his pockets with shotgun shells, knowing that it was an unorthodox method of hunting ducks, wondering if Jean would someday learn to shoot ducks in season, with license, decoys, retrievers, brandy—romantic like in Hemingway's *Across the River*—if she'd learn that after she'd filled out, after she was a nurse in the army or a fashion model—would she remember this day, his method, and think him mean? But his method was necessary, Ira told himself, because the small flocks only stopped for a few hours, and they would flush only once—when they were fired upon they would circle high and move out. With such a flock there was the possibility of only one surprise, and not even that, if they weren't properly stalked. Perhaps she'd remember the stalk, he mused, if he made it a good one.

She pulled her knit cap over her ears while Ira buttoned all of his pockets. He was thinking that it would keep the snow out when they crawled, but he'd have to remember to unbutton one pocket so he could get to the shells when it was time to shoot. Then Jean buttoned up her coat, and Ira took two .22 bullets out of the box. She wouldn't get more than two shots, because she had to pull the bolt and reload after her first shot. He told her to put the shells in her mouth and handed them to her. He opened the bolt on her rifle and checked to see that it was unloaded. She would be crawling behind him, part of the way. Then he did the safety ritual of showing her that the breech of his gun was broken and clear. Ira went out the back door and let the screen door close gently on her shoulder, so she could keep it from slamming.

They walked quickly past the hen coop and began a wide circle that would bring them into the hollow and then down to the little running stream that fed the pond.

Ira kept walking fast, even after they entered the trees, and only slowed when they were about a hundred yards from the pond. They walked carefully for another fifty yards through the muffling snow and jumped a big swamp rabbit. Ira followed him with the empty shotgun and could have had him easily, but they were after ducks. It was very still. He wished for a breeze to give them some concealment, but there was none.

Ira started the stalk. He put Jean in front, and she understood exactly. She moved forward, step by step, always keeping a tree between herself and the pond. When they were close she stopped. They waited, listening. Ira's breeze came up. It blew in their faces, from the direction of the pond, and that was good, he thought. She looked at him, and he got down on the snow and began to crawl. When he passed her she followed, crawling in the path that he broke. Perhaps with the breeze crawling was unnecessary, but it made the hunt more exciting and meaningful for them to lie in the snow and push themselves forward, holding the guns in the crooks of their arms. The Mississippi snow was rare enough to be shocking with its freshness.

They'd been crawling for about twenty minutes when the breeze stopped. Ira waited a few minutes and nothing happened. He slowly raised his head and saw the ducks. Then he carefully pushed up a parapet of snow, toward the front, and signaled to Jean to crawl up beside him. She peeped over the wall of snow and saw the birds, close together and still, resting. They were quite close, and occasionally one would make a low, quarrelsome quack.

There were seventeen. Ten big ones and seven small ones—and they were calm. Ira was completely satisfied with the hunt. The sun was bright and, sure enough, the big ones were mallard males with bright green heads.

He rolled over onto his side and slowly, carefully, checked the barrels for snow. Then he unbuttoned his pocket and loaded both barrels with the shells, shot size four. He carefully moved the shotgun up over the parapet and took Jean's rifle. Opening the bolt, he blew through the muzzle. It was clear. She took it and put one of the shells in the little slide and slowly closed the bolt. Ira nodded to her, and she wiped off the rear sight. He rolled back on his stomach, pulling up his right knee so that he could stand quickly for a wing shot. Jean was sighting over the parapet, and she looked ready, so Ira took another look. He waited until three or four of the mallards were in a close bunch, and then he touched her shoulder and got ready.

Ira heard the little spitting crack of the .22, and immediately pulled off one barrel at the bunch of three or four. Birds flew, and with his second shot Ira dropped one that was about twelve feet in the air. The rest of them flew straight up, circling out of sight.

As they ran down to the pond to get the birds, Ira's knees were stiff. He couldn't feel his toes as he stumbled down the icy slope. Jean didn't seem to feel the cold. Her duck floated dead on the water, along with two of the bunch that Ira potted. His wing shot had fallen on the ice, just at the edge of the pond. Jean beat him to the bank. When he got there he saw a cripple rise and try to fly. It ran across the water and scooted into the frozen stubble of weeds at the far bank, but Jean was ready. When it stopped she killed it with a head shot.

They had five big ducks, and she grinned at Ira. That part of the pond was shallow, about knee deep, so he put his gun down on the ice and waded in. Jean retrieved his wing shot, while he retrieved the others. It was cold, and Ira waded out of the water as soon as he could. They started walking quickly back toward the house, with Jean carrying both guns, and Ira carrying the ducks. Ira was thinking that he'd have coffee first, then clean the birds. They could have a big one for supper, and he'd pack the other four in snow for tomorrow and the day after that.

They were halfway up the slope. Jean was walking ahead of him. The snow was deep for her, five inches or so, and she stopped. "Let me carry them," she said, handing Ira the guns. He dropped the five ducks onto the snow and took the rifle and shotgun. She divided the birds into two groups, turning their heads in the same direction, so that she could circle their necks with her small hands and lift them waist high to carry home.

"What do you say?" Ira asked.

She looked at the ducks' heads. The heads of the males were bright green, cocky. "Beautiful birds," she said. "But let's not shoot any more for a while."

"Well—we didn't lose any cripples," he said.

"Yeah. And we didn't kill too many," she said, turning from him, starting to walk up the snowy hill, lifting her feet high out of the snow and putting them straight down, so that she didn't drag her heels through the snow but instead left neat tracks like a fox or a deer.

CHAPTER 19

AFTER THEY'D EATEN ALL THE DUCKS AND TIED BUNDLES OF THEIR bright feathers with string and hung them from the mantelpiece, and after the snow melted (it doesn't stick long in Mississippi) it was Christmas vacation. It seemed to Ira that Jean changed. The weather was bleary cold, wet, and being cooped up so, Ira did everything he could think of to pass the time. He helped Jean make a quail trap out of thin pieces of split-pine shingles, stacked in a pyramid, crossed like the logs in a cabin with a spring-stick tied across the top to hold them tight, spaced half an inch apart so that there would be plenty of light inside the trap. A corn-baited tunnel lured the quail up into the trap. If there was enough light in the trap, he explained, the birds would go in, and once inside they'd become confused and walk around the sides, poking their heads at the slats, not noticing the dark opening of the tunnel in the center where they'd entered. They would try to escape, so the trap had to be heavy enough to hold five or six if they flew against it from the inside. It was a pleasant job of handwork and whittling. Eating the good ducks gave Ira the idea of building it. He remembered that Delaney had helped him make one like it when he was about Jean's age.

It was while they made the trap that it seemed to Ira that she changed. She stared sadly at the quail trap, poking her fingers in the holes between the slats. She was melancholy.

"We ever going back to Texas?" she asked.

"No," he answered automatically, without thinking. "You want to go back to Texas?"

"No. I like it here. I'm glad you bought this farm."

"OK."

She was quietly crying. She looked away from him. "Can I hug your neck, Ira, sometime?"

"I guess so, sure."

"I get scared."

"There's no one to be afraid of—here."

"I'm not afraid of anybody." She put her small arms around his neck.

"Jean, everybody gets afraid sometime. And lonely. Do you miss your mother?"

"No."

"Do you think you could go back to Texas and find your father?"

"No, Ira, I couldn't find my father."

"What is it that scares you?"

"Sometimes I remember what you said to that lady in Fort Worth. Sometimes I get afraid you'll send me away."

"I won't do that." Ira put his arm around her waist. He'd never held her in his arms before. His throat tightened. He found it difficult to talk. He pulled her close. "That's why we left the fishing camp—and went to the Gulf—and sold the car and bought the truck—that man in Tongs said if we didn't leave he would have the police take you back to Texas."

"You didn't want them to?"

"No, honey. I've gotten used to having you. You're a nice kid."

She kissed his cheek.

❀   ❀   ❀

When her trap was finished they took it up above the house to an old cornfield and baited it. Jean spent the day running out and checking it. When she came to the house she'd try to do something for him, to show her appreciation, but there was nothing to do, for Ira had swept the house, washed all the dishes, and cut a big pile of firewood.

He had an urge to drive somewhere, alone. It was too damp and cold to walk around the farm, and it was too confining in the little house. For the first time since he saw her in Texas, Ira felt uneasy being with Jean. With the drizzle and clouds he couldn't even watch the sunrise. Always before, he'd taken her with him on shopping trips to Beauville, but now he devised a hasty plan to excuse himself for going alone. She was warming her knees by the stove, smiling so prettily that he almost lifted her from the chair and kissed her mouth. Ira said, "Do you know that it'll be Christmas in four days?"

"It is?"

"Sure is. What do you want for Christmas?"

"I don't know."

"Don't you have any idea?"

"No."

"Then I'm going to drive into Beauville and look for something for you."

"What can I get you for Christmas, Ira?"

"You might make me something."

"What do you need?"

"Well, can you sew?"

"No."

"I'll try to think of something then, while I'm in Beauville."

"OK."

"Oh. That reminds me," Ira said, "did I overlook your birthday? When is your birthday?"

"April seventh."

"I'll remember that," he said. "What year were you born?"

"Nineteen hundred and forty-five," she replied. "I'm exactly eleven."

"OK, kid. Keep the home fires burning," he said. "I'll be back—probably after dark. Lock the door."

" 'Bye."

The old truck was cold and hard to start, and then when he got it out of the driveway, the gravel road was slick from the cold rains, so Ira hunched over the wheel and concentrated on his driving, concentrated on keeping out of the ditch until he got to the WPA road. By that time, the cab had warmed up. The WPA road was asphalt paved. If he'd turned left on that road he would have gone straight to Tongs, but Ira was afraid to do that. He was afraid that even in the strange Whitton's Egg Farm truck he might be recognized.

Ira turned right and drove northwest, toward Beauville. About halfway to Beauville the WPA road crossed a wooden bridge. The stream under that bridge had to be Mill Creek, he realized, and it was strange for him to think that there was a bridge across Mill Creek where it was only a bushy stream, only a foot deep, for always before he'd thought Mill Creek came from an unknown place, a place with no roads or trails, a place where man did not live, could not survive, but he saw that the holy creek of snakes and fish and beavers that passed Melissa's house and then flowed down to his aunt Essie's place came from here, a known place, quite civilized. There were fences and houses. There were cold, windblown mules standing in the lee of tarpaper shacks—Ira even saw a jet airliner fly over, pushed across the sky by its own vapor trail—like the finger of God. The old truck was warm, so warm that he turned off the heater before he got to Beauville.

Ira had hot solitary coffee in a new chrome and glass cafe just across the Okatoma bridge. He tried to think of something to get for Jean's Christmas present and ended up getting her two bottles of Coke and some candy bars. Ira got different kinds of candy, because he didn't know what kind she liked. He remembered wanting to kiss her. Then he drove around Beauville for an hour, passing the big theatre, the Belle Arms Hotel where they lose messages, and the funeral home, thinking it strange that they call it a home. He saw the new Tanglewood Addition with big brick houses, the offices of the REA, the courthouse. "When you've seen that," he thought, "you've seen Beauville." Then Ira stopped at Mason's Department Store where he saw a big display of bicycles, in front, on the sidewalk. He thought that a bicycle would make a fair and traditional Christmas gift for Jean and bought a blue one, a twenty-four-inch girls' model with a white basket and a squeeze-bulb horn.

On the way home Ira started thinking about women—trying not to think about Jean. He thought about Melissa, and Janet, and the welfare woman—and then he knew that he'd stop, when he thought about Melissa, for he'd known, subconsciously, from the moment when he realized that the little stream under that wooden bridge was Mill Creek, that he would stop there.

*   *   *

It was marshy by the bridge. Ira could barely get the truck far enough off the road to allow traffic to pass. There was no way to lock the candy and Cokes in the truck, so he looked up and down the road to see that no one was in sight, and then he hid them in the brown weeds by the bridge. He pulled armloads of dead grass to cover the bicycle. As an afterthought, he put the candy and Cokes in the bicycle basket. If anybody saw the truck, he reasoned, they'd think it belonged to someone hunting in the creek bottoms and leave it alone, knowing that hunters were quiet, with guns, and might walk out of the trees at any time, returning to their truck. He crossed the little bridge, left the road on the east side of the creek, and entered the vine-thick tangled bottoms.

The only good thing about the weather, Ira was thinking, was that there wouldn't be any snakes crawling around.

He couldn't tell for sure, if indeed it hadn't been there all along, exactly when the idea of Melissa came into his head, but he thought about seeing her while he walked several miles, brushing through the tangles sometimes, sometimes cutting across abandoned fields, cutting bends off the creek. In the process he walked up and down a lot of round hills that had been planted in corn, and he climbed or descended them row by row using the horizontal rows for steps. On the round hills the dry stalks stood in file, and sometimes when Ira stepped down he would place his foot close beside the base of a stalk so that when he stepped onto that foot it would sweep the stalk forward and down. He found that he could pretty much control the direction in which the stalks fell, and he made a game of it, like the lumberjacks' competition when they try to cut and drop fir trees on pegs that the judges have put in the ground.

It might have been the round uncultivated hills covered with soft blowing broom sage that kept reminding him of Melissa, round hills sometimes remind men of women, or it might have been that before he left home he'd been looking at Jean. Maybe it was because he'd thought of kissing Jean.

Ira opened his shirt at the collar, for he was sweating from the walk, and he thought—Old Man Natale is dead, one sister is married to Paul Jacobs—that would leave the mother, Melissa, and the younger sister there on the farm.

From the top of a hill he saw a curl of blue smoke, and then from the next hill he saw the house and the corrugated-tin roof, the brick fireplace and chimney, and the barn. Ira could see the barn well, for he was coming up on the farmhouse from the back. The barn sat there with a cavelike black eye, the hayloft door, staring from its forehead, and Ira stared at the impoverished slope of its tin roof. In some parts of the country, barns are painted and have hipped, puffed-out roofs that make them look like they've just eaten enough Thanksgiving dinner to last all winter, but on the red-clay farms of Mississippi the barns are built with skinny roofs that don't even go straight from roofbeam to eave, but are pinched in, as if they're starved. He saw the ladder rungs nailed to the back wall leading up to the hayloft, where he'd had to duck his head as he crawled in to dodge the rusty iron pulley that hung from the gable above the door.

Once when Melissa met him at the beaver blind they found that a cottonmouth had chosen the closeness of their blind for a den. Not disturbing the snake, they went to the loft, for they could climb the ladder on the back side without being seen from the house.

Then he felt it, it was as if he'd known it all along, there was no question in his mind that he would go to see Melissa. Ira cut down to the creek, expecting to find the beaver pond, but there was no pond. There was just the ditch, slightly larger than it had been at the bridge, yet still small enough for a boy to jump. He found the place where the beaver blind had been, but a freshet must have washed it away, he supposed, for there were high-water marks on the trees. The dam was gone. Maybe it washed out, he thought, or maybe the beavers had died, or maybe they'd been run off or killed.

From there he had to climb the bank to see the house, where there were no signs of life, except a constant light-blue smoke coming from the chimney. The faint smoke, however, made the un-painted bleached-gray house stand out warm against the dark green pines beyond it. He would see Melissa, Ira told himself, he would say hello, but not just yet, he thought, not until he could talk to someone and learn what the situation was—whether she had a fel-low. That doctor would do, if he was still staying down at Essie's place, but before Ira turned to follow the creek downstream the back door of the house opened, and a girl ran out to a pile of fire-wood, grabbed a stick of wood in each hand, and ran back in the house. Ira froze, staring at the house. He thought, "Why not stop for a minute and say hello? It couldn't hurt." Thinking, "What could it hurt, I've known them all before, I'll just say hello," he climbed up the shoulder of the creekbed through gnarled mountain laurel, skirt-ing a grove of pine and sweet gum. There were spined balls on the sweet gums, but no leaves, and their ash gray limbs contrasted to the rich green of the pines. One sweet gum was the host of a climb-ing vine—probably a fox grape. Ira advanced to the house. There were no dogs at the house, and he was glad of that. He didn't want a bunch of scared dogs yapping at his heels, and he remembered that there were dogs before, black and white ones with short ugly muzzles.

At the steps he kicked the red mud off his boots, then he crossed the hollow porch and knocked on the door. As he knocked, Melissa opened the door; it was as if she'd been standing there the past six years, expecting him. It was dark and cold inside. They all wore sweaters, and even though Ira had his blood up from the long walk, it chilled his backbone to sit on the split-cane chair that she offered. The old woman didn't talk. She hovered in the kitchen and sucked her teeth. Ira imagined that she was thinking, "He's the one who lived in the big store, and his family was too good to be connected with any Natales, and when Mike said make a wedding they gave him a new green suit and sent the boy away. Paul is a good boy. Paul came to work with us and help us. Paul came and married to us before there was the money. Paul is nice, but this one was too good to marry a Natale, and now his store burned down he comes to see if there's any money here for him. Paul has it in the bank. Paul has it in the bank. Paul has the money."

Melissa was dressed like her mother. She was pretty in spite of, or maybe because of, the plain dress and cotton apron and black sweater. The sweater had a small hole in the right shoulder, and she wore it unbuttoned. It curved over her shoulders to her breasts, and then hung straight down from there. As she faced Ira, he saw the row of buttons on the left side of the open black sweater and the corresponding row of buttonholes on the right side. He held his eyes away from the tented, full sweater. She stood with her back to the fireplace, warming her hands. She raised her head and looked straight at him, defiantly, like she did the time he met her at the beaver dam.

Ira remembered that she was never afraid. Even in school, when she was a child, when the third-grade boys called her Palmolive, she'd silenced them by the way that she would look at them, unafraid. The younger sister came from the kitchen, pretty like Melissa, with a long neck and long dark hair, streaked with brown. It wasn't as dark as Melissa's, but it was as long. The younger sister sat on a stool by the fireplace and tucked her knees up under her chin. Hugging her folded knees, she looked down at the floor. He could see her long eyelashes. Her body was the same size as Jean's —two-thirds grown.

Melissa smiled at him, and then she looked at the old woman, who continued to suck her teeth. The house was dark and cold. There was no smell of money in the house.

Ira smiled at her, thinking, "Why did you give it away, why did you give it away, it was your only chance, you're beautiful, but you're too quiet to catch a man without the farm, why did you give it to Paul Jacobs?" But it's not a question for asking, so he smiles, and the younger sister smiles at him, and he says something to Melissa about nice to see you, and goes back outside, stepping lightly with his heavy boots while she says something like, "Why don't you stay or come again some other day," but he's going down the steps backwards and trying not to trip and fall. The younger sister is peeping out the front door, smiling, while Melissa is wiping her hands on a print apron as if they are wet or something. Ira stops and looks up at her. She sweeps her hands toward the door and shoos the girl and her mother inside, like chickens.

"Are you going away again?" Melissa asks, her eyes moist.

"I don't know."

"I waited for you, a long time. I kept your money."

"You weren't supposed to wait. You were supposed to get married and live on that farm."

"Nobody asked me to marry. I was afraid of that house. I was afraid to live there alone."

"That didn't mean that you had to give it to Paul Jacobs, I didn't want that. That's not why I gave it to you."

"It was mine. You gave it to me. You didn't even come and give it to me yourself, the *bank* wrote a letter. The letter had your name in it, but you weren't in it. You have forgotten what I told you at the beaver dam the first time we talked. None of us own this land. This land was here before us. There are Indian flints in the fields. This land will be here after us."

"What happened to the beavers?"

"They died, or went away." She lied. "Besides, if you wanted me to be married, why did you leave me?"

"It was my fortune. That summer Delaney took me to County Line. An Indian fortune-teller told me that I would know three women. It all came true."

"Am I one of three?"

"Yes."

"Do you believe in fortune-tellers?"

"Of course not, but it came true."

"Which one did you marry?"

"I didn't marry."

"Paul said you married and had a little girl?"

"Paul lied. I have a girl, but I didn't marry."

"Paul lied. I'll tell Mother. No, I won't tell her, she trusts Paul. She says he wasn't too good to . . . I thought you went back to Texas when Mr. Delaney died? I tried to find out about . . . you."

"No. I couldn't leave, because of Tongs. They must have named this place for the way it grabs people and holds them. I'm like a bullet on a string, but you don't know about that, do you?"

"No. Tell me about it."

"It's too cold here, it's been too long to begin."

"Then I'll visit you. Where do you live?"

"In a cave, behind a rock."

"Where?"

"Under a bridge with the girl."

"Where?"

"Possum up a gum tree."

"Where?"

Ira dropped his head, caught and victorious. He smiled, "Seven miles out the Danville Road in a house by a pond with the girl. She's a good girl, you'd like her."

"Your eyes are watery, Ira. I still love you."

"Then come see me sometime. But don't let Paul Jacobs know where I live. I've been careful to sell my car and hide my tracks. I've stayed out of Tongs and not seen anybody who knows me— until you."

"Why? It's a free country."

"It's a long story about the girl. It's too damned cold to stand here and tell it now, but Paul ran me out of town. We ran. He threatened to have her put in an orphanage. Still, my fortune isn't complete. I don't want you to hate me. Don't tell Paul Jacobs where I live, please, don't tell him."

"No."

"I'm going to walk on down the creek and look at Aunt Essie's place."

"Ira, I didn't thank you for it, when you gave me the farm—I couldn't thank you—I didn't know you cared for it."

"I didn't care, then, not that day. I've changed, but I've bought another farm, it's OK. Like, I didn't care for the girl when she first came to me. It was only after she was forced on me, after I had to come back to Tongs, that I cared, and the coming back, somehow, made her important, and having her made the land here important —that's why I bought the farm."

"I see." She smiled at him, putting the back of her hand to the side of her head, brushing back her hair, shielding her eyes from the cold wind. "I want to talk with you longer—maybe I could come see you. But Paul has the only car I know. I can't get him to take me to your place. I could walk."

"No. Don't walk in the cold."

"Then I'll meet you somewhere."

"Up by your mailbox. Tomorrow. I'll pick you up. We'll drive over to Beauville to a movie, or out to our farm. You can meet my girl."

"Good. I'm glad." She smiled again, open-faced.

"OK. Tomorrow?"

"What time?"

"About noon. Noon at your mailbox." Ira turned away from the porch, toward the creek. His legs were numb and slow to start. Stiff-kneed, he'd lost the balance he'd had before, when he crunched the dry cornstalks with precision. But he warmed up by the time he got to the creek, and he was hot by the time he'd walked half a mile.

Ira walked like a bear. In the summer, when green vines and grasses and leaves made solid curtains of light and shadow, on days like the day he discovered the beaver dam, Ira imagined that he moved like an Indian, silently gliding from tree to shade, watching the water for fish, the plants for poisonous or edible leaves, the ground for snakes, and the chunks of sky for unusual birds. Sometimes he held his breath, listening for sounds of animals or men, smelling the air for snakes, or rain. But on Mill Creek, in December, frosts and the early snow had sered that sappy green, leaving leafless brown and gray twigs and stems and branches. Head down, straightforward, Ira crashed through them. A bear makes his money overturning fallen tree trunks, Ira thought, smashing bee gums, splashing elbow-deep for fish, not creeping and gliding. The summer is the time of the fox, but the winter is the time of the bear.

Ira was like a bear in another way, for he'd been in both social and spiritual hibernation. Although it was winter, he'd come out of his hibernation, and he'd come out hungry. Vines and branches tangled his feet and shoulders, but he bowed his neck and broke straight through, telling himself that he was no longer a masked coon who sat on his heels and washed his crawfish in the darkness, but a stand-up, thick-haired, hungry bear who would have, by God, dignified, stand-up, mature Melissa Natale.

When Ira got to Essie's house he found the doctor there—absolutely drunk. Ira noticed, when he knocked on the door, that the doctor had smashed a fifth of Old Crow on the front porch. From a distance, Ira had seen black smoke pouring from the chimney.

The front door was ajar. It opened to his knock, revealing a tremendous fire in the hearth. In his drunken extravagance, the doctor was burning pure heart-pine kindling. Ira went through the fireplace room to the study, where the doctor greeted him from one of the overstuffed chairs, peering through an alcoholic haze. "Hello, Ira King. Fancy seeing you today. Want a drink?"

"Sure," Ira replied. The doctor gestured with a grand sweep of his arm to an open bottle on the shelf.

"No stale amenities, Ira King. No glasses either."

Ira took the bottle from the shelf. Apparently the doctor had thrown the cork away. "I see you dropped one on the porch."

"Threw it, King. Threw it. I've a phone for emergencies," indicating the black phone on his desk, "I can have my bootlegger chap down here in five minutes with another." He reminded Ira—his hair had grown longer—of all of the pictures Ira had seen of Edgar Allen Poe, and it fascinated Ira that when drunk he spoke precise English, because when Ira was drunk he talked Mississippian.

"You're pretty deep in the sauce, Forsythe," Ira said, feeling an impulse to get just as deep as the doctor was. Recoiling from his pull on the bottle, he added, "A bit of chaser wouldn't hurt."

"A chaser, King, is as worthless as the tits on a boar hog."

"OK." Ira spoke softly, yielding to the burn in his throat. "Why's this you're so deep in the sauce?"

"Shock—massive shock, King. We'll never be the same—I know too much about humans—should have stuck to frogs—embryo pigs. My wife lost her baby—we lost it." He sank deeper in his overstuffed chair, his arms hanging over the sides of it.

Ira could only say, "No."

"Yes." He took the bottle from Ira. "If she had been another man's wife, well—I'd not understand, I'd say"—he took a shot—"you're young, you can conceive again. But I know my wife. I understand her. We'll never be the same."

"When was it?"

"Last night. Midnight. It was time. I was taking her to her doctor in Beauville. I've a good car. I knew I could make it. There was no traffic. Halfway to Beauville a tire blew out. I was afraid to dirty my hands trying to change the tire in the dark, so I continued driving on the rim, but she couldn't stand the jolt and clatter of the iron rim digging into the pavement. I stopped on the shoulder and waited. A car came—but refused to stop. Then it turned in the highway and came back, but too late. Perhaps I could have saved the baby in my office, even, but not in the dark car."

"But it's true, what you said about being young—able to conceive again?"

Forsythe pulled up his socks, as if that mannerism was a ritual never to be forgotten. "She's lost confidence in me. She didn't want to come to Tongs. This is a bum practice. I once told her, a year ago, that I should have been a mechanic. She remembered that. She kept crying that I was no doctor, that I should have been a mechanic. I had to leave her, unconscious, in the Beauville hospital. Maybe I should have been a mechanic. I couldn't help her."

Ira was beginning to feel the drink, and his friend's story saddened him, for he'd been feeling good after his talk with Melissa. He told himself that he didn't even know the doctor's wife—but that didn't help him feel any better about it. Ira knew something about women, and he knew something about loss. He stared at the bottle, avoiding the doctor's eyes.

"I need a drinking partner, King."

"Sure. You got one," Ira replied, feeling that he needed drink too. It had been too much for one cold December day, Jean's outgrowing her dress that he bought in September, seeing Melissa, and with seeing her wanting her, even more than he'd wanted Janet when she undressed by candlelight, and feeling good about Melissa—for the first time in six years—and then the doctor's wife. "Sure, Forsythe, ring up your bootlegger"—the doctor smiled gratefully—"and tell him to bring some goddamn 7UPs—I can't hack this stuff straight —and some ice."

CHAPTER 20

Ira stayed with the doctor while they both got drunk, or rather while he got drunk and the doctor got drunker. Forsythe kept all the electric lights on, he insisted on it, and they moved into the fireplace room to watch the roaring fire. He told Ira about the trivial garments that his wife had bought for the baby. She'd bought blue, but the store in Beauville would exchange them for pink, if need be. Ira tried to get him off that subject, but as they drank Ira's own mind followed morbid thoughts of Kings being cut and killed up Mill Creek. That reminded him of Tongs Bridge. In his mind he kept seeing Stanley pinwheeling off the river bridge, turning end-over-end in the air—and then he saw, in slow motion, Cassfield go stiff and topple forward from his old cane-bottomed chair where he'd sat staring into the fire, right where the doctor sat, to smash his head once more on the hearthstones.

"Don't look so sad, Ira. It's not the end of the world for you, you know."

"I was jes thanking, hour ago, that I might git married myself, Forsythe."

The doctor's smile was crooked, but warm. He spoke slowly, his words tangled, "Don't missurstand me, King. Marriage is a wonderful instution."

They both stared at the fire.

"Who is the lucky girl?"

"Changed mind—I think," Ira said, staring at the fire, remembering his old truck parked miles up the creek and the new bicycle hidden under brown grass with Cokes and candy in its basket.

Then neither man spoke. Deep in their second bottle, the bootlegger returned, having finished his night's work, to drink with them. Forsythe passed out, so Ira and the bootlegger hauled him into his lounge, where they put him in the big chair. The fire had burned low when they finished the bottle. Ira asked the bootlegger to drive him around the WPA road to his truck.

The bootlegger drove his Mercury fast, with savage confidence, telling Ira that he'd only lived in Tongs three years, that he'd been a stock-car driver until "it got t'where it didn't pay."

Ira was too drunk to find Jean's hidden bicycle and Cokes and candy bars. He knew where they were, but he couldn't make his feet go that way. He leaned on the old truck and breathed the cold night air, debating with himself whether it was pointed in the direction of Beauville or his farm. Then he decided in favor of the latter. He got in and started the truck. He released the clutch with studied nonchalance and drove slowly, staring at the asphalt road that looked, to him, like a black ribbon unrolling from a large, black spool.

Jean woke him early the following morning, right at dawn, by casually dropping, again and again, what sounded like the same saucepan in the kitchen. It was too early for her to be awake, Ira knew. He covered his head with the blanket and played possum, but she was relentless—he smelled hot coffee brewing. Seeing that he'd slept in his clothes, Ira rolled from his shelf and took his toothbrush and paste from the top of her neat chest of drawers.

"Good morning, Jean." Ira spoke to her as he went through the kitchen to the outside well. He splashed his face with well water and brushed most of the whiskey-stale from his teeth. As he went back through the kitchen, she asked, "You want me to cook eggs?"

"No, honey. Let's drink our coffee in the living room and watch the sun rise."

"OK," she said.

Ira started a fire in the heater.

She brought in the coffee, asking, "Did you find what you went for?"

"The treasure?" He took his coffee. "Yes, but I was kidnapped by pirates on the Okatoma River—I had to hide the treasure before they caught me." Ira sipped the hot coffee and felt better.

"Where did you hide it?"

"Beside the road. Hand me a pencil, I'll make you a map." Jean brought him paper and a pencil and he drew a sketch map of the house, the WPA road intersection, and the bridge on Mill Creek. He put a ⊹ near the bridge, where the bicycle lay. "Here it is, here, right here, Jean. They gave me an amnesia injection—I'm apt to lose my memory, completely, at any moment! Take this map and guard it with your life!" He handed her the map.

"What sort of treasure is it?" she asked.

Ira dropped his jaw and rolled his eyes from side to side. "Dunno, girlie, can't remember nuthin' since this mawnin', where am I at?"

She laughed—"I think the amnesia injection is taking effect— poor fellow—what's your name?"

"Dunno," he groaned.

"Where are you?"

"In a house, that's all I know."

"Who am I?"

"Dunno, girlie, complete stranger t'me."

She giggled. "Can you still drive?"

"Dunno, girlie. When I finish this here coffee and it gets sunup, I'll try. But you'll have to tell me where to go."

"Oh, I can. I've got a map."

"What kind of a thing is it I have to drive?"

"A pickup truck."

"What kind?"

"A Ford."

"OK, kid, think I can handle that."

She went in the bedroom, and he warmed his coffee from the tall pot in the kitchen. The sun rose right on the money, right on top of a tall pine—where it was supposed to. There was no wind. It was clear, so Ira knew it would be a nice warm day. When Jean was ready, they went to the truck, and Ira started it up. At the mailbox he made her tell him which way to turn, also at the WPA road intersection. She followed the map intently, moving her finger along the line on the paper while her eyes searched the roadside for a bridge. When they finally got to the bridge, she told him to stop. She leaped from the truck, and while he pulled onto the side of the road he watched her quickly walk straight to the hidden bicycle. She scratched aside the brown dewy grass and lifted it by the handlebars, while he got out of the truck.

"There's some candy and Cokes in the basket." She nodded, rolling it up to the pavement. "Can you ride a bicycle?" he asked.

"Sure." She put the candy and Cokes in the truck, stepped through the foot-gate, and aligned the pedals. "Watch." She stepped down on the right pedal and rode off toward Beauville. Ira followed her for a mile in the truck, until she stopped, then he put the bicycle in the back of the truck.

"Do you like it?"

"Sure, Ira. It's brand new." She was hot from riding the bicycle. She sat close to him on the truck seat and kissed his cheek.

"Let's go on to Beauville for breakfast. Wouldn't you like a cafe breakfast?"

"Sure, Ira. Thanks a lot for the bicycle. I never had one of my own before."

He ordered big breakfasts at a new, clean cafe. Jean asked him to move to a table by the window so she could keep an eye on her bicycle. The food came. While he salted his grits the voice in his mind recalled the blues lyrics, *If I don't love you, Babeee—Grits ain't groceries—Aigs ain't poultries—And Mona Lisa WAS a man!* He remembered his date.

"I have another surprise for you, Jean."

"Oh! I hope it's a movie!"

"It is," he replied. "That's part of it."

✿   ✿   ✿

At noon he stopped the truck on the road beside Natale's mailbox. Melissa wasn't there, so Ira turned off the motor to wait. Jean asked, remembering her promised Beauville movie, "What we doing here?"

"We're going to meet someone," he said.

"Who?"

"You wait and see. It's a surprise."

Jean looked around the truck. It was a bright day, not too cold. Ira read the dim MIKE NATALE stenciled on the mailbox and saw that the flag was down, telling the mailman that he needn't stop to pick up a letter. A bored or disappointed hunter had put four small .22 holes through the box. He watched the path to the house. Melissa appeared on the path, then stopped and turned, saying something back to the drab house. She waited, said something else, turned, and came up smiling toward the truck. Awkwardly, Ira got out of the cab and went around to open the door for her. She was dressed well. She had her hair straight, caught at the back of her neck with a silver clip. She wore red lipstick. Jean looked at her with wonder, like she'd looked at the welfare woman, Delaney, and James Goff. Melissa got in beside Jean. Ira closed the door, went back around the truck, opened his door, and got in.

"Melissa, this is my friend, Jean."

"Hello, Jean."

"Hello," Jean said, looking straight into Melissa's eyes. Then she looked ahead, down the WPA road, knowing that they were headed away from Beauville and her movie.

Melissa asked, "Do you know where we're going, Jean?"

"I *think* we're going to the movie in town."

Ira started the truck and turned back toward Beauville.

"Is that where we're going, Ira?"

"That's right, we're going to the movies."

"What's showing?"

"*The Adventures of Ira King.*" As he said that, Jean's eyes flashed up at him. "*Pot Luck, The Adventures of Pot Luck.*"

Melissa smiled. "Don't you know what's showing, Jean?" she asked.

"Same one's been on for two weeks."

Melissa didn't know what that was. She asked, "What's been on that long?"

"*The Ten Commandments.* We saw it when it first started, I've been wanting to see it again. It's a good movie."

Since the first feature at Beauville didn't start until four, Ira drove them back to show Melissa the farm and to brew a pot of coffee. They all drank coffee, and then they walked down to the pond to look at the water. Jean wore Delaney's binoculars, dangling in their battered case, the straps too long for her body. Ira told Melissa about the ducks, and he showed her where they'd been feeding. He explained to her how the meadow below the pond was seeded with clover so that it would be green and blooming next spring. "I'm going to get three or four white-faced heifers to put in the meadow," Ira said. Jean looked at him curiously, for he hadn't told her about the calves. They walked around by the hollow and up to the cornfield so Jean could show Melissa her quail trap. She told her that it worked real good, but she'd stopped baiting it because the bobwhites were too pretty to eat. She told Melissa, "They're called a covey—when they're all together. When they're feeding, with their heads down, they make one bird be the lookout. He stands up on a fence post or a bush."

"When does he get to eat?" Melissa asked.

Jean squinted. "That's something I haven't figured out yet. I think they take turns being lookout, but I'm not sure."

They went down to the house, checked the stove to see that it was banked, had another coffee, and then drove in to Beauville.

When they entered the theatre there were only five or six people waiting for the early feature. Ira chose seats near the back of the lighted theatre, knowing that Jean liked to sit close to the screen. As the house lights dimmed, she slipped into the aisle and went to the front row. She snuggled deep in a front-row seat, gazing up at the screen. When the feature started, the reflected light from the screen gave her yellow hair a halo. Ira put his arm around Melissa and touched her hair, feeling the softness of her shoulder. He smelled her shampoo, or perfume. They watched *The Ten Commandments* until his arm ached. He wanted to kiss her. He whispered to her, "I want to kiss you." She drew away from him, and in the faint light he saw her smile.

"Let me rub off this lipstick." She got Kleenex from her purse for that. She put her arms around him and they kissed, unmindful of the movie, the six strangers in the theatre, or Jean on the front row.

After the long movie, they ate in the Cranfield Cafeteria and then drove back out the WPA road to drop Melissa off at Natale's mailbox. Ira didn't say that he'd see her soon, because he knew that she knew he would. Relaxed and confident, she'd chatted with Jean on the way home about the movie, about school, and about the ducks.

*　*　*

The weather was cold and bright the following morning when Ira stood in his front yard drinking coffee and staring at the ugly stump of the chinaberry tree. It reminded him of that sumbitch stump in Cassfield's yard, the one Cassfield tripped on daily, and daily cussed. Ira kicked it with the toe of his boot, stared at its black, hollow middle, and thought that with imagination it could be a giant's rotten tooth. Charred from his several attempts to burn it out, first with motor oil from the truck, later with kerosene, it was too alive to burn. Ira admired its tenacity, but he hated to leave it like it was, charred and ugly, an emblem of his failed attempts, and to dig around it and chop it below the ground would have taken three or four days, maybe even a week.

In truth, Ira mused, it reminded him of the burned store in Tongs, his birthright that he sold to Paul Jacobs.

While he meditated on the black stump, a car drove up the hill with the quiet, impatient whine of a late-model, new motor. Ira knew by the sound that it wasn't a truck or a tractor or an old worn-out car, even before he saw it. It slowed and stopped beside the mailbox, and he thought that maybe the mailman had a new car, but the driver stayed at the mailbox only long enough to check the name. Then he turned into the driveway and pulled up to where Ira stood, near the stack of stovewood that he'd cut. Ira looked closely at the driver, trying to identify him as the mailman, or Forsythe, and the car had stopped before he noticed the other occupant, a small man with a khaki uniform and a khaki uniform hat. The driver cut his motor and waited for the small man to get out and approach Ira. When the man in khaki was about three steps from Ira, the driver got out. He wore a light miracle-fabric suit and glasses with clear plastic frames. His jaw was square with a dimpled chin, and his teeth were bright. He came up beside the little man and faced Ira, saying that he was "Mr. Cantwell of Jackson" and that the little man was a constable. Ira smiled at Mr. Cantwell of Jackson's self-introduction, remembering a calling card that he'd once seen in a museum in Texas. The card was set in clear black type, and all it said was *Samuel Houston of Texas.* Ira thought the pair might be lost, they looked lost.

"I'm Ira King," he said.

"How do you do, Mr. King."

"Just fine, Mr. Cantwell. But I'd feel better if I could think of a way to get this stump up." Ira looked straight at Mr. Cantwell and smiled at him, thinking that he probably wasn't a native of Mississippi, waiting for him to ask directions for some place.

"Well." Cantwell took a step to the other side of the stump. "I was up in Neshoba County and saw they were blasting out pine stumps with dynamite. Big virgin pine stumps."

"Dynamite would get the stump out, all right," Ira replied, "but it would play hell with the curbing of my water well, it's right over there." He pointed.

"Oh, I see, that's right, it might. Well, the last thing a man would want to do is attack it with an axe."

Ira smiled at Cantwell, thinking he was a decent sort, liking him for making the suggestion about dynamite. He liked his honest face. The constable cleared his throat. He was the only one of the three wearing a hat, and he pushed it back on his head and squinted at Cantwell. He said, "Mr. Cantwell, we drove since seven this morning to get here, made two wrong turns and got plumb lost once. Here we are. Let's get on with it!"

The warm, friendly aftertaste of Ira's coffee turned bitter in his mouth. He realized that they knew they were at the right place—for some reason they'd come to find him.

Cantwell looked at the constable, and then he looked down at the stump. He wet his lips. "Wish I knew what to tell you about that stump, Mr. King," he said. Then, turning back to the car and opening the door, he took a black plastic briefcase from the seat. He returned to where he could prop one foot on the charred stump. He took a printed form from the case and spoke softly to himself as he began to fill in the form, confirming the date with the constable. "It's the twenty-first?"

"Yes. Yesterday was the twentieth, Mr. Cantwell."

"Your full name is Ira King, no middle initial?"

"That's right," Ira replied involuntarily.

"And the girl's full name?"

Ira moved half a step closer to Cantwell. He tried to mask any anxiety in his voice. "If this is for life insurance, or an encyclopedia, Mr. Cantwell, I'm not interested."

Cantwell lowered the form. "Oh, Mr. King. I thought you'd been informed of this action—you should have been. We've an extradition for the girl. A Jane Doe document. It's a strictly civil procedure, but it could turn nasty, if there's any indication of—mistreatment. I'm assuming there isn't."

"OK. That's fine by me, but this girl is no Jane Doe. She's Jean Harlow King. She's my daughter," he lied.

Cantwell wet his lips. "There are strong indications to the contrary in our report, Mr. King. Could we talk with the girl?"

Ira was scared. He wasn't sure that Jean would tell them he was her father—she would try to do what he wanted, but she might guess wrong. He hoped that she was listening from the house. Trying to make a plan, he said, "Sure, but she's shy." He turned to the house and spoke her name loud. In a minute she came out on the porch. "Come here, honey," he said to her. She came from the house slowly.

"Hello, young lady," Cantwell said, "how are you?"

"Fine," Jean answered.

"How old are you?"

"Eleven."

"Do you go to school?"

"Yes. But it's Christmas vacation."

"Oh, that's right. What grade are you in?"

"Fourth grade."

"Who's your teacher, honey?"

"Miss Jerri Bradley."

"Well, you are certainly a fine girl. Who's your father?"

She looked at Ira. He waited.

"Ira."

"Where's your mother?"

"She died last year." She looked at the ground, crying.

The constable fished a kitchen match from the outside band of his hat and deftly stuck it deep in the corner of his mouth, with only the sulfur and phosphorus tip extending beyond his lips. He swept it to the other side of his mouth and bit down, breaking it with a mean snap. He said, "It's not much of a trick to teach a kid to tell lies. That don't prove our report is wrong."

"Hold on." Cantwell spoke softly. "If we subtracted eleven years from your age, Mr. King, what would we have left?"

Ira wet his lips, avoiding the beady eyes of the constable.

"Seventeen."

"You're twenty-eight?"

"Yes," Ira lied.

"Do you have a copy of the girl's birth certificate?"

Ira cursed himself for not getting, from somewhere, for Jean's Miss Bradley, a forged birth certificate. He decided they were from the state education agency, that Miss Bradley had reported him for being tardy with the birth certificate. His heart raced— "No. I've written to the hospital in Texas for one. I know, I keep getting notes from Miss Bradley that you need one—it should come any day now —I wrote them weeks ago. And I wrote a reminder just last Friday."

Cantwell nodded pleasantly while he listened to Ira. Then he asked the question that Ira knew he would ask. Ira knew when he'd asked his age that Cantwell would think of it.

"Do you have a copy of *your* birth certificate, Mr. King?"

Ira tried to keep his voice low. "No. I lost it in the move."

The constable spat out his match. "You ain't no twenty-eight-year-old, *Mister* King. Let me tell you what we know about you. We know you and the girl lived in a fishing camp with Tom Delaney, a deviate, and we know you took her from there to live with a James Goff, another deviate! And we know you hid out here so we couldn't find you, but we outsmarted you, we did. And on top of all that, we *know* this ain't your kid. We know you been doing all sorts of perverted trash with this child. Why, I can just imagine what you and Tom Delaney and James Goff made her do!"

Ira stooped for a piece of the chinaberry that he'd sawed and then split for stovewood. Cantwell looked hard at his companion. "Go to the house, Jean," Ira said. *A stick of stovewood.* His mind recalled old aphorisms. *Grab a holt, girl, grab a holt.* He dropped the stick and grabbed up a longer, heavier one, feeling the blood sing in his ears, hearing in his mind, *Tar up your ass wid a tater vine.* Ira stood up straight. *You can't get blood out of a turnip.* He licked his lips. *The salt of the earth.* "Get the hell off my property!" Ira yelled. *You can lead a horse to water, but you can't make him drink.* "Get the hell out of here!"

"That's a threat of assault, King." Cantwell batted his eyes. "You have to let us take the girl—until you can prove that she's your own daughter."

"Git. Right now!"

"We'll just have to come back later, with the county sheriff."

"Git!" Ira raised the stick of stovewood as if it were a hand axe.

The little constable mocked a sarcastic smile as he and Cantwell backed, crab-fashion, to their car. They got in and shut the doors, but the window on Cantwell's side was down. Ira followed Cantwell to the car. Holding the stick of stovewood down, parallel to his leg, Ira put his left hand on the door as if he intended to hold the car back. Cantwell jabbed the key into the ignition. The motor spun quickly and started. Cantwell was nervous, but he wasn't afraid. Ira's knuckles were white where he gripped the car door. His left hand was clamped across the top of the window opening of the door, his right hand gripped the stovewood—knocking it softly but impatiently against the car door. All his knuckles were white. His throat was dry. He looked down at Cantwell's face, and something made him remember Paul Jacobs's threat.

"Have you ever heard of Paul Jacobs of Tongs?" Ira asked.

Cantwell's toe patted the accelerator just enough to keep the motor from dying. "Yes," he replied.

"I see. Don't you come back, Mr. Cantwell of Jackson. Don't send the sheriff, either. I mean it. It's not worth it. I'm like a bear in a cave. I'm a snake under a rock. Go back to Jackson. This is not a threat. It's just advice. It's that I'm at the end of my rope. I'm tied to this place like a bullet to a string, and I'm not gonna run again. Have you ever been at the end of your rope, Mr. Cantwell?"

"No. I mean, maybe—"

"Have you ever been tied like a bullet on a string?"

"I don't know about that."

"I like you, Mr. Cantwell of Jackson. Don't come back."

"But—"

"No buts. Don't fool with a bear in a cave, it's not worth it."

"You're up against the law, King. Don't make things worse for yourself. Think about the girl."

"That's exactly what I'm doing. That's what I'm thinking about. You think about yourself. Would you pick up a rock if you knew there was a snake under it? No? I'm like a snake under a rock. There's a story about a man who picked up a frozen snake on a road in January and put it in his shirt, and it thawed out and bit him, and he hollered and cried, but the snake said, 'All right. You knowed I was a snake when you picked me up.' Doesn't that make sense to you, Mr. Cantwell?"

"It's difficult to follow your logic."

"But it's true logic. It's a true fact—think about what I said. Think about it."

Cantwell put the car in reverse and started backing out the driveway. Ira followed for two halting steps, until he realized that he was holding the car. He let go and turned to the house. As he passed the pile of stovewood, his hands and shoulders and knees were weak. He dropped the stick on the pile.

Ira found Jean in the living room, wanting to talk. He poured another cup from the tall coffeepot and wished for a phone so he could call the bootlegger. "Ira, how did they find us?" she asked, following him to the living room table. Ira couldn't answer her. He was trying too hard to guess that, himself. It could have been through the Beauville school, Paul could have checked there—or the bootlegger could have told him about drinking with Ira night before last. Or the doctor could have mentioned it in town, Ira didn't tell him not to. The doctor didn't know that Ira was hiding from Paul Jacobs. "I don't know, honey." He was sickened by the notion that Melissa had told where he was hiding, but he quickly forced it from his mind—like a man can refuse to think about his wife's being unfaithful—knowing that she wouldn't. "Perhaps Paul followed us," he thought, "after I met her at Natale's mailbox. I remember her stopping on the path and turning back to the house and speaking back to it. Maybe she was answering her mother's question, 'Who are you going with, where are you going?' Maybe her mother told Paul—but do they even have a phone? No."

"I don't know, honey. But they've got us. You're in the middle of a school term. I've used all of my money to buy this farm—I don't see how we can run off and leave it—"

"Ira, how do they *know* you're not my father!"

"They know. You're too old to be my child. They know that."

"Let's stay right here, Ira." She cursed, "Hell-fire! They can't *make* us move. Let's stay here. You bought this place."

Nobody else came that day. Jean and Ira drove into Beauville just before the stores closed, and he parked the truck beside the loading dock of a feed store. He entered the feed store and went quickly to the cash register counter and said that he wanted twelve sacks of chicken feed and four blocks of cattle salt. He paid with two crisp twenties, tapping them impatiently on the counter while the clerk said that the sacks were pretty, would make nice dresses or aprons, wife would be glad to see them. Ira thought—"I have no wife. I want Melissa for a wife. I want Jean, too. I don't want any of Paul Jacobs's large fortune, but I do want Melissa—put her on the shelf—and I want Jean." The clerk carried the yellow blocks of salt to the truck, dropping them on top of the sacks of dusty feed. Ira thanked him.

Then Ira drove to the supermarket and bought three big sacks of food, a lot of canned meats and fruit juice and several boxes of saltine crackers. He gave Jean a dollar and told her to get a snack in the cafe beside the supermarket, knowing that his stomach would accept no food. He went into the hardware section and bought three boxes of shells: for the shotgun, slugs—longs for the .22, and .38 specials for Delaney's pistol. The clerk tried to sell him a hunting license, but Ira said he was just going to do target practice. He could think of no other supplies for the siege, so he waited in the truck for Jean to finish her hamburger. He thought about going out of this life like a bear in a cave, rather than like Delaney had gone, like Joe had gone—old.

They didn't see any cars on the way back, and when they got to the farm the house was dark. Jean helped him carry the brown paper sacks of food into the house and light the lamps. Ira unloaded the sacks of feed on the porch and stacked some of them in the front and back doorways, like sandbags, putting four at each door and one in each window, on the sill, and then he lowered the windows until they rested on the sacks. On top of the crisscrossed sacks in each of the doors he put two of the salt blocks, forming a loophole in the middle, thinking, *salt of the earth.* Then he cleaned and oiled the guns. He stacked a neat assortment of the three types of ammunition beside each window and each door. And he filled the big enamel water bucket at the outside well and put it, with its enamel dipper, inside the front door. The well was shallow and old, but it had sweet water. He put Delaney's binoculars right beside the water bucket, thinking, "This door will be my command post." The metal dipper floated on the water.

It was past eleven o'clock when Jean got hungry. She opened a can of chopped ham, dividing it between two plates, along with a handful of crackers. She gave him one plate and then she put the coffeepot on to boil. They ate all of the chopped ham, so she opened a can of sausage for dessert, and Ira remembered what Clyde Ponder had said about canned sausage, the night before he brought Jean to Ira's cabin. It seemed to Ira that all those things had happened years ago, a lifetime ago.

About one-thirty Jean fell asleep beside the heater. Ira turned off the lamps, moving from the front door to his chair by the east window, where he watched the dark downhill slope below the pond. Remembering the army, he thought, "It's the third man on the match who gets it." That, in turn, reminded him of the story they told at the packinghouse about the pigsticker. Ira remembered when his battery first got the claymore mines and fired them on the training range at Ft. Sill—he remembered how effective they were against the cardboard silhouettes of crouching and kneeling and standing men. Other violent images came to his mind—army talk, military formations—two on a line, one back—support mission—fire for effect: Gentlemen, over your heads at this time there are approximately seven hundred pounds of flying, flaming steel . . . if you will observe the red tank hull eleven hundred meters to your left-front, you will see, at any moment now, a direct hit. Our mission is to provide close-in fire support. The claymore mine may be triggered manually or electrically by the friendly forces, or by the enemy walking into carefully concealed trip wires. Let the enemy do the dirty work for you, make him kill his own self, use the claymore mine to cover likely avenues of approach to your defensive position. "It's a pretty good barricade we've got on this house," Ira thought. "This is a pretty good defensive position, but we still could use a few claymore mines. I've heard some country people say bear cave for barricade. It makes more sense, in a way. I'm a bear in a cave."

It was a clear sunrise. The sun poked up just north of the big pine, over the water of the pond. The chickens came out of their coop making jerky little movements, for they were stiff from sleeping. Ira was stiff from not sleeping. He watched the sun break free of the trees and float up over the pond, but he didn't start coffee until Jean woke up. She had to go outside. Ira checked out all the windows, and seeing nothing suspicious, told her to hurry. He had an idea. Ira rolled her bicycle to the front door, stepped over the feed sacks onto the front porch, and pulled it out after himself to the front porch, thinking that it was so new and blue they'd have to notice it—they knew Jean was with him—but the bicycle would emphasize that fact.

While she was out back, a truck rattled by, but it was an old familiar truck that passed daily, taking someone to work in Beauville. She hurried back inside, there was a heavy frost, she said. She asked how long they would have to wait, thinking it was exciting. Ira told her he didn't know, but most likely they'd come before noon.

Two hours later the mailman passed without stopping, and it was three hours after that when the two black cars stopped at the mailbox. There were several men in each car, and they looked at the little gray house with sacks of feed bulging from its windows and a parapet of sacks at the front door, topped with two of the yellow blocks of cattle salt. One of the men had binoculars, and he could see the barrel of Ira's shotgun yaw slowly between the salt blocks. Ira made sure he saw it, but he shielded his own binoculars, not wanting the men to know that he could see them as closely as they could see the house. The man sitting in the front seat of the first car waved to the car behind him, motioning for it to back up. Then his driver backed up also, following the rear car for about twenty yards to a wide place in the road. He got out and walked to the rear car where he talked to the men in it for a few minutes. Ira recognized none of the men. Paul Jacobs was not with them, he saw. After they talked for five minutes, the first car turned in the road, pulling forward and backing twice to make the sharp turn, and went back toward town. The other car sat still in the road, like a tank, and watched the house.

It was late afternoon when the first car returned, bringing three other cars in convoy. Ira imagined that the cars were filled with men who had pistols and rifles and shotguns and tear gas grenades, and he saw that they'd brought Dr. Forsythe. He guessed they anticipated they'd need the doctor, and Ira was sorry for that. Their foresight in that detail, and their delay, frightened him. He told Jean to lie down on the kitchen floor. "If they throw in gas that makes you cry," he said, "get in the pantry. If you smell wood burning, run out the back door."

"OK, Ira," she replied, "but I could help you shoot. I did good with the ducks, didn't I?"

"They're not ducks, honey. I'm not going to shoot them," he said. "I'm just going to bluff them off. But I want you on the kitchen floor, OK?"

"OK, Ira," she replied.

Paul Jacobs joined the convoy in his car, a big tan and brown Oldsmobile, and Ira was sure, then, when he recognized Paul's face through the binoculars, that they'd been waiting for Paul. Mr. Cantwell of Jackson was with him. Mr. Muncey got out of another car. He looked like he was feeling proud, like he looked the day Delaney drowned. The Winslow boys were with him, Gappy was there too—so was Tommy Ethling, the regular deputy who met Ira at The Falls and stood on the red cliffs in his wet undershorts to tell him about Delaney being down in the maw of The Falls.

Sweat stung Ira's forehead and neck. He reached himself a dipper of water, without taking his eyes off the carnival, and when he returned the iron dipper to the bucket of water it floated, bobbed, reminding him of the iron boat at The Falls.

The sheriff walked to the front of his car, put his hip against the front fender to steady his position, and stared at the house through his binoculars. Forsythe walked up to the sheriff and stood beside him. He spoke to the sheriff. The sheriff lowered his binoculars and looked at Forsythe. He listened. Then the doctor started walking toward the house. Ira put down his glasses. Forsythe was coming to talk to him, he realized. He knew that Forsythe was his only trump, his only hole card. For he cared, perhaps he alone, of the men in the road, cared what happened to Ira and Jean, but Ira realized, too, that he couldn't trust the doctor—because the doctor was a poker player—Ira couldn't tell him that it was a bluff. He would let the doctor see, he decided, the guns and ammunition. He'd let him see the food supplies and water.

The doctor passed the mailbox. Ira decided to let him see Jean huddled on the kitchen floor.

He passed the broken chinaberry stump. Ira decided to tell him it was the end of the road.

He stepped up on the porch. "Ira."

"Hello, Forsythe," Ira said, putting the shotgun aside.

"Drinking partner, this is getting scary. They've got an extradition. Let them take the girl."

"No."

"You can file suit in the courts," he said, looking in the front door, leaning over the block salt and sacks of chicken feed.

"Thanks, Forsythe. Go back and tell them I'm at the end of my rope. Tell them the law makes this my home—"

"But Ira—" he wet his lips.

"This is my land. Tell them that common human dignity makes Jean Harlow King my daughter. Tell them to believe we're blood kin, or else they'll see blood. Tell them to leave us alone."

"Is that all you want?"

"That's all. To be left alone."

"Gappy told me it all comes from Paul's property, your moving in on his wife's sister. Is that true?"

"No. I don't want his damned property. I have this. But I do want to be left alone."

"I'll tell him that, that you don't want his property."

"OK."

"Let the girl go with me?"

"No. She's not a hostage. She lives here."

"Ira King—"

"No. No more words, Forsythe. Please just tell them all what I say." Ira bit his lip, convincing himself that he meant what he said, remembering claymore mines and the army, remembering *Blood is thicker than water, an eye for an eye, a tooth for a tooth,* then knowing that he meant it, when he tasted the blood of his inside lip. Knowing that he'd known it all day, since the previous night, that she wouldn't leave, and he wouldn't let them take her out of the little house, away from the farm.

"It'll be dark soon, Ira. They'll come from all sides."

"I know."

"What will you do?" Forsythe looked around the living room.

"I'll hope they have more sense than to come."

"Don't do it, Ira. It's possible that—"

"Go." He spoke softly. "Please go." Ira lifted the barrel of his shotgun, not against his friend, but to finalize the talking. The doctor wet his lips, turned his head to observe the cars in the road, shrugged his shoulders, and then slouched from the porch.

While he returned, slowly, to the cars, Ira looked past him at the sheriff, using Delaney's binoculars, telling himself that he'd spent more time staring through binoculars than that sheriff ever had—there was a saying in the army—to emphasize time—that came to his mind, *I've spent more time in the pay line than you have in the chow line,* like saying a month of Sundays.

Ira knew the magic of binoculars. Sometimes he'd gotten the sensation of travelling through the binoculars to the place he was observing, of being drawn through the tubes to another place. He got that same feeling once by looking down a well and seeing the round bright reflection of water at the bottom of the well. He felt that dizziness in the stomach, like looking down a well, when he saw, with magnified clarity, the men talking in the road. Ira saw Mr. Cantwell of Jackson's mouth stop moving, and Ira counted, one thousand, two thousand, three thousand, four thousand, while Mr. Cantwell of Jackson's eyes bored into the side of Paul Jacobs's face, for it took Mr. Cantwell of Jackson those four seconds to realize that Paul Jacobs was not even listening to him—didn't even care what he said.

* * *

Slowly, with difficulty, as when one recalls forgotten names, Cantwell perceived the nature of the shabby little drama in the dusty road. As his realization grew, he felt that he could even smell the sweat of lynching fever, and that taste, or smell, or touch of feeling in the air changed his very expression. The hairs on the back of his neck stood up, and he kept hearing Ira King say, from their conversation of the previous day, "I'm a bear in a cave. I'm a snake under a rock." He backed away from Paul Jacobs, sidestepping down the road, but he couldn't speak, he just looked at the faces of the men in the cars. He was thin-lipped and white around the mouth, almost comic, for his arms hung limp in the sleeves of his shiny, cheap, light summer coat already two months out of season. He remembered the horrible, dusty, sickening carnival he'd visited in Knoxville when he was five, and six, and seven—when his mother bought him taffy that was stretched, automatically, inside a glass cage, stretched by chrome rods that turned, slowly, meshing with other chrome rods, stretching the taffy that he later ate until it made him sick at the foot of a platform that he later learned was properly a platform for the fat lady who ate no taffy, herself, but three chickens, two dozen biscuits, two pounds of bacon, or fifteen hamburgers each and every day of her natural life.

Then Dr. Forsythe reached the side of Paul Jacobs, where he could, himself, speak directly into Jacobs's ear and tell him that that man, Ira King, refused to come out, refused to send the girl, said that she was his daughter, that they both lived there, that they would not come out. Forsythe moved close to the cup of Paul Jacobs's ear, where the sheriff couldn't overhear his words, and then he told Paul Jacobs that Ira had said he just wanted to be left alone, that he didn't want any part of Paul Jacobs's lands or timber or trucks or other investments. Paul's expression didn't change. He wasn't at all the officer in charge (although he really was); he was merely there as a private citizen.

Dr. Forsythe waited thirty seconds, feeling fever in his scalp and the burn of blood in his ears, while Paul Jacobs did not respond to his appeal. Then he turned abruptly and walked over to Mr. Cantwell of Jackson, caught his elbow, pulled him around, away from Paul Jacobs, and looked into the pupils of his eyes (as he had done to the Winslow boys when Delaney drowned), looking for a spark in Cantwell's eyes that said he understood, or cared.

Cantwell said through his teeth, without moving his lips, "Yes, I know, they're going to kill that man, Ira King. Jacobs has known for weeks that he was hiding here. He pulled big strings in Jackson to get me down here. This is a piddling affair—there's no harm with Ira King and this girl. Jacobs came here for a shoot-out, to burn the house and smoke them out, that's what he wants, it's his show, completely."

Forsythe replied, "I know that, I know that, what can we do?"

Cantwell put both his thin hands on the doctor's right arm, softly kneading the doctor's biceps, imploring, "Talk them out of it, quiet and quick before he knows what we're doing, he's just waiting for the right time to get 'em started. If King was to fire one single shot out his front door—that's all it would take. If anybody starts shooting, that will be the end of it—everybody will shoot—that's the way it will happen. Nobody will even know who killed them. It's dusk. He'll start them soon."

"Yes," Forsythe replied, eagerly, "I'll tell them to leave him alone. I'll tell them I know him. I *know* he's not mistreating the girl —because he brought her to my office, like a good father—she's my patient—we doctors have privileged information."

The two men parted on the gravel road, and each went to a different car. And they did it, talking soft and slow to each man. And then Gappy helped, too, and Tommy Ethling, and even Mr. Muncey, after he thought about it for a minute. The men searched Paul Jacobs with their eyes, questioning his authority over them.

When Jacobs saw what was happening, that they didn't want to shoot it out, he spat in the ditch and said to hell with it, if the crazy son of a bitch wanted to pervert a child, and if they weren't men enough to do anything about it, then to hell with the lot of them, for all he cared the son of a bitch could sit in his dirty house until he rotted and went to hell, and they—that ragged deputation in the road—could take their gear, their paraphernalia, and cram it, for all he cared.

※　※　※

There was only room on the narrow road for one car at a time to turn around, so they all had to wait their turn. They reversed and pulled forward, repeatedly, in tight, jerky circles, crunching gravel into the shallow ditch. Some of the cars flicked on their headlights, and there were three nighthawks flying, like crazy boomerangs, north of the house, silhouetted against a cloud bank that lit itself, periodically, like a jack-o-'lantern, inside itself, with distant, silent lightning.

CHAPTER 21

WHEN THE LAST CAR HAD LEFT, DR. STEPHEN FORSYTHE STOOD ON THE
gravel road, alone in the darkening twilight, watching the flight of
those three nighthawks. Their flight seemed to him, the human observer, to be a haphazard, jerky, drunken pattern of interrupted
banks, chandelles, rolls, and suicidal dives—but then the scientist
in him spoke, telling him that the birds, like fish and grass and
men, were moved by complex and invisible forces, too easily simpli-
fied into sentimental nonsense.

He then turned to face the small, unpainted frame house of Ira
King, thinking that maybe Ira would give him a drink, at least
coffee, in exchange for the news that Paul Jacobs had backed down,
called off his attack on him and the girl. He walked toward the
house, toward the chinaberry stump, wondering if King would have
really shot it out with that ragged deputation, knowing that he
would visit with King as long as possible, to avoid going to his own
wifeless, childless brick house. He paused at the chinaberry stump
and lit a cigarette. The match in his cupped hands reflected orange
light back onto his rather pleasant face, so that Ira, watching from
the front door, could see that the tiny muscles at the corners of his
mouth had relaxed, that his brow had smoothed.

Stephen Forsythe hesitated, postponing the last ten steps to the
porch. He looked back, over his left shoulder, at the flying nighthawks. Then he put one foot on the chinaberry stump and leaned

from the waist so that he could rest his elbows on his raised knee, like one weary. The cigarette was in his lips, and his hands hung down, wearily, from his wrists. He looked past the nighthawks at the evening star, twinkling *Star bright, first star I see tonight.*

Then he straightened up. Taking the hot cigarette from his mouth, he started walking toward the house, where Ira stood in the front door, waiting for him.

"They've gone, King."

"Yes."

"I'll help you pull those feed sacks inside. It looks like it might rain, tonight."

"It does. Yes, it does."

Jean came out onto the porch to retrieve her new bicycle. She smiled at her friend, the doctor. Ira, knowing that he had no drink in the house, thought that after they put up the feed, he and For-sythe would drive the old truck over to County Line.

EPILOGUE

On a warm afternoon in August, of the following summer, an old, friendly, family-type Ford truck drove quietly west on the main street through Tongs, Mississippi. It had a faded Whitton's Egg Farm sign painted, in a crescent, on the doors. It passed the steepled Baptist Church, went down the big hill, passed the turnoff leading to Dr. Forsythe's remodeled cabin, and drove onto the Okatoma bridge.

The steel arches of the bridge were painted silver, and they looked like giant, serious lovers who'd waded out from opposite banks to stand, facing each other, in the river to hold hands, unmindful of the little rafts of gray driftwood jammed on the upstream sides of their legs, drifts that wash away and are replaced each time the river rises but which always look the same.

The old truck drove across the bridge and then slowed to turn and park at a place called Shiloh Crossing. Ira and Melissa and Jean got out of the truck and started undressing, revealing that they all wore bathing suits under their clothes. Three turtles fell, like rocks, from their sun-bleached log into the water of the river. Melissa wore an olive-green suit. The color of it set off her complexion well. She smiled at Ira and walked beside him, following Jean who had already run through the dry grass, kicked the white sand, and splashed into the water.